The Triumph of Grace

Everyone should read *The Triumph of Grace* by Kay Marshall Strom for an inspiring and exhilarating journey to freedom. Kay draws us into a historical moment for slavery and emancipation through the evolution of key characters—slaves, owners, freedom advocates, historical figures, and humble Quakers. Your heart will pound for the perils of enslaved Grace Winslow. And you will yearn for her freedom and for all who know a similar plight. If you want to know what it takes to free the slaves of today, you can glimpse the key components of God's sovereign workings in *The Triumph of Grace*.

—Michele Rickett, president of Sisters In Service and co-author of *Forgotten Girls* with Kay Marshall Strom

The Triumph of Grace

Book 3 of The Grace in Africa series

Kay Marshall Strom

 Abingdon Press fiction
a novel approach to faith
Nashville, Tennessee

The Triumph of Grace

ISBN-13: 978-1-4267-0213-6

Published by Abingdon Press, P.O. Box 801, Nashville, TN 37202

www.abingdonpress.com

Published in association with the Books & Such Literary Agency,
Janet Kobobel Grant, 5926 Sunhawk Drive, Santa Rosa, CA 95409,
www.booksandsuch.biz.

Cover design by Anderson Design Group, Nashville, TN

Library of Congress Cataloging-in-Publication Data

Strom, Kay Marshall, 1943-
  The triumph of Grace / Kay Marshall Strom.
    p. cm.—(The Grace in Africa series ; bk. 3)
  ISBN 978-1-4267-0213-6 (alk. paper)
  1. Women slaves—Fiction. 2. Slave trade—Fiction. 3. Passing (Identity)—Fiction. 4.
Africa--Fiction. 5. Women—England--Fiction. I. Title.
  PS3619.T773T78 2011
  813'.6—dc22

                                        2010023968

Scripture quotations are from the King James or Authorized Version
of the Bible.

Printed in the United States of America

1 2 3 4 5 6 7 8 9 10 / 16 15 14 13 12 11

I dedicate this book to the memory of millions
of Africans whose lives were destroyed by
the disastrous slave trade,
and to the men and women who fought to bring
the wretched practice to an end.
May we dedicate ourselves to see a time when
slavery is no more on this earth.

Acknowledgments

My grateful thanks to the many people who
helped make this book possible.

Thank you especially to Rene Mbongo in Senegal
and Raymond Peel in England
for helping me bring West Africa and London to life.

A special thank-you to my editor, Barbara Scott, who
refused to echo others who shrugged and said,
"Don't stir up the past,"
and to my agent, Janet Grant, who
worked out all the details.

Thank you, Jo Jeanne, for encouraging me
throughout my entire life.
Thank you, Lisa and Eric, for encouraging me
throughout your entire lives.
Kathy Force, you are a great first-line editor.
Thank you so much.
And to my husband, Dan Kline—well,
I am more grateful than words can express.

1

London

1793

"Who is it? Who is out there?" Nurse Hunter demanded. She rushed down the hall of the Foundling Hospital. "Must you knock the door completely off its hinges?"

Even in the best of times, Nurse Hunter was not a patient woman. And now, with her nerves already taxed by two weeks of unrelenting rain, the persistent pounding on the front door pushed her to the point of exasperation. Her characteristic staccato steps clicked through the halls with even more haste than usual.

Grace Winslow paid Nurse Hunter no mind. She extracted another bedsheet from the bundle young Hannah held in her outstretched arms. With an expert hand, Grace stuffed the sheet alongside the soggy heap already jammed into the corner where the dining hall floor connected to the entry hallway. She dropped to her knees and forced the padding firmly into place.

As Nurse Hunter tugged the water-swollen door open, Grace straightened her back. She sighed and brushed a stray lock of auburn-tinged black curls from her dark face, now glossy with sweat. "Whoever you are, do not trail mud over my freshly scrubbed floor," she murmured—but not loud enough for either Nurse Hunter or the newcomer to hear.

A worthy concern it was, too. With the road outside an absolute quagmire of muck, first one person and then the next tracked the mess inside and down the hallway faster than Grace and the girls could clean it up. Even courteous people carried the foul outside into the building. And whoever it was raising such a row at the door was obviously no courteous person.

Through the open front door, a rough voice demanded, "We's come fer Grace Winslow!"

"And just where do you fancy yourself taking our help in the middle of the day?" Nurse Hunter demanded. "The children sweat in their beds with the fever, and every corner of this building has sprung a new leak. I'd be a fool to hand our best worker over to you, wouldn't I, now?"

"Takin' her to Newgate Prison, is wot," came the sharp reply. "On orders of Lord Reginald Witherham hisself."

Grace stiffened. Lord Reginald Witherham? Charlotte's husband? An entire year had passed since Grace made her escape from that dreadful man's house! Lord Reginald had been frightfully angry, but so much time had passed. Surely by now—

"And what right does Lord Reginald Witherham have to remove our help from this charitable establishment?" Nurse Hunter demanded, her long, thin arms akimbo on her spare body.

"Grace Winslow be a thief, is wot," the irritated voice replied. "Now, kindly step aside. Elsewise, we be taking you along with her."

A *thief!* Grace could not believe what she had heard. She was no such thing! Charlotte would tell them as much. Yes,

Lord Reginald's wife knew everything that had happened that day at Larkspur Estate.

A tall burly man in a shabby greatcoat pushed past Nurse Hunter and forced his way into the entry hall. Right behind him was a short man with bushy eyebrows and an overgrown mustache.

"Hannah!" Nurse Hunter ordered. "Run and find Nurse Cunningham and bid her come immediately. Hurry, now!"

The child dropped the bedsheets. She looked uncertainly from Nurse Hunter to Grace to little Phoebe, whose arms were still piled high with folded cloth.

"Go!" Nurse Hunter commanded.

As Hannah bolted down the center hall, little Phoebe screamed to Grace, "Wun, Gwace! Wun away fast!"

The burly man pointed to Grace and called, "That be her!"

Before Grace could get her wits about her, the men were upon her. The tall burly man held her firmly in his grasp, and the bushy one bound her wrists with a rope.

"It is all a mistake!" Grace protested. "I never stole anything!"

Without bothering to respond, the men shoved her toward the door. Phoebe shrieked and Nurse Hunter scolded, but the men paid no mind. They hustled Grace out into the rain toward a waiting carriage with doors that bore the golden letters **WL**—the unmistakable monogram of Witherham Larkspur, Lord Reginald's estate.

"Here, now!" Nurse Cunningham panted as she ran up behind Hannah. "What is the meaning of this?" When she saw Grace in the grip of the two ruffians, she ordered, "Loosen our servant this instant! I insist!"

Nurse Cunningham might as well have been speaking to the trees.

"We are a charitable house for orphans, sirs!" she exclaimed. "Have you no concern for the welfare of poor children?"

The burly man shoved Grace through the open carriage door and hefted himself in beside her. The bushy-faced man scurried up after them, settled himself across from Grace and the large man, and yanked the door shut. Not one word was spoken. Not one word was needed. The driver whipped the horse. The carriage jerked forward and rattled onto the cobblestone street.

Grace tugged herself around in time to see the two women and a clutch of children staring after her. Wide-eyed, they huddled together in the driving rain.

"I am no thief," Grace said.

"Save it fer the magistrate," the burly man told her. "It's him wot will hear yer plea."

Grace started to object, but the bushy-faced man glared hard at her and growled through his mustache in such a terrifying way that she closed her mouth and sank back in miserable silence.

A year of schemes and plans. A year of saving every shilling of her pay from the Foundling Hospital. Months of gathering bits and pieces of men's clothes.

"When may I go back to the Foundling Hospital?" Grace ventured.

The burly man barked a sharp guffaw. "The Foundling Hospital, is it, then? Be there a graveyard out back? One with a poor hole, perchance? 'Tis the only way you will be seein' the likes of that place again."

"Should've said yer good-bye's afore the door closed on this carriage," said the small man with the bushy face. His stony voice unnerved Grace. "You won't be seeing them children again. Not in this life."

Grace shivered in her drenched dress and sank further into the seat. Each clomp, clomp, clomp of the horse's hooves was like a hammer driving a spike of despair deeper into her heart. Why now, after all this time? Surely, with his powerful connections, Lord Reginald Witherham could have found her at any time during the year she had worked at the Foundling Hospital. Why now, just when everything was almost ready?

For the past year, at the end of every exhausting day, Grace took off her only dress, laid it over the single chair in her room and slipped into the loose cotton garment Nurse Hunter had given her for sleep. She lay down on her cot and in the darkness carefully traced Cabeto's face in her mind. She recalled its every curve—the laughing tilt of his mouth, the broad shape of his nose, the spark of assurance in his eyes. When her husband was firmly fixed in her memory, she whispered again the promise she had called out to him on that awful day in Africa: "*I will see you again. I promise!*"

Cabeto, in chains. Cabeto, forced onto the slave ship. Cabeto, the slave. Oh, but Cabeto, in America, waiting for her!

Unless . . . unless she couldn't get to him in time. One year, Captain Ross had told her. Maybe two. That's how long it would be before whatever slave owner bought Cabeto would likely work him to death.

One year, maybe two.

"Don't you worry yerself about Newgate Prison," the burly man taunted. "Lord Witherham be in such a state, I guar'ntee you won't be lingerin' there fer long."

Mistakes happen. Grace understood that. Misunderstandings occur. If she were in her village in Africa, she and her accuser would simply sit down under the baobab tree—the spirit tree—with the wise old man in the village, and they would all talk together. The wisdom of the ancestors would rise from the spirit tree and fill the mind of the old man, and he would guide the disagreeing sides to a place of understanding. In Africa, the two would walk away in harmony. But this was not Africa. It was London, where no baobab trees grew. Even if a spirit tree did exist in London, it would be lost among the crush of tall buildings and chimneys that clogged the city and church spires that reached to the sky. Nor could the wisdom of the ancestors hope to pierce the unyielding shroud of thick, smoky fog that held London in its relentless grasp.

"Lady Charlotte—I must speak to her!" Grace said.

The burly man burst out in a great guffaw. "You? And what would the likes o' you say to so fine a lady?"

"I know her, you see, and—"

"If you knows anything at all, you knows to shut yer mouth while you still can."

"Exceptin' to beg fer mercy," interrupted the man with the bushy face. "Surely you knows that. Elsewise you be about to gift all London with the pleasure o' watchin' you dance at the end of a hangman's rope."

2

The charge?" asked Magistrate Francis Warren.

Attired in a long black robe and with a white powdered wig on his head, the magistrate looked frightfully official even though he sat at his own desk in the parlor of his own home and rubbed his hands warm before the fire in his own hearth.

"What charge do you bring against this woman, Lord Reginald?"

Magistrate Warren peered over the wire-rimmed spectacles perched on the bridge of his nose and squinted with filmy eyes at Lord Reginald Witherham, who sat stiffly on the opposite side of the fireplace. With great show, Lord Reginald set aside the teacup he so expertly balanced on his knee. He rose to his full unimposing height and bowed low to the magistrate. Lord Reginald artfully posed himself to one side of the opulent marble mantel—head high, left hand behind his back for a touch of elegance, right hand free for gesturing. For an entire year, he had bidden his time. After so great a display of discipline, this moment was far too sweet to pass by without indulgence.

Slowly, deliberately, Lord Reginald turned his attention to Grace Winslow. Miserable and shivering in her wet dress, she stood some distance from the fire, flanked by the same two men who had brought her from the Foundling Hospital.

"Your Lordship," Lord Reginald began with a most dramatic flair, "this African woman who stands before you—" here he paused to look at her with disgusted pity "—is naught but a wanton thief!"

"I see."

The magistrate heaved a wearied sigh.

Grace caught her breath.

An air of victory settled over Lord Reginald's pale face. He lifted his narrow jaw and fixed Grace with as searing a glare as his weak features could manage.

"Sir," Grace said, but not to Lord Reginald. She searched the magistrate's craggy face for understanding. "Are you the wisest man of this town? Are you the one who hears disagreements and leads your people to a way of healing?"

"Your Lordship!" Lord Reginald interrupted with a great show of indignation. "I really must protest this display of insolence!"

Ignoring Lord Reginald's incensed huffs and allowing the trace of a smile to push at the corners of his mouth, Magistrate Warren answered Grace.

"I should be most pleased to think of myself in such lofty terms," he said. "But, to my great misfortune, I fear that such a calling is not mine. You stand before me today for one purpose alone: to make it possible for me to determine the quality of the case brought against you. With that single intention in mind, I am required by my office to insist that you remain silent as I hear Lord Reginald Witherham state his charges against you. Afterwards, I shall determine whether you shall be bound over for trial."

With a sigh of impatience, Lord Reginald abandoned his carefully orchestrated pose and strode to the magistrate.

"I took pity on the wretch," he informed Magistrate Warren. "That was my downfall, Your Lordship. Out of naught but kindness, I allowed her to enter my house, and she repaid my benevolence with blatant thievery. She took my goodwill as an opportunity to remove from my estate as many items as she could secret under her skirts. Of that I have not the least doubt."

Grace gasped in disbelief. She had been inside Lord Reginald's estate house, that much was true. But only one time, and she was never left alone. No, not for one minute.

"Sir, that is not true!" Grace protested. "I never—"

"Madam, you have no right to speak," the magistrate cautioned. His voice was kind, yet firm. "This is an official hearing."

"If you just ask Lady Charlotte, she could tell you—"

"Hold your peace, madam! If you do not, I shall have no choice but to have you removed forthwith straight to Newgate Prison!"

Lord Reginald allowed himself the indulgence of a satisfied smile. All was proceeding precisely as he had meticulously planned. Justice wrought would surely be worth the year's wait.

"Your Lordship," Lord Reginald continued. "I ask permission to submit for your excellent consideration one particular piece of evidence."

Here Lord Reginald reached into his pocket and pulled out a fine linen handkerchief, sewn with the daintiest of hands and most delicately trimmed in an elegant lace border.

Grace cried out in spite of herself.

"Please note the quality of this piece of finery," Lord Reginald continued unabated. "Embroidered flowers throughout, all done in the most perfect of stitches. This piece is easily worth six shillings. Perhaps as much as eight."

"Missus Peete gave me that handkerchief when I left her employ!" Grace cried. "Where did you get it?"

"Silence!" Magistrate Warren ordered.

"It was in my room, sir! I kept it under the pillow on my cot!"

"I shall not repeat my injunction," insisted Magistrate Warren. The kindly creases in his face hardened into angry resolve.

"The handkerchief was indeed retrieved from the cell where the accused has lived for the past year," said Lord Reginald, "but not from under the cot pillow where she lays her head at night. No, no. Some days past an associate of mine found it hidden away behind a loose stone in the wall." Lord Reginald paused dramatically. "I ask Your Lordship, does that not provide ample proof that Grace Winslow is nothing but a common thief? That she is only using the Foundling Hospital as a convenient place to hide herself, cloaked in the guise of a nurse caring for homeless children?"

Magistrate Warren ran his hand over his face and heaved a weary sigh. "A six-shilling handkerchief, then. Have you evidence of further thievery, Lord Reginald?"

"Even such a one as she is not fool enough to keep stolen goods lying about," Lord Reginald answered. "Undoubtedly she visits the rag fair regularly and offers for sale whatever she has pilfered. This particular piece, however, she evidently determined to keep for herself." Here he held the handkerchief high, as though it were a great trophy. "Perhaps such a dainty allows her to believe that she truly is a lady . . . and not merely an escaped slave from Africa."

"None of that is true!" Grace cried in exasperation.

"Silence!" ordered the magistrate.

"And I am not a slave!"

"Have you any witnesses to call, Lord Reginald?"

"No, Your Lordship," replied Lord Reginald with a deep bow. "Taking into consideration the obvious circumstances of this case, I did not deem it necessary to inconvenience such witnesses."

Since Magistrate Warren would not permit Grace to speak in her defense, he most certainly did not extend her an invitation to call witnesses.

"I am certain you will find that I have set before you a case most worthy of trial," Lord Reginald continued.

Magistrate Warren knew perfectly well what he had before him: an African woman—a mere cleaning maid—one of a multitude of her kind to be found in London. She faced a charge brought by an exceedingly wealthy lord, an aristocratic gentleman of great power and influence. A servant of foreign extraction could disappear into the depths of Newgate Prison—or worse—and never be missed. On the other hand, Lord Reginald Witherham had it in his power to do much to propel a cooperative magistrate forward politically, or he could wield equal influence to destroy an uncooperative one. Magistrate Francis Warren could ill afford to subject himself to such a risk. And, really, why should he? There was, after all, that expensive handkerchief to consider. What further evidence did he require?

"Grace Winslow," Magistrate Warren pronounced, "I commit you to Newgate Prison to await trial on the charge of thievery."

Forgetting himself, Lord Reginald Witherham allowed a whoop to escape his thin lips. He looked triumphantly at Grace, who had dared bring such ridicule and humiliation down on him, and crowed, "If you thought you could hide from me, you were indeed the greatest of fools!"

Magistrate Warren's shoulders slumped. He swiped at the sweat that glistened in the crevices of his tired face.

Grace looked neither at the uneasy magistrate nor at the gloating Lord Reginald. She shut her eyes tight and desperately tried to trace Cabeto's face in her mind. His mouth . . . his eyes . . . his brow. . . . But this time, she could not.

After all Grace had endured, after all she had survived, it had finally happened—Cabeto had slipped away from her.

3

*Y*ou don't thinks you can keep on livin', but somehow you do," said Kit as he attacked the endless expanse of weeds with his hoe. "My woman, she be gone. My children, dey be gone, too. Everyone already be ripped away from me. You don't thinks you can keep on, but here we be sloggin' in de swamp."

"Here we be," said Caleb. "Together . . . all alone."

Caleb.

Yes.

In another life he was Cabeto, but now he was Caleb. Caleb, who wore a mud-splattered white man's shirt and breeches soaked to the knees. Caleb the slave, that's who he was now.

"Do you remember Africa?" Caleb asked Kit.

"No, and if'n you knows what's good for you, you won't, neither."

No African names were allowed on the plantation. No words in any of the tongues of Africa. No drums, no dances, no talk of the ancestors. And no Grace. No Grace. Aching homesickness tore into Caleb's heart, which was precisely why he did his best to block Grace from his mind. He could not endure the memories.

"Dis here be like de islands of home," said Kit.

Caleb never knew the rice fields in the coastal swamps of Kit's Africa. Caleb hailed from the parched savanna, the flat grasslands. The rich bottomland marsh at White Jasmine Plantation, which lay just up the Ashley River from Charleston, South Carolina, brought no recollections of home to him. Certainly the dank swamp, overgrown with cypress trees and sweetgrass, didn't, either. To Caleb, it was nothing but the land of masters and slaves.

"Folks like me, we's de ones what knows when to plant de rice seeds," Kit said. "We knows how to strap up de water so's it drowns de land with de tide. After de harvest, it be our womenfolks what know to use fanna baskets to throw de chaff to de winds. And dey's de ones what knows how to pound de last bit of hull off de rice grain, too."

Africans using African ways to grow African rice to make the white master richer still. Caleb plunged his hoe into the thick mud with such vengeance that the head flew off. Growling with frustration, he dropped to his knees and groped in the weed-strewn mud. When he located the metal head, he laid it aside, then thrust his hands back down into the muck to feel around for the piece of stone he had carefully chiseled to fit under the cracked head and make the broken tool usable again.

Be a good slave. Fix de massa's useless tools. Den take dem to de field and work, work, work. Work hard like a good slave.

Caleb's first master, Silas Leland, had bought both Caleb and his brother, Samson, from the auction block, fresh off the ship from Africa. Silas Leland's only thought was to get a couple months' hard, unending labor from the two maimed Africans before they sank to their deaths in the snake-infested swampland. But then Macon Waymon came around, his head full of big ideas for his own rice plantation. When he saw the strapping Caleb knee-deep in the soggy swamp doing the work of two men, it caught his attention.

"Silas," Macon said as he lounged with his host in the gathering twilight and sipped apple cider. "What did you pay for that slave with the lame leg?"

"Ha!" Silas laughed. "Him and his brother cost me 300 shillings and 20 gallons of rum for the both of them. His brother already lies dead in the field."

"I'll give you five gold eagle coins for that lame one," Macon said. "Take it or leave it."

Silas took it. When Macon Waymon set out for home, Caleb limped along behind his new master's horse.

Fool! Silas Leland laughed to himself. *That man just bought himself a cripple!*

Fool! Macon Waymon smiled. *That man doesn't know a prize worker when he sees one!*

ℒ❧

"Over yonder!" Kit called out to Caleb. "It be Juba, and he be comin' our way. Best look busy."

Because he already was busy, Caleb paid Kit no mind.

"You almost be done with your section, Caleb!" Juba shouted over. "You plannin' to quit early so's you can work dat garden of your'n?"

Caleb nodded.

Juba strode across Caleb's field and on to Kit's field. He looked at Kit, but he kept right on going to the field on the other side.

"Him bein' boss over us! It ain't right!" Kit scowled. "He gets a cabin all to hisself and shoes to wear on dem big black feet of his. We gets boiled pig's feet to eat and he gets smoked bacon."

"And he ain't welcome among his own people, neither," Caleb said.

"Amongst folks he done whupped? Whose ears he's sliced off? No, he shore enough ain't welcome amongst dem!"

"Juba ain't sliced off no ears, and you knows it," Caleb said. "Bein' driver of us does keep his wife comfortable in de cabin and de whip off her back, though. And his children—dey still be alive. Massa ain't sold dem away, neither."

Caleb thrust his hoe into the ground. Sweet Grace, grabbed up by the slavers, and him bound in chains and helpless to fight back. Then little Kwate pulled out of her arms and dashed against the rocks. Caleb would be a driver like Juba if he could protect his family. Oh, yes, he surely would. A kind driver, though. And fair. Always he would be fair.

Caleb thumped the hoe against a tree stump—just hard enough to shake the worst of the mud clods loose, but not hard enough to knock off the broken head.

To keep water moving in and out of the low-country rice paddies, many slaves had to labor constantly at clearing the swamps. On Master Macon's plantation, tides brought fresh water in to irrigate the swamps. Dikes held the salt water back—except when muskrats or alligators undercut them, which happened all too often. Inside the large, walled-up areas, drainage and irrigation canals set off smaller fields and divided them up. "Rice trunks"—heavy gates—regulated the canals.

As driver, it was Juba's responsibility to assign individual slaves to work specific fields. Caleb had the field farthest from the slave quarters, and Kit's field jutted up beside Caleb's. Slaves who worked hard and efficiently, as Caleb did, could finish early—which is why Caleb had been able to plant and successfully tend a vegetable garden. Those who spent too much time talking and complaining, the way Kit did, didn't finish their fields until dark.

When Master Macon first bought Caleb from Silas Leland and led him home to his plantation, the slaves had just begun to prepare the fields for planting. Kit showed Caleb how to yoke the oxen and use them to plow and harrow the soft ground. After the fields were flooded and drained, Kit demonstrated the proper way to plant the rice. As the plants sprouted, Kit had shown Caleb how to work his hoe through the mud.

"Soon now, Massa Macon be leavin' here," Kit called over to Caleb.

If Kit hoped to get Caleb's attention, he succeeded. "Leavin'?" Caleb asked. "Where Massa be goin' to?"

"Takin' his family to his fine house in de city. Massa Macon don't want to be out here when de weather turns hot."

"Why not?"

"Mosquitoes. Dey swarms everywhere in de hot season," Kit said. "People gets jungle fever."

Kit laughed at the troubled look that crossed Caleb's face.

"When dem white folks be gone away, it be good for dem and it shore enough be good for us!" Kit said. "We be left to work de fields alone. Den we can be Africans again. We can talk our talk and sing our songs and cook our food anytime we wants to. If ever de ancestors can find us, it be in de summer time."

Alone! Without the master! Long-forgotten shards of shattered hope began to piece themselves together in Caleb's heart.

"When do Massa come back again?" Caleb asked.

Kit shrugged. "About de time de rice birds come swoopin' in to gobble up de rice. We all so busy, no one pays him no mind. We gets us out in de fields, swingin' de rice hooks and we does our best to cut down de sheaves before dem birds can gobble all de rice away. Can't be bothered with Massa, so wild is we in de fields. Women and children and old folks, dey all shoutin' and poundin' drums—doin' anythin' to scare off dem birds. And we men . . . we works like crazy folks to get de rice sheaves cut and bundled and stacked for dryin'."

Caleb tossed the hoe over his shoulder and climbed up to the road.

"Ain't you goin' to help me finish my field?" Kit entreated.

Caleb shook his head. "No, sir. Gots me a garden to tend."

It wasn't just the garden patch filled with collard greens and okra, squash, and bean sprouts that brought such a special joy to Caleb—although when the women threw fresh vegetables into the cook pot, the porridge did smell mighty rich and inviting. What Caleb really liked was being a part of the bustling slave quarters. Small children chased after each other, laughing and playing—it reminded him of his own little Kwate toddling about in their village in Africa. Older children, already at work, wrapped straw into brooms and swept the cabins clean. The old women, whose job it was to watch over the little ones, gathered up the sweetgrass the men had carried back from the swamp and coiled it into baskets. Sweetgrass, bull rushes, and pine needles—the women bound them with cabbage palm and stitched them all together, their sewing bones flying. Even though Caleb was not from the coast, the fresh-cut-hay fragrance of sweetgrass brought a rush of Africa to his mind—the smells, the sounds, the porridge bubbling over the cook fire.

"Set down and rest yourself," old Tempy called out to Caleb as he walked into the slave compound. "You deserves it. You already done a full day's work in dem rice fields."

Caleb smiled. Just like Mama Muco, she was. He walked around behind Tempy to the other side of the slave shack where his garden grew.

"Tempy," Caleb called back, "can the ancestors see us here in dis old swampland?"

Tempy barked a deep-throated laugh. "What you think? Dat Nyame can't watch over his people? Just because things ain't de way dey used to be, just because dey ain't de way dey's supposed to be, dat don't mean Nyame forgot about us."

"No spirit trees grow here," Caleb said to the *chop chop* rhythm of his hoe.

"How does you know dat?" Tempy shot back. "Just because you can't see a spirit tree don't mean no spirit tree grows here."

Caleb looked around him—up at the lacy mimosas, over at the gnarled arms of giant oaks with their long finger trails of Spanish moss, past them to the mysterious humped-over cypress trees that grew alongside the swamplands.

Yes, Caleb thought. *Who's to say no spirits live in any of dem trees?*

Slowly, deliberately, Caleb straightened his back and stood tall. He dropped his hoe to the ground, unbuttoned his white man's shirt and pulled it off his back. He moved to the cook fire and slowly began to dance around it.

Tempy watched as Caleb dipped sideways on his bad leg with a haunting gracefulness. She laid her basket down and began to clap out a rhythm for his steps, raising her voice in a tune unfamiliar to Caleb's ear. Although he did not recognize the melody, or even the language of the words, the meaning was perfectly clear to him. Just as Tempy knew the meaning of Caleb's dance. Honor to Nyame, the Creator, the God Supreme. Tribute to the author of life, maker of everything. Praise to the one from whom comes strength and inspiration and wisdom.

Honor to the one who gives hope in a world of hopelessness.

Whatever his name.

Wherever he might be.

4

Has ye naught to give to recompense me fer yer keep, then?" the jailer demanded of Grace. "'Tis me wot kin make yer life at Newgate easy or hard, miss. But ye can't expect me to do nothin' fer ye unless I gets me rightful pay."

Grace stared at the expressionless face of the grizzled jailor. Obviously he managed to secure enough pay from the prisoners to keep his belly plump and round. She looked from him to the grated window in the locked door. On the other side Grace could see the prison cell. And a dismal sight it was, too—hoards of wretched men and women in dirty rags, all crowded together without so much as a bench to sit on. A smattering of the prisoners, their hands and feet bound in heavy chains, sat fettered in chairs bolted to the floor. "Are they all slaves?" Grace asked in confusion.

"Criminals they be, same as ye," the jailer snapped. "All waitin' fer trial, too. Now, I asks ye again—Is ye goin' to pay fer yer keep, or does I toss ye in with the rest of the refuse?"

"I have no money," Grace said.

The jailer turned his key in the lock and pulled the heavy door open.

"In with ye, then!"

The jailer shoved Grace inside and banged the door shut behind her.

Grace ducked in time to avoid a man throwing wild punches into the air. But in her effort to stay clear of him, she stumbled into two women huddled together on the floor.

"Watch yerse'f!" snapped the younger woman. Much younger, as a matter of fact. She looked to be hardly more than a child. "Don't be tryin' to take over our space."

"Ye kin take yer daily mail elsewheres," added the older, more disheveled of the two. Grace realized with a start that the older woman was probably no more than her own twenty-six years.

Grace stared at the woman. Her words made absolutely no sense.

"Daily mail?" Grace asked.

"Don't ye know nothin'? Yer stories and tricks, o' course!" came the impatient reply. "Liar's tale, is what it be . . . Daily mail!"

Grace pushed past the two. She forced her way around an old man who chanted incomprehensibly at the bare wall. She pressed through a knot of men and women huddled around a couple of ragged children. Choking in the terrible stench of the packed room, Grace lifted the hem of her skirt and pressed it against her nose and mouth. Even so, she could only breathe in short gasps of the foul air.

"Wot crime has ye done?" asked a pale woman with straight hair that hung wild and undone to her shoulders. With shaky hands, the woman grabbed up the two ends of a brightly colored scarf draped around her shoulders and tied them at her neck in a knot.

"I did nothing," Grace answered. "I am no criminal."

"Ha!" the woman laughed. "Jist like the rest o' us in this place. We all be innocent, we do!"

A man in chains threw his head back and laughed wildly. "That be me! Innocent is what I is! I took the iron bars off the cellar window of a rich man's house and robbed the bloke blind, I did. But no one's the wiser because I nailed them bars back on like I found them. The poor little maid went to the gallows for me crime."

"But . . . but you are in prison, and in chains," Grace said.

"Me mate, he picked a rich man's pockets. When the constable grabbed him, he grabbed me too, though I never picked a pocket in me life."

"So ye be innocent on both sides," said the woman in the bright scarf. "But ye will hang from the gallows all the same!" The irony of the man's predicament struck her as so funny that she laughed uncontrollably.

At the far wall, a man with no teeth moved away from his place and stumbled toward the water jug in the front of the room. Quickly Grace slipped away from the laughing woman and into the vacant spot, where she sank down onto the filthy floor. Shivering in her still-damp dress, she leaned back and closed her eyes.

Could it be that just outside these dismal walls life continued as usual? That peddlers still called out their wares, that people continued to whistle in the lanes, that children yet laughed? Was it possible that outside Newgate Prison, hope lived on and people still dared to dream?

❦

"Up! Up wi' ye now!" The jailer punctuated his order with a stiff kick to Grace's side. "It's to the court fer ye, missy."

Back to stand before the magistrate, Grace supposed. But instead of heading to Magistrate Francis Warren's house, the jailer led Grace across the street to the Old Bailey, into a room packed with people. Fine people they were, too—mostly men dressed in silk frock suits, elaborate waistcoats, and white silk stockings, their heads covered with powdered wigs. But there was also a smattering of women in lovely dresses, proud to show off their towering hairstyles. After a night on the filthy floor of Newgate Prison, Grace—looking every bit as wretched as she felt—was led up to the dock and left to stand alone to face a solemn judge. The room fell silent.

Sir Geoffrey Phillips—Grace recognized him immediately. He was seated on the front row. Sir Geoffrey had treated her kindly that day at Lord Witherham's estate. In fact, Grace recognized many of the men on the front row with her accuser. They were all his friends. What Grace could not know was that each one of them had received an engraved invitation to the trial a full week before the two miscreants had ever banged on the door of the Foundling Hospital looking for her.

Grace scanned the room for Lady Charlotte, the one person who could vouch for her, but she was nowhere to be seen. Certainly she was not seated beside her husband.

Lord Reginald Witherham sat quite comfortably in the chair nearest the Lord Judge as the clerk read the charge.

Grace stood straight in the dock and listened to the proceedings in bewilderment. So totally excluded was she from the verbal exchange that shot back and forth between Lord Reginald and the Lord Judge that it quite alarmed her to hear the Lord Judge suddenly demand:

"To the charge of theft, Grace Winslow, how do you plead?"

Lord Judge Aaron North, squat and flush-faced, looked as though he had long ago wearied of hearing complaints and excuses.

Grace stared back blankly.

"Come, come!" Lord Judge North said impatiently. "What do you plead, guilty or not guilty? Speak up!"

"Not guilty!" Grace said.

"Not guilty, you say? Well, we shall soon see about that."

Not a line of compassion creased Lord Judge North's hardened face. This was simply one more trial for one more thief on one more long and tiring day. Criminals such as Grace Winslow came before him in a constant stream, often twenty in a day. Sometimes as many as twenty-five. All were felonies, of course, although not all were found guilty. Still, by the time the sun set, many who passed before Lord Judge North that day would face the gallows. With a criminal code that listed two hundred forty offenses punishable by death, the law of the Crown was uncompromising. So was his Lordship, Judge Aaron North.

"Lord Reginald Witherham," the judge said, "would you be so kind as to describe the location of the theft you suffered, as well as the manner of the crime committed against you? Also, please describe for the court the goods stolen from your estate. Place an approximate value on your loss, too, if you will."

Slowly, purposefully, Lord Reginald rose from his seat. As he turned to face the assembled crowd, he assumed the singular pose he had so carefully practiced in front of his own full-length mirror. For this most important of occasions, he had donned a striking embroidered velvet waistcoat of a deep scarlet hue. Because he'd had this garment specially made for the purpose of dazzling the court, he had carefully rehearsed his speech complete with flamboyant gestures, each one timed to accent the clever turn of a phrase or to emphasize an important point he intended to make.

In a forceful voice, Lord Reginald Witherham began: "On the fifteenth day of May, in the year of our Lord 1792, a slave, brought to London by my faithful employee, Jasper Hathaway, did escape. My poor Mister Hathaway was at the time suffering a most compromised state of health, yet with no regard for him—or for any of us who had gone to great lengths to see her safely to this blessed country—she callously forced herself onto the grounds of my estate and into my private residence. The guilty person of whom I speak is the very same disreputable woman who now stands in the dock before your Lordship, one Grace Winslow."

Here Lord Reginald paused in order to gesture dramatically to Grace.

"This escaped slave managed to completely confound my poor wife, Lady Charlotte, who most regretfully has not been of sound mind for some time. Once in my house, Grace Winslow proceeded to toss about wild accusations that not only caused me severe humiliation, but completely distracted and confused my invited guests. Several of these selfsame upstanding men have been good enough to accompany me here today."

Lord Reginald nodded to Sir Geoffrey Phillips and the others seated with him on the front row.

Pacing across the front of the courtroom, Lord Reginald continued, "Out of kindness, I did not order the intruder out of my home, though I am certain that few would have blamed me had I done so. Rather, with tolerance and patient forbearance, I attempted to entreat her to leave of her own free will. So confused and upset was my household by the outrageous actions of this slave, that it was not until later I ascertained my loss. Only then did I realize she had taken advantage of the disturbance she herself had caused to steal valuable items from my home. I am absolutely certain she accomplished this feat by concealing the objects amongst her skirts."

At this point, Lord Reginald paused, plucked his handkerchief from the pocket of his elegant waistcoat, and dabbed dramatically at his eyes. For good measure, he sighed deeply and patted at his brow as well.

"Being the generous gentleman I am, I have waited with exceptional patience for this woman to return the goods she stole from my estate. I am only here today because I now acknowledge, to my great distress, that this is not to be. Most certainly, my valuable belongings have already been sold for a pittance at the rag fair. I have no doubt but that many other unfortunates have also suffered a similar loss at the hands of this heartless thief."

"You have evidence for your account of the matter, Lord Reginald?" Lord Judge North inquired.

"I most certainly do, Your Lordship," Lord Reginald replied with a deep bow.

From his chair he picked up the same handkerchief he had displayed before Magistrate Warren the day before. Lord Reginald held it high for all to see.

"It would seem that this . . . this *slave* woman . . . was not able to release her grip on this one fancy—a valuable lace-edged handkerchief, embroidered with a fine and steady hand. Therefore, it remains behind to testify against Grace Winslow!"

"I see," Lord Judge North said thoughtfully. "But, if you please, what evidence have you that the thievery of the accused reached beyond your own estate? Or that she did indeed sell any of your belongings?"

"Most certainly she sold my belongings!" Lord Reginald snapped. But he quickly recovered himself and continued in a much more gentle voice. "I have with me witnesses prepared to testify to that precise fact, Your Lordship. And as to the question of further thievery . . ."

From underneath his chair, Lord Reginald produced a wrapped packet. He untied the string and unwrapped the papers in a most dramatic fashion. First he pulled out a newly sewn man's shirt, which he held up high for all to see. A crisp new pair of breeches followed.

"Both are items of men's clothing, as you can well see, and both are sewn with a fine hand," Lord Reginald proclaimed. "Most assuredly these are not garments expected to be found in the possession of a wretched slave girl . . . or even, of a *servant* girl. These items of clothing—along with leg stockings, cap, and shoes—were retrieved from a hiding place in the wall of Grace Winslow's cell at the Foundling Hospital. They were so carefully hidden away behind a loose brick at the rear of her cot that a good bit of investigation was required to locate them."

Whispers and murmurs arose throughout the courtroom.

"No!" Grace protested. "Missus Peete made those clothes for me—"

"Silence!" the judge ordered. "You have no right to speak in this court, madam. You are not under oath, nor shall you be."

"But Missus Peete—"

"Silence! Everyone here can clearly see clothing found in your possession that could not possibly be yours. I caution you, miss: do not make your situation worse than it is already."

A satisfied smile danced at the edges of Lord Reginald's fragile mouth.

"Does Your Lordship desire to see further evidence of the fruits of this woman's thievery?"

Without waiting for an answer, Lord Reginald triumphantly held high an embroidered silk purse.

"I ask you," he boomed to the entire assemblage, "is there any legal way that a wretched servant, such as the one you see before you in the dock today, could honorably obtain so fine a silk purse?"

He opened the flap and turned the purse upside down. One by one, Grace's hard-earned shillings clattered to the floor.

". . . Filled with thirty-eight shilling coins?"

"Captain Ross gave that to me!" Grace cried.

"You will not speak!" the exasperated judge roared. "One more time and I shall see you locked into restraints! Had you desired to present a defense, you should have written it out properly and submitted it before the trial began. Had you done so, I should have read it on your behalf. As I was presented with no such document, I consider your rights duly waived."

Grace clenched her fists in silent exasperation.

"I should say, however, I cannot see that such a statement would have done you one particle of good," Lord Judge North added. "Not in the presence of so profound a mountain of evidence."

"As to value," Lord Reginald said, "the fine handkerchief is in itself worth a minimum of six shillings. The silk purse must surely be worth another eight. The shirt and breeches? A full twenty-eight shillings for the set, I should say. That brings the total to forty-one shillings. When one adds the thirty-eight shillings hidden inside the purse—which can be nothing other than the fruits of thievery—the Crown must of a certainty agree that Grace Winslow committed thievery with a value greater than forty shillings. Therefore, Grace Winslow most certainly committed a crime for which the sentence is death!"

A frown crossed Judge North's face. Off to his side, the men of the jury fell to murmuring their opinions to one another. Valuable goods, without a doubt—yet not of so great a value.

That they were stolen from the rich estate of a powerful Lord was a fact that must weigh heavily in the decision, most assuredly. Furthermore, the theft was perpetrated while the master of the house performed an act of charity toward the accused—which he most certainly must have done, for why else would so ragged an African as now stood before them even have been in Larkspur Estate?

It was these final two points that made it an offense that absolutely could not be tolerated.

"Your Lordship," Lord Reginald said with a deep bow, "I can provide further witnesses for the Crown. I assure you that each in turn will attest to Grace Winslow's dealings in stolen goods. Each will also—"

"Yes, yes," the judge said with a dismissive wave of his hand.

Lord Judge North was growing impatient with the endless talk. Many other thieves awaited trial that day, and he had no wish to be late for his dinner. Anyway, the judge knew all about "witnesses for the Crown." Like as not, those very same men had stood before his bench more times than he could count. They always waited outside the courts, ready to swear to anything on behalf of anyone who had the money to pay them. One only need look for a straw stuck in the heel of a shoe to identify a man ready to give testimony to anything in exchange for money.

"I see no need to prolong this trial," Judge North stated. "Have you a final summation to offer, Lord Reginald?"

"I do, indeed," Lord Reginald replied. "While I have no doubt but that the crime before you warrants public execution, I most respectfully submit that merely hanging such a one from the gallows is not enough to satisfy the blight that has befallen our fair city. London is overrun with foreigners—refugees from Africa, India, Ireland, America, France. . . .

Who can say from what all distant shores they hail? Foreigners come, and they bring impudent ideas and uncivilized behaviors along with them. Our laws mean nothing to such as these. It is imperative that we make an example to any who would wish to live among us but not within our laws. Your Lordship, I submit that for her crimes, Grace Winslow must burn at the stake!"

The courtroom erupted in confusion as people shouted out their opinions to the men of the jury. But Lord Judge North shouted for silence.

"We are not here to make an example of this woman, however wretched she may be," he said. "We are here to exact justice for a crime committed against the Crown."

The courtroom fell silent.

"One week from today," decreed Lord Judge Aaron North, "at the gallows at Newgate Prison, for the crime of thievery, Grace Winslow will hang by the neck until dead."

5

*G*race did not shed a tear. Not when the judge pronounced the sentence, and not when the jailer shoved her into the women's room of Newgate prison to await execution. She gagged at the sickening stink of the cell, but she did not cry. Women lay sprawled on the floor, sick with the fever and delirium of typhoid . . . women, crazed with desperation, clawed their fingers raw on the stone walls . . . women sat straight and still, like statues of rock, their hopeless eyes fixed on nothing at all. Grace did her best to shrink away from all of them. She searched until she found an empty spot on the mucky floor, and there she settled herself. But she did not cry.

"Good Shepherd," Grace breathed, "lift me up onto your shoulders and carry me. Take me away to a place of safety, in this world or the next."

The jailer held up hunks of bread and pieces of cheese and a ladle for the covered barrel of fresh water. He even had a few apples. But all those were available only to women with money to pay. Most prisoners, like Grace, had none.

"We ain't given to charity here!" the jailer snapped to a lame woman who made a grab for the food.

Sometime before twilight, a shadow passed by a second grated window, one that opened out onto the street, and it lingered there. Immediately, the women roused themselves. In a sudden rush, the prisoners rose up and pushed toward the window. As many as could force their way close enough thrust their hands and arms through the grating.

"Bread, bread!" they begged. "Please, bread!"

Grace dared not relinquish her place on the floor, but she did stand up and try to see what was happening. She could make out someone on the street outside the window—or maybe it was several people, she couldn't quite tell. He—or they—looked to be putting hunks of bread into the hands of the most fortunate of the prisoners.

Although Grace watched in fascination, she made no move toward the window. Why should bread interest her? Why should a dying woman care?

She sank down again onto the floor, leaned her head back against the rough stone wall, and closed her eyes. The rub of the uneven blocks flooded Grace with memories of that other prison dungeon. It seemed so long ago and faraway. Yet she would never forget Zulina slave fortress.

❦

"Grace! Grace Winslow!"

Curled up on the floor, shivering with cold and scratching at the crawling lice, Grace opened her eyes. She shook her head to clear away the voices of her nightmare dreams.

"Grace, where are you?"

She pulled herself upright, ran her fingers through her wild hair, and blinked into the dank shadows of the cell.

"Grace—"

This time a choking cough cut the call short.

Now Grace's eyes were wide open. She jumped up and stared in disbelief. It was Charlotte!

Lady Charlotte lifted the skirt of her fine linen gown and gingerly picked her way through the throngs of unseemly women stretched out on the filthy prison floor. She walked on tiptoe in an effort to protect her finely embroidered kidskin slippers. Although she clutched a perfumed handkerchief over her nose and mouth, she still found it a struggle to breathe.

"Charlotte!" Grace exclaimed. "Whatever are you doing here?"

"Oh, my dear," Lady Charlotte cried. She rushed to Grace and threw her arms around her. "I came to help you."

"You are too late," Grace said.

"I tried to warn you about Lord Reginald," Lady Charlotte implored. "You should not have made him look the fool in front of his friends. He cannot bear such humiliation."

Oh, how angry Lord Reginald had been that day. "*If you are Christian men, where is the justice?*" That's what Grace had demanded of him and those he had assembled to destroy the fledgling group of abolitionists. "*Where is the mercy?*" Lord Reginald had tried to stop her, but the other men told him to sit down and let her speak. "*And I ask you, with your pride as thick as the London air, how can you begin to see the pathway your God walks, let alone walk beside Him with humility?*" She used the words she had read in Captain Ross's Bible against them, and Lord Reginald had not been able to stop her. Finally, in furious exasperation, he had tried to grab her. Grace had escaped, but only because of the help of the very men Lord Reginald trusted the most. In his eyes, it was the ultimate betrayal.

In the dusky shadows of the prison cell, with her arms around Grace, Lady Charlotte wept. "I am so sorry," she said.

"I am sorry for my husband . . . I am sorry for the pompous way I treated you when we were young girls . . . I am sorry for the sins of my people."

"You were not at the trial," Grace said.

"No," said Charlotte. "I had intended to be there, Grace . . . I wanted to be there . . . but Reginald forbade it."

Grace said nothing.

Charlotte dropped her arms to her sides. "I felt I must obey him, you see. Oh, how dearly I regret my cowardice."

Still Grace said nothing.

"Reginald came home from the trial with that cur Jasper Hathaway at his heels, and I heard Reginald laughing and bragging on and on about how quickly and efficiently he had maneuvered the proceedings against you. It was then that I made up my mind to come and stand alongside you."

Grace shook her head and said again, "You are too late."

"Maybe not," said Lady Charlotte. "I have already talked to Lord Judge North. If we can show him evidence that merits something less than the gallows, he will listen. He promised me as much."

A spark of hope lit Grace's eyes.

"Missus Peete can tell you about the handkerchief," Grace said. "She gave it to me. The servant of some wealthy lady left it behind when she picked up the wash, and no one ever came back to claim it. Missus Peete gave it to me as a gift."

"But what of the men's clothing found in your room?"

"I paid Nurse Cunningham for the cloth left over from sewing the children's uniforms," Grace said. "Missus Peete sewed me the shirt and breeches with her own hand. The stockings and hat I bought at the rag fair."

"Whatever for?" Lady Charlotte asked.

"So that I could at long last get myself to America," Grace said. "So that I could find my Cabeto before it is too late!"

Lady Charlotte stared at her in disbelief.

"I planned to pass myself off as a sailor boy from India and sign onto a ship bound for America. One leaves London in five days' time."

At Lady Charlotte's incredulous gape, Grace insisted, "I have to find Cabeto, Charlotte! I have to find a way to help him. I thought if I could just get to America . . . Oh, why did this all have to happen now, just when everything is finally ready?"

Tears flooded Grace's eyes and her shoulders trembled.

"An entire year has already gone by," Grace sobbed. "Unless I can do something very soon . . . Oh, Charlotte, Cabeto needs me *now*!"

"Tell me about the silk purse," Lady Charlotte said. "Tell me about the shillings they found."

"When I came to London from Africa, just before I got off the ship, Captain Ross gave me that purse with fifteen silver shillings in it. Missus Peete can tell you as much. I had to spend most of the shillings. But Nurse Cunningham paid me one shilling each week for my work at the Foundling Hospital, and whatever of it I could save went into that purse."

Lady Charlotte nodded thoughtfully.

"Charlotte, everything your husband says I stole was already mine!"

Before Lady Charlotte took her leave, she gave Grace a bundle that contained a cloth to clean herself with, a comb for her hair, and a clean dress. She also gave Grace a fresh meat pie and a crisp apple. And she slipped two shillings into Grace's hand. "For the jailer," Lady Charlotte said.

Two shillings bought Grace a clean space on the floor, water for washing, two ladles full of clean drinking water, and a blanket for the night. And the next morning, it was not the rough jailer who called out her name, but a man of a most respectable appearance. Dressed in a black suit of clothes and a broad-brimmed hat, he could have been taken for a clergyman come to comfort those on their way to the gallows, rather than the turnkey who ran the jail, were it not for the jangle of keys he wore at his waist.

The turnkey personally led Grace outside the prison doors. He walked her across Newgate Street, where they passed directly under the gallows. She followed the somber man in black all the way back to the courtroom where, just the day before, Lord Judge Aaron North had sentenced her to death.

"Grace Winslow?"

Lord Judge North started in surprise when he saw the young woman who stepped up into the dock.

Clean and combed and dressed in Charlotte's green silk frock, Grace did indeed look to be an entirely different person.

The courtroom was not nearly as full as it had been the day before for her trial. Lady Charlotte was there. She smiled encouragingly at Grace as she entered. To Grace's delight Missus Peete was also in attendance, seated in self-conscious discomfort on Lady Charlotte's left. Nurse Cunningham sat on the opposite side, to Lady Charlotte's right.

Lord Reginald Witherham had reclaimed his seat nearest the judge, but now the chairs around him sat empty. Lord Reginald crossed his legs, then he uncrossed them. He folded his arms, then he unfolded them. Nervously he laid his hands in his lap, one on top of the other. Lord Reginald cast a vicious stare across the witness box to his wife. He turned to Grace and glowered at her as she stood in the dock.

In the back of the courtroom, out of Lord Reginald's sight, Joseph Winslow crept in and sank down in a back-row seat. Grace didn't see her father enter.

"I have before me a declaration of evidence that concerns the conviction of Grace Winslow, who yesterday in this court was sentenced to death by hanging," said Lord Judge North. He glanced up at Lord Reginald, but only for an instant. Quickly he recovered himself and proceeded to read aloud Charlotte's written explanation for each of the charges made against Grace.

As Lord Judge North read the final words, Lord Reginald jumped to his feet.

"Please, Your Lordship, if I may prevail upon the Crown to speak!" he demanded. "This document is merely an obvious attempt on the part of a practiced thief to gain the Crown's sympathy. I do not place blame on you, Your Lordship, for mistaking the defendant's word as truth, for her words have even deceived my own wife. But, as I am certain you can see, her explanations are most preposterous. The very idea that a handkerchief of such quality would remain unclaimed at the hovel of a washerwoman stretches the credibility of any sensible person beyond—."

"It is not my handkerchief."

Lady Charlotte stood up from her chair and faced her husband.

"The handkerchief does not belong to me, and I will testify to that fact under oath. Surely, Husband, you do not claim such a dainty to be your own. If it is not a gift from Missus Peete, how exactly do you explain its presence in our house? If, indeed, it ever was in our house at all."

"But . . . the handkerchief most certainly is yours, my love," Lord Reginald insisted through clenched teeth. "Surely, in your present state of emotional confusion, and with the multitude of lovely things you have in your dressers and chests, you have forgotten this one."

In a moment of inspiration, Lord Reginald continued in a most animated manner, "Ah, indeed, I do believe I remember now! It was a gift from me to you. Yes, a token of my affection which I presented to you before our wedding."

Lady Charlotte turned her attention to Lord Judge North.

"Your Lordship, that is not my handkerchief!" Lady Charlotte declared. "I request that you allow me to so swear under oath."

Lord Judge North waved his hand in a dismissive gesture of exasperation. He had heard quite enough.

"I have considered the evidence," the judge said. "Moreover, I have duly noted, and taken into consideration, the many kindnesses attributed to this defendant in a sworn statement presented to me by one Priscilla Cunningham, most respected head nurse at the Foundling Hospital. Therefore, by the mercy of his Majesty, King George, I hereby grant Grace Winslow a conditional pardon."

Lord Reginald sprang to his feet. "Your Lordship!" he exclaimed. "I must indeed protest most strenuously!"

"Protest noted," said Lord Judge North. He did not look at Lord Reginald. The judge cleared his throat and continued: "The stated request is for transportation to our overseas penal colony in America. I shall grant the request for transportation."

Grace gasped out loud.

Lady Charlotte, crying with joy, hugged the ladies on each side of her. Both Nurse Cunningham and Missus Peete cheered wildly.

But Lord Judge North was not finished.

"However, inasmuch as the American colonies have recently declared themselves to be a free and independent country, they are no longer willing to accept our prisoners on their shores," the judge continued. "Therefore, the defendant,

Grace Winslow, shall be placed on a ship even now being made ready to sail in a fortnight to our new penal colony at New South Wales. She will remain there for the rest of her life."

Then Grace wept.

6

*N*ow, then, so ye doesn't know yer own mate, eh?"

Joseph Winslow, his clothes rumpled and his chin adorned with four days' growth of white bristle, positioned himself squarely in front of Jasper Hathaway. He paid not the slightest mind to the well-dressed ladies and gentlemen who hurried past him on their way to Sunday services. Joseph scratched at his greasy hair, knocking his stained hat askew.

"I know you well enough," replied Jasper Hathaway with undisguised disgust. He grasped the two sides of his silk coat and did his best to tug them together. As in his days in Africa, his coat strained at the seams. During the past year he had regained every bit of his former girth. "I simply do not care to pass my time with such a one as you. Now, kindly step aside and allow a gentleman to attend to his Sunday obligation."

Joseph let burst a cackle of sarcastic mirth. "Oh, so it's a gentleman ye be, is it?" he asked. "And if ye be sech a gentlemen, why is ye forever grovelin' at the feet o' that dandy, Lord Reginald Witherham?"

"You would do well to refrain from showing yourself to be so great a fool, Joseph Winslow!" Mister Hathaway blustered in disgust. "Pray move yourself to one side and allow me to pass."

"Me Grace is set to be shipped away to the prison island at the bottom of the world," Joseph said.

"Move aside, you drunken dupe!"

Jasper Hathaway tried to push his way past, but Joseph Winslow was determined to hold his ground. This turn of events took Mister Hathaway by surprise. He assumed the most threatening stance he could manage, balled his hands into fists, and swung his right arm back with every intention of punching Joseph full in the face. But the side seam of Jasper's coat, stretched beyond endurance, chose that moment to burst open. It thoroughly disconcerted Mister Hathaway.

Joseph, taking advantage of the moment, grabbed the man's extended arm in a vise-like grip and twisted it backward.

Jasper Hathaway yelped like a wounded hound.

"Look me in me eyes, Jasper 'athaway," Joseph ordered.

Mister Hathaway would not.

"Look me in me eyes and tell me ye is ready to send me girl to 'er death!"

Joseph gave Mister Hathaway's arm a cruel yank. As Jasper gasped and lurched, his artificial teeth popped out of his mouth. This unexpected turn of events so startled Joseph that he dropped his hold on the man's fleshy arm. Joseph gaped from the set of teeth grinning up from the street to the toothless man before him.

Jasper Hathaway snatched up his teeth and sucked them back into his mouth.

Joseph Winslow was not used to thinking quickly. So the clarity that suddenly crossed his mind astonished even him.

"It be ye!" he accused.

Mister Hathaway tried to push past Joseph, but Joseph blocked his way.

"Ye still be fast in Lord Reginald's employ, don't ye?" Joseph insisted. "But ye ain't at Zulina fortress anymore. Ye ain't in Africa at all. So what is it ye be doin' fer Lord Reginald, Jasper?"

Jasper Hathaway opened his mouth but said nothing.

"Ye be 'is 'ired rat!" Joseph exclaimed. "Ye spies on pretty young ladies fer 'im, doesn't ye? It be ye wot digs among their private things at 'is biddin'!"

"I have not the least idea about what you are going on about," Jasper Hathaway sputtered.

Once again he tried to push past Joseph. Once again, Joseph blocked his way.

"It were ye wot found me Grace's belongin's and gave them to Lord Reginald to wave about before the judge!"

"Grace was rightfully mine!" Jasper Hathaway shot back. "That is the truth of the matter. You know it to be so. Grace should have been my woman! She should have been my wife!"

Joseph stepped back. His face twisted to a disgusted scowl, as though he stood face to face with a pile of two-week-old garbage.

Right there was Jasper Hathaway's opportunity. He could easily have skirted Joseph Winslow and gotten away, but he did not. Instead, his shoulders slumped, his face sagged, and he stood still.

"I wanted to make her pay for leaving me," Mister Hathaway said. "I wanted her to pay, but I did not want her to die."

Joseph stared at the doughy man before him. So proud and haughty . . . so weak and pitiful.

"I needed the money!" Mister Hathaway said.

Now he was pleading.

"You know how it is without slaves to trade!"

Joseph's face hardened.

"Never once did I lay a hand on her, Joseph. That I swear to you."

Jasper Hathaway's tone approached desperation.

"I pressed coins into the hands of unsavory men, the kind who can follow in the shadows and sniff out trails and whisper questions that demand answers. When I found Grace at the Foundling Hospital, I passed along a shilling here to a doorman and two shillings there to the handyman, and it bought me access to everything I needed."

"Ye followed Grace the entire year?"

"Ever since she left Lord Reginald's estate that day. But I tell you the truth, Joseph, all the while I wished things were different. I surely did wish so."

"And now she be gone," Joseph said. "Onliest part o' either of us that be any good, Jasper. And now she be gone."

Joseph Winslow turned his rumpled back on Jasper Hathaway and walked away.

Mister Hathaway, the would-be gentleman, slumped in the doorway, alone and miserable, on a fancy street, in the fancy part of London.

⌇❧

There had been a time when Joseph Winslow's name had brought grudging respect from those around him. When he owned the slave fortress Zulina off Africa's Gold Coast, when he and his wife Lingongo controlled the slave traffic in the entire area, Joseph could walk the dusty streets outside his compound and white people would doff their hats and bow at the waist. In those days, even when he came to London, people allowed him to call himself a gentleman. He would go into a bookshop and lay down a gold piece to pay for a leather-bound volume, and the proprietor would call him "Sir." Out on the street, with a new book clutched under one arm and a recently purchased London frock for his daughter, Grace, bundled under the other arm, ladies curtsied and men bowed deeply as he passed by.

But that was then. That was before his disgrace at Zulina . . . before he lost everything and everyone . . . before he was forced out of Africa . . . before gambling and drink engulfed his life.

Further up Lombard Street, bells chimed from high atop the steeple of a most impressive church. Back when he was a young lad, Joseph Winslow had learned his catechism. All English children with any semblance of a decent upbringing did as much. But that was a lifetime ago. He had long since ceased to think of himself in religious terms. For all his talk of raising his daughter to be a proper English lass, he had been so spiritually remiss that she knew nothing of even the most basic catechism. Now, however, with the church doors flung open before him, with the church bells calling out and people streaming in, Joseph was overcome with a sudden longing to once again sit in a church pew.

Joseph moved hesitantly toward the church steps. The men and women of the downtown parish were well-dressed in silk and taffeta frocks, and lavishly turned-out silk topcoats. Joseph Winslow tugged at his own disheveled coat and did his best to mingle unobtrusively as he followed the aristocratic worshippers inside.

What astonished Joseph was the crowd of people that managed to pack into the small church. Nor were all the worshippers well-to-do. Oh, the ones who paraded on up to the front pews most certainly were. But many others—the ones who sat in the back of the sanctuary and those who stood in the aisles—looked to be more the working-class sort of folk.

Joseph eased himself into a corner with others who looked to be more like him.

"Ye likes the sea captain preacher, does ye?" whispered a man with a sun-leathered face.

Joseph stared at the stranger. Because some answer seemed expected of him, he shrugged his shoulders and shook his head evasively. But as it turned out, Joseph did like the sea captain preacher. He liked him very much, indeed. John Newton, that was the preacher's name. And what a story he had to tell: a story of wretchedness, of redemption, of amazing grace.

"I was the worst of the worst," the Reverend John Newton proclaimed from his pulpit. "The Lord God sent a storm from on high and He delivered me out of the deep waters. And though my sins be too numerous to count, the Lord God saved my soul. Today, even the most wretched and hopeless of souls can look at me and say, 'If God can save John Newton, He can save anyone!' That He can, too. For God's grace is greater than all our sins—mine and yours."

It was a shaken Joseph Winslow who walked out of St. Mary Woolnoth Church. It was a changed Joseph Winslow.

$\mathcal{L}$❤

Stealth and cunning were not words commonly applied to Joseph Winslow. Even so, he did manage to approach Heath Patterson's barn unnoticed, even by the vigilant young man who stood guard with a musket over his shoulder. Joseph folded himself into the shadows until he was thoroughly concealed beside a window with the cover slid open a crack. The crack was just wide enough to allow him to take in the entire discussion of slavery in America, and its emerging position as a serious social issue.

"Theirs is not a call for immediate abolition," Sir Thomas McClennon explained inside. "Few in that land ask so much. But many—and this includes some slave owners—do express genuine concern about the issue of the slave trade. Not only over its morality, but indeed, about its very utility."

"The Americans show a willingness to talk about slavery? That alone is a great change!" snapped Jesse, a young Negro man.

Joseph recognized Jesse. The first time Joseph had seen Grace in London—the time she had sought him out and things had gone so badly—Jesse had been outside on the street waiting for her.

With the discussion taking so energetic a turn, the would-be guard abandoned his post and moved up to the barn door in order to better listen. He grabbed up the musket he had rested on the ground and strode on in to join the others.

"Talk, talk, talk! That's all the Americans will ever do!" the young man chided as he walked. "Slave trade is their bread and milk. They will never allow real change on their soil. Why should they? It would prove too great a threat to their purse strings!"

Joseph Winslow chose that moment to slip back around through the shadows of the barn. Then he, too, walked in through the open door. So engaged in their heated discussion were the members of the group, that not one noticed his presence until he was directly behind them.

"I do beg your pardon!" Lady Susanna exclaimed when she spied the intruder. "Who might you be? And how did you—?"

"I be father to me darlin' daughter, Grace Winslow, wot loved the lot of you," Joseph said.

At Grace's name, the entire group caught a collective gasp.

"Ye 'as no call to trust me," Joseph continued. "I set fire to yer coffee 'ouse. I admits as much to ye, and I be sorry fer me actions. But I does repent of it with me 'eart and soul. And I must say that I warned the lot of ye afore'and. Not one 'air on yer 'ead was touched by the fire, was it? That's because I warned ye, ever'one. Though I could 'ave died fer squealin', I warned ye."

Ethan Preston stepped forward and bowed deeply before Joseph Winslow. "That you did, sir, and I thank you for it."

"Me Grace wot was to die on the gallows is bein' sent away to the bottom of the world," Joseph Winslow said.

Ena covered her face and wept.

"To me shame, I admits that in Africa I tried to kill 'er," Joseph said. "I tried to kill me own girl, God fergive me. Yet she stepped up and stood twixt me and death."

Joseph wiped his watery eyes with his sleeve.

"Grace saved me life," he said. "Now it be me turn to save 'er life. I 'as no money to give ye, but I will gladly forfeit wot remains of me own life and be a slave to any man or woman amongst ye wot will rescue me Grace."

7

"We profess to be a land of laws!" Lord Reginald Witherham insisted to Sir Geoffrey Phillips, who sat before him most impatiently. "It is that precise hypocrisy that stirs up such a fury within me. For were we truly a land of laws, we would actually *abide* by the laws we have established. Is that not so?"

Lord Reginald paced the floor. Each time he turned on his heel, his steps grew more furious. Sir Geoffrey extracted a handkerchief from the pocket of his waistcoat and mopped at his forehead.

"Were we truly the law-abiding people we claim to be, a penalty of death would mean that a criminal so sentenced would actually die for his crime . . . or her crime, as the case may be. Surely it does not require a person of great intellect to grasp so simple a concept. Do you not agree?"

"The Crown has spoken," replied an exasperated Sir Geoffrey. "And, in all truth, Lord Reginald, the punishment of transportation is far greater than almost any person could bear. I say . . ."

"You say! The Crown says! What do I care about such endless rhetoric?"

Lord Reginald paused in his pacing. He grabbed the knob on the parlor door and flung the door open. A young maid happened to be passing along the hallway at that precise moment, and he grabbed hold of her by the arm.

"Let us see if the concept of law and punishment is indeed as simple to grasp as I imagine it to be," Lord Reginald said,

Bronze skin, auburn hair, dark eyes . . . the young maid Lord Reginald held in his grasp bore a fair resemblance to Grace Winslow. This girl, like Grace, looked to be of mixed parentage.

"Here now, Ena," Lord Reginald exclaimed, "do join us and give us the benefit of your wisdom."

The girl's dark eyes widened in terror. She frantically searched before and behind for a way of escape.

"Really, Reginald, you do force a point much too far," said Sir Geoffrey.

"No, no, not in the least," Lord Reginald argued. "My point is that it does not take a person of great intellect to grasp the concept I purport." To the girl he said, "Ena, what does a legal sentence of death mean?"

"I . . . uh . . . please, sir, it is not my place to say, I'm sure," Ena stammered.

"Come, come, I asked you a straightforward question. Surely even such a one as you is able to provide me with a straightforward answer. A legal sentence of death . . . what does it mean?"

"I suppose that . . . well, that a person . . . that a person must die, sir."

"There, now!" Lord Reginald announced. "Even a foolish servant girl understands the meaning of a legal sentence of death. Grace Winslow was sentenced to hang from the gallows for her crime, and hang she should."

"Oh no, sir," Ena said. "Not Grace."

Lord Reginald stepped back. His eyebrows arched on his tight face. In mock amazement he exclaimed, "No? So now you fancy yourself wiser and filled with greater insight than His Lordship the judge who pronounced Grace Winslow guilty and worthy of the gallows?"

"No, sir," Ena pleaded with increasing desperation. "I would never fancy myself in such a way as you say. But, sir, people do change their minds, don't they? The Lord Judge—his Lordship . . . most surely he changed his mind. Why, even Grace's own father changed his mind, didn't he?"

"Grace's father?" Lord Reginald responded.

"Yes, sir. He once tried to kill Grace, he did, but now he wants to save her from the transportation. He's even willing to make himself a slave to do it, too. He said as much to Mister Ethan and the others."

Cold fury wiped all traces of jovial mockery from Lord Reginald's face. He grasped Ena's arm in a vise-tight grip and through clenched teeth demanded, "Did you say Mister Ethan Preston?"

It was at that moment that Ena realized she had said far too much. She covered her face and sobbed.

"Ethan Preston and his pieced-together band of criminals who call themselves an abolition group?" Lord Reginald demanded. "Are they the ones Joseph Winslow approached?"

Ena fell to her knees and wailed.

"For God's sake, Reginald, let the girl go!" Sir Geoffrey said.

With a low growl, Lord Reginald kicked Ena away from him.

"Leave my house!" he ordered.

Ena scrambled to her feet and stumbled for the door.

"Joseph Winslow is a simpering ingrate!" Sir Reginald raged. "He is happy enough to take my money, but when the days grow dark, he slithers away behind my back and crawls into the enemy camp to betray me. Well, I will not be made into a laughingstock again, not by a half-breed slave girl and not by her drunken fool of a father. I pledged my vengeance on that little wretch, and I was as good as my word. Now I pledge my vengeance on Joseph Winslow, as well. Let his daughter languish on the far side of the world. What does it matter to me? Joseph Winslow will hang from the gallows in her place."

Sir Geoffrey Phillips stared in astonishment at Lord Reginald. He saw fury ignite the man's eyes and set his face aflame. Sir Geoffrey had not the least doubt that Lord Reginald Witherham would do exactly as he had said.

Slowly Sir Geoffrey shook his head. "What has happened to us, Reginald?" he asked. "What have we become?"

ℒ❧

When next the abolition group met in Heath and Rebekah Patterson's barn, Oliver Meredith stood guard at the door with far more vigilance than he had done at the previous meeting. He did admit Joseph Winslow, although not without a fair bit of trepidation. And as Joseph walked forward and took a chair next to Heath Patterson, more than a few in the assembly cast uncomfortable glances his way. The meeting got off to a slow start since no one seemed of a mind to say much of substance in Joseph's presence.

"William Wilberforce continues to press forward in Parliament with his select committee," Thomas McClennon reported. "And I must say, it is most fortunate indeed that he is able to proceed with the good graces of Prime Minister William Pitt. In no small part due to this happy alignment, the cause of abolition of the African slave trade continues to win political support. It is imperative, therefore, that we be outspoken in our own support of those efforts."

Murmurs of agreement arose from the group. Still, no one suggested a specific action. The murmurings drifted off and an uneasy silence settled in the barn.

Finally, with a decidedly irritated sigh and a flounce of her full skirts, Lady Susanna abruptly stood up and stepped forward. The power of her elegance immediately demanded attention.

"If not one of you brave men will speak to the question that hangs heavy in every mind here today, I shall do so myself," Lady Susanna said. "Our dear Ena was set upon by Lord Reginald Witherham. Now he once again threatens to use his influence and wealth to ready the gallows."

"So long as Lord Reginald's wounded pride continues to fester, not one of us is safe," Heath Patterson said. "He is a vengeful man, and he—"

"And he has wealth and class on his side!" Oliver Meredith's words rang hard as the young man swung the musket down from his shoulder and once again strode into the barn to add his impassioned opinion to the discussion. "Wealth and class he has, which means he also wields the power."

Sir Thomas McClennon raised himself to his full aristocratic height and addressed Oliver. "Wealth and power are indeed formidable attributes, my dear sir," he agreed with a polite bow. "But they are far from everything. It is my considered opinion that—"

But Sir Thomas's considered opinion was not to be heard, for at that moment the unguarded barn doors flew open and Sir Geoffrey Phillips stepped inside.

Rebekah Patterson screamed in alarm. Oliver Meredith rushed for his musket, and Jesse did the same.

Sir Geoffrey made a deep courtesy to the group, stretching his leg forward and tipping his hat with the most gracious of manners. He reached for the barn door and held it open for Lady Charlotte, who followed behind him.

"There is no need for apprehension, dear sirs and madams," said Sir Geoffrey. "Most certainly there is no reason to take up arms. Lady Charlotte Witherham and I pose not the least danger to any of you."

Sir Geoffrey's eyes went from Oliver and Jesse to Lady Susanna, then to Joseph Winslow and on to Ethan Preston. But when he saw Sir Thomas, who sat beside Ethan, a smile of friendly recognition crossed Sir Geoffrey's face.

"We have come on behalf of Grace Winslow," Sir Geoffrey said. "I pray we are not too late."

8

$\mathcal{C}$harleston is not the city it once was," Macon Waymon lamented as he stepped over a dead dog sprawled across his path. With a shudder, he patted down his perfectly pressed white cotton shirt and straightened the lay of the already impeccable waistcoat under the unadorned knee-length coat of his suit.

"That it is not," agreed Samuel Shaw. He preferred lace-trimmed garments with puffy ties at the neck and white silk stockings, all of which he wore with easy comfort despite the filth of the streets. Mister Shaw sighed and shook his head in disgust at the rivulets of stinking sewer waste that seeped from a street drain up ahead and befouled the entire road. "That it most assuredly is not."

That his friend also so fondly recalled the glories of pre-war Charleston—or Charles Town as it was called then—certainly strengthened the case Macon Waymon had prepared for their afternoon together. And, indeed, much had changed. Thanks to a booming indigo industry and the area's world famous sea-island cotton, South Carolina had been one of the wealthiest of the American colonies. But then came the war for independence, and it had indeed been cruel to the state. More battles were fought on South Carolina soil than in any other state, and those battles had left both the land and the people deeply scarred.

In the past handful of years, literally thousands of folks had crowded into the constricted peninsula south of Charleston's Boundary Street. Many of them were now packed into the tenements and shacks that lined countless narrow streets and alleys.

Samuel Shaw scowled at the piles of refuse that littered the street. Obviously, the city scavenger had not found it convenient to collect for quite some time. "My dear sir, why must you insist on strolling along these putrid streets?" he reproached Macon. "I do find it most objectionable! And with the cow yards and hog pens up ahead, too. Really! Can we not remove ourselves to a more pleasant locale?"

"Philadelphia . . . New York . . . Boston . . ." Macon said. "I do believe that those are the only great cities of these United States other than Charleston. Do you suppose they suffer such degradation as we?"

"I'm sure I do not know," Samuel groused. "I certainly would not think it of Philadelphia. Not with the country's capitol still located there."

"But you will agree that the situation here is desperate."

"Undoubtedly so. But come, come, Macon. Surely you did not call me away from my work to talk over the hard times!"

Macon Waymon turned in at an unremarkable traveler's inn and proceeded straight through to the small garden out back. Samuel Shaw had little choice but to follow him. The garden had a table and two chairs situated in the far corner, and the table was already set for two. Macon headed directly for it. No sooner had he sat down than a colored man hurried over with two cups of hot tea. Without a word exchanged, the man set the tea before the two, bowed slightly, and hurried off.

"The fortunes of Charleston . . . indeed, of all South Carolina . . . rise and fall with the planters," Macon said. "Unfortunately, the planters are failing."

Macon took a sip of his tea.

"But a great revolution is just around the corner, Samuel," he continued. "And if we act quickly and wisely, both you and I can soon be extremely rich and powerful men."

Samuel raised his eyebrows. "Goodness me," he said. "This sounds to be another terror tale involving African slaves. I'm sure I cannot see how that would concern me, however, seeing as how I am neither a landowner nor a slave owner."

But the story Macon Waymon told Samuel Shaw was not one of slave rebellion. No, it was the story of a Yankee boy who left Massachusetts for Savannah, Georgia, and took a job as a tutor on a plantation owned by one Missus Greene, the widow of a war hero.

"Talk on that plantation was the same as talk here," Macon said. "Hard times. Even worse there than here, though, for they had no money crop at all. Just that useless green seed cotton they waste their time raising. Little better than a weed, that is."

Samuel shook his head in sympathetic understanding. "They say it takes a full ten hours of painstaking handwork to separate one pint of cotton lint from three pounds of those tough little seeds."

"Yes," said Macon. "Well, this Yank watched the slaves as they cleaned the cotton on Missus Greene's plantation. As he watched, he studied the particular way those slaves moved their hands as they worked. When he went back to the plantation workshop, he built himself a machine that copied just what their hands did!"

Samuel took a deep drink from his teacup and carefully set it back down on the table. "I do not see the importance in that," he said. "We have available to us many devices that separate cotton bolls from the cotton seeds."

"That we do," Macon allowed, "so long as we concern ourselves solely with the smooth-seeded, long-staple cotton we enjoy on the coast of South Carolina. But not one of those devices will work with the upland short-staple cotton. Those seeds are too sticky and the cotton fibers too tightly attached to the seeds. Which is precisely why this new cotton engine design is so full of possibilities."

"If this new machine is so wondrous, why are people not already making use of it?" Samuel asked.

"For the simple reason that hardly anyone knows about it yet," said Macon. "See, this particular Yank—Eli Whitney is his name—agreed to keep the whole thing hushed up until he and his partner in the venture got a patent on it. But Missus Greene, she just couldn't keep quiet. She invited a group of her friends and relatives up to Mulberry Grove and persuaded the Yank to give them a demonstration. My wife Luleen's sister's husband, Edward, was right there to see it all, which is how I came to know about it. Edward told me that in one hour's time, that little engine turned as much cotton as a whole passel of slaves hard at work could do in a full day!"

Macon Waymon picked up his teacup, but in his excitement he set it back down without taking a drink. "New days are coming to South Carolina, Samuel," he said, "and I aim to be the one ready to usher them in!"

Of course, ushering in a new day was not something that would happen automatically. Macon Waymon's vision required that he own vast fields—all planted in green seed cotton growing tall in the South Carolina sunshine well before other people became aware of the significance of Mister Whitney's cotton engine. The fields were available, all right, but two small matters stood between Mister Waymon and his dream: first, some of those fields were already planted in other crops, and second, the fields all belonged to other growers.

Still, both of those matters were subject to change. Take the indigo plantations, for instance. Before the war for independence, much of the state's prosperity depended on indigo, especially since the British government had been so willing to subsidize it. But now that the United States was free from England, that subsidy had been cut off. To make matters worse, chemical dyes were now available. The result was that indigo growers were losing a great deal of money on a crop no longer profitable. Even rice cultivation had become more difficult and undependable. Scot-Irish settlers in the upland regions had cleared so much land in the red clay hills for their crops of corn and beans that the natural flow of the Santee River was completely disrupted. Now the river flooded during planting and harvest time, and in the growing months, the water level was too low to do its job.

If Macon Waymon wanted to buy land, he would find no shortage of indigo and rice growers in such financial pain that they would be most eager to sell. Or even short-staple cotton growers, for that matter. Most of them could not earn enough from their crops to pay their bills.

But, of course, it took money to acquire land. Waymon was rich in slaves and muscle power, wealthy in ideas and willingness, but his financial fortunes had suffered in recent years. He simply did not have the money to buy up the fields and get them planted immediately. And for this venture to succeed, immediacy was most definitely required.

Samuel Shaw, on the other hand, came from a well-moneyed family in Virginia. He also had a strong incentive to acquire land in South Carolina. Nine months earlier, amid great fanfare, President George Washington had laid the cornerstone for the new national capitol building in the swampland between Maryland and Virginia. The new location would be called Washington, the District of Columbia. Ever since that momentous day, Mister Shaw had dreamed of being elected South Carolina's representative to Congress and going to Washington, the District of Columbia, to serve in the new capitol building.

But as things presently stood, Mister Shaw could not even run for a local office. For in South Carolina, to stand for any elected office at all, one must not only be an adult white male, but must own fifty acres of land. While Mister Shaw easily met the former requirement, he owned only a single house in the city of Charleston. Certainly he could well afford to purchase a large plantation, but he had not the slightest interest in doing so, nor would he have any idea how to manage it if he did.

Macon Waymon leaned in close, his face hot with excitement. "Together we can build up the richest cotton plantations in the state of South Carolina, Samuel. Perhaps in the entire world!"

Certainly, Macon had Samuel's attention. And yet, Samuel Shaw was not entirely convinced.

"Even if all you say were true, even if the cotton came through the new engine undamaged—it still would be nothing but short-fiber cotton," he pointed out. "The whole world knows sea-island cotton is fine and strong and soft and desirable. And the whole world also knows short-fiber cotton is inferior in every way."

"True," agreed Macon. "But sea-island cotton will always be scarce and expensive. Few growers have the sophisticated knowledge and experience needed to grow it. And fewer still have access to the rare, exquisite sandy soil its cultivation requires. So even if the cotton engine does do some damage to the cotton, even if the short-fiber sells for just half the price of sea-island, consider the amount of cotton we can produce! Even with those limitations, Samuel, our profits cannot help but be enormous."

"You assume that European manufacturers will accept the crop. Remember, they have always considered short-staple nothing but worthless weed cotton," said Samuel.

Macon smiled and winked. "When they see the low price tag attached to it, they will be overjoyed. I guarantee it!"

For a long time the two men sat in silence, each lost in his own thoughts.

"If I put up the money by week's end . . ." said Samuel.

"If I pull my best workers away from the rice fields . . ." said Macon.

"If I lay my hands on the deeds of the growers most in distress and therefore most likely to sell . . ." said Samuel.

"If we get the cotton crops in now . . ." said Macon.

"If you get Eli Whitney's cotton engine in your hands . . ." said Samuel.

"If I get the right man to work it . . ." said Macon.

Both men fell silent. Planted in the spring, cotton was picked in September and October. Despite starting a bit late, with good fortune and dollars placed in the right hands, the entire crop could all be run through the cotton engine, compressed, packed, and stacked at the Charleston ports by early the following spring.

Macon and Samuel sank back in their chairs, twin smiles lighting up their faces.

This time next year, Macon Waymon thought, *I will be a rich man.*

By the time the swamp on the Potomac River is turned into a city and the capitol building is completed, Samuel Shaw thought, *I will be seated as a representative of the state of South Carolina.*

9

A ray of early March sunshine forced its way through the city's fog and misty clouds, and planted the hope of spring into the hearts of winter-weary Londoners. But in Abraham Hallam's heart it struck nothing but dread.

"How many men do we still lack to fill the crew?" Captain Hallam barked to Archie Rhodes, his first mate.

"Five, sir," Archie replied. "At bare minimum."

"Well, then, fetch us five men today!" the captain ordered.

"Where from, sir?" Archie asked.

"I don't care!" said Captain Hallam. "Scour Newgate Prison, if you must. Already winter's deprivations are too long past. Unless we sail immediately, the hurricanes will be upon us before we can catch the trade winds!"

Ever since the thirteen United States had gained their independence from Britain, filling up a crew docket had become a matter of frustrating difficulty on every ship bound for America. As tales spread, fewer and fewer men were willing to risk the journey into what was now widely considered wild territory. To make matters worse, Britain was again at war with France. It was well known that the newly independent United States cast a more favorable eye toward the side of the French than the side of the English. The Americans aligned themselves with France's revolution against the monarchy. This made it harder still to assemble a decent sailing crew.

Still, the American demand for British goods remained strong, which meant there was plenty of money to be made from a full ship.

The promise of spring set Captain Hallam in a foul and impatient mood, a perfect time for Sir Geoffrey Phillips to meet with him and propose that he take on a young Indian sailor willing to work in exchange for passage. Before Sir Phillips made his appearance, however, he made certain that a full leather purse was on display in the front pocket of his expensive woolen waistcoat.

✍

In his private chambers, Lord Judge Aaron North pulled off his wig and caressed his throbbing head. At the sharp knock on his door, he growled impatiently, "Who is there at this hour?"

"Two fine ladies, m'lord," his servant replied.

Lord Judge North hesitated. But with his wig still tossed aside on the desk, he called out permission for them to enter.

"My lord," Lady Susanna cooed as she performed the most perfect full curtsy before the judge. Her pink and white frock floated around her in a sea of silk and lace as she bowed low.

Lord Judge North's eyes bulged.

"With our deepest apologies and most sincere appreciation for your indulgence, Lady Charlotte and I beg a few minutes of Your Lordship's most valuable time," Lady Susanna entreated.

Lord Judge North snatched up his wig and shoved it onto his head.

"Of course, my dear ladies," he said. "The pleasure would, indeed, be all mine."

Lord Judge Aaron North cleared his throat nervously. In his rush to his feet, he almost knocked his chair over.

"Do sit down, my ladies," he insisted. "Tell me, please, how may I be of assistance to you this fine day?"

"It is about the servant girl, Grace Winslow. She stood before you yesterday in the dock," Lady Susanna continued in her soft purr of a voice. "Lady Charlotte and I both know you to be a man of singular justice and mercy, Your Lordship, which is the only reason we are able to gather the courage to come before you now. But it is also why we feel so certain that you will desire to set a cruel injustice aright."

"I have already reconsidered Miss Winslow's case," Lord Judge North said warily. "I cannot think what more might be appropriate for me to—"

Lady Charlotte held in her hand a drawstring purse cut from the same yellow-gold silk as her gown, woven through with black figures and trimmed with hand-made lace. It was a most captivating ensemble. At this precise moment the purse slipped from her hand and clattered noisily to the floor. With a wide-eyed gasp, Lady Charlotte scooped up the purse and laid it on Lord Judge North's desk.

"Oh, I do apologize, Your Lordship!" she exclaimed. "This purse is quite simply too heavy for me, I fear."

Lord Judge North stared at the purse, but what he saw was not the matching silk of Lady Charlotte's fetching ensemble. What he saw were gold crowns visible through the loosely tied drawstring.

Throughout his entire plea for Grace Winslow's release, Sir Thomas McClellan stood before Jonathon Cartwright in Cartwright's cabin aboard the transportation ship, *Albatross*. Sir Thomas stood for the simple reason that Captain Cartwright never offered him a chair. When Sir Thomas finished his petition, the captain stared at him.

"And why should a gentleman such as yourself take such an interest in the predicament of a servant girl of African descent?" he asked.

"Purely to correct a grievous injustice," Sir Thomas replied. "Of course, I shall make the inconvenience worth your time."

Sir Thomas retrieved a coin purse from the pocket of his waistcoat and laid it on Captain Cartwright's desk.

"You can put that purse back where you got it, sir," the captain said. "I do not accept bribes."

Sir Thomas smiled as he re-pocketed the gold crowns.

"Very good, sir," he replied. "It seems that you are in a class by yourself."

"No, sir," said Captain Cartwright. "That I most assuredly am not."

"As you are obviously a man of high principles, I am certain you will understand my concern for a prisoner I know to be innocent of all charges leveled against her."

"She may well be innocent," the captain replied. "In that, she would not be alone. And I shall be most pleased to transfer her to the hulks on the Thames, or to another ship, or even to hand her over to you. You need only provide me with the appropriate documents from the Crown."

"And if such documents are not forthcoming?"

"In such a case, sir, in a fortnight the prisoner shall sail to New South Wales on my ship. I shan't waste any more of your time. Good day, sir."

Lord Judge Aaron North, still in his chambers although it was well past the dinner hour, imagined himself riding in great comfort over the roughest of London's cobblestone streets in the fine new carriage he would now be able to afford. He dipped his quill into the ink pot in order to write a note in his own fine hand. In it, he gave explicit instructions to Captain Jonathon Cartwright to release prisoner Grace Winslow forthwith into the custody of Sir Thomas McClellan, who would then be responsible to see that the prisoner paid her debt to the Crown. Carefully Lord Judge North folded the letter and slipped it into a creamy linen envelope. Making use of the candle flame before him, he softened his sealing wax just enough to allow a single large dollop to fall across the flap of the envelope. He pressed his official ring firmly into the melted wax.

When the letter arrived, sealed with the authority of His Lordship the Judge, Captain Cartwright opened it and carefully read the message. Without comment, he instructed his second in command to fetch the prisoner Grace Winslow and to deliver her into Sir Thomas McClellan's care.

"Sir . . . Sir Thomas—" Grace stammered when she saw McClellan standing before her.

"Not now," Sir Thomas cautioned as he rushed her toward his carriage. "We have not a moment to waste on dallying."

When the carriage arrived at the Pattersons' barn, Grace's heart leapt with joy. Although she had only minutes to enjoy her reunion with her abolitionist friends, she gasped in amazement to find that Charlotte and Sir Phillips were among them.

"Quickly now," Ethan Preston insisted. "This is an imperfect plan at best. Our success depends upon swift and precise timing."

"And on th' grace o' God," said Joseph Winslow as he stepped forward from the shadows.

"Father!" Grace gasped.

But already the women were rushing her out to the back where a bucket of water and a piece of soap awaited her. After a good wash down by Rebekah Patterson, Lady Susanna and Lady Charlotte dressed Grace in an oddly cut pair of men's pantaloons. Then they tightly bound her chest with strips of cotton.

"What are you doing?" Grace demanded. "I can hardly breathe!"

"Hush, Grace. We are preparing you for your voyage," said Lady Susanna.

"According to your own plan, since we have no better one," added Lady Charlotte. She slipped a loose-fitting tunic over Grace's head.

Grace had never before seen such a garment. She held out her arms and inspected the strange costume.

"My voyage to where?" Grace asked. "The prison at New South Wales?"

"No!" Lady Charlotte whispered with a smile. "To South Carolina. So you can search for Cabeto!"

Cabeto! No, it could not be! How could such a miracle be possible? And yet, why would Charlotte tell her this if it were not true?

"Come, Heath!" Rebekah Patterson called to her husband.

Using a long red scarf, Heath Patterson secured Grace's hair in a neatly wound red turban.

"It's called a *rumal*," Heath told Grace. "I brought it back with me from India when I sailed for the East India Company."

When the women brought Grace back into the barn, the men gasped at the change in her appearance. But Grace took no notice of her old friends. Her eyes were only on one person—Joseph Winslow.

"Father?" she asked incredulously. "Can it really be you?"

"Aye, 'tis yer pap," Joseph said. "But I be a changed man, Daughter. I be in this place t'day to 'elp ye git away, to go find yer man. Like ye 'elped me git away."

For the first time in more years than she could remember, Grace threw her arms around her father and hugged him.

"Bygones be bygones, then?" Joseph Winslow asked hopefully.

But time was precious, Ethan Preston reminded the two.

"From this day forth, you are Ashok Iravan, a boy of fourteen from India, too young to see the first of your beard," Mister Preston informed Grace. "You have some sea experience and are willing to work for nothing but free passage. Sir Geoffrey Phillips, whom you have met before—" Here, Sir Phillips doffed his hat and bowed deeply to Grace. "—Sir Phillips has secured you a position on the last merchant ship to leave for South Carolina this season."

Sir Geoffrey handed her an envelope sealed with his personal seal. "Your papers of identification. Guard them well."

"This letter of introduction is for your use when you arrive in America," said Sir Thomas McClelland as he handed Grace another envelope, this one sealed with his seal. "It is addressed to one Reverend Francis Asbury. He is a traveling preacher of the Methodist persuasion, and I am told by mutual friends a man of considerable influence and connections. He is well known, so ask after him in Charleston. It is my hope that he can assist you in your search."

"I am still of the opinion that I should accompany her," said Oliver Meredith, the boisterous young member of the abolitionist group. "I, too, could sign on as a seaman. I would welcome the adventure. Once in the colonies, I could mix with the peasants and keep an eye out on the situation there. It would provide me with a perfect vantage point from which to make certain no one takes liberties with Grace."

"You?" scoffed Jesse. "You be too English to blend easily with Americans!"

"Not at all!" Oliver shot back.

"Americans do not call their fellow men 'peasants,'" Jesse replied with disdain. "And should you speak the word 'colonies' there, you'd be fortunate to escape with naught but a sound flogging!"

"Jesse is right," said Ethan Preston. "In America, everyone who bears arms considers himself fully equal with his neighbor. This is no time for you to pursue an adventure, Oliver, however noble your motives."

"It is me that knows America," Jesse said.

"As that is so, you most assuredly must understand that in that country it is every *white* man who is considered equal, do you not?" responded Sir Thomas. "You may be a free man here in England, but on the other side of the Atlantic Ocean, you would almost certainly find yourself a slave once again."

"And what of Grace?" Jesse demanded.

"I must go," Grace said, "whatever the cost."

"Charleston is indeed a most dangerous place for one such as you," said Sir Thomas. "Keep yourself to yourself . . . Ashok Iravan. Mister Preston and I will do everything we can to arrange for someone to meet you."

Heath Patterson called the others to join him in a circle, then he raised his voice in prayer: "Almighty God in Heaven, we beseech Thy mercies on behalf of our sister Grace. We entrust her into Thy bountiful protection on this perilous voyage. Mayest Thou look upon her with mercy, and mayest Thou grant her Thy safety and Thy protection."

One by one, the others joined in, each offering a prayer.

Sir Phillips's carriage rolled through the streets of London and out to the docks. Already a crowd of men and boys busily loaded boxes and barrels into boats for transport out to the merchant ship, the *Ocean Steed*, which lay at anchor beyond London Bridge. Grace's head pounded with all the advice her friends had thrown out to her:

"Accentuate your accent and insist it is Indian."

"Never, ever take off your clothes."

"If you cannot answer a question, pretend you don't understand the language."

"Speak no more than absolutely necessary."

"In all things, at all times, be a man."

But it was the final words from Joseph Winslow, called out as the carriage lurched forward, that pierced her heart most deeply: "God be gracious to ye, Daughter. I'll be prayin' fer ye ever' day of me life. That be me vow to ye."

10

"*A*shok Iravan! What kind'a name do that be?" Archie Rhodes sneered as he tossed a rolled-up hammock toward Grace.

"Indian, sir," Grace replied. *Accentuate your accent.* "I come from India."

"I know where Indians be from," Archie snapped. "Does you take me for a fool?"

"No, sir," said Grace.

Speak no more than absolutely necessary!

Archie carefully scrutinized the dark-skinned addition to the ship's crew. "What's that you be wearing? A court jester, is you, now?"

"A tunic, sir. The clothing of my people."

Insist it is Indian.

"Well, I don't like it. Take it off and throw it overboard," Archie ordered. He tossed a worn seaman's blouse to Grace. "You dress in civilized clothes like ever'one else on this ship."

Never take off your clothes!

Panic rose up in Grace. The tight cloth that bound her chest felt as though it would smother her.

"Quick now!" Archie ordered. "Change outta that costume and do it right fast!"

Grace gasped for breath.

If you cannot answer a question, pretend you don't understand the language.

Grace forced the look of panic off her face and carefully replaced it with perplexed confusion. "*Degguna*," she pronounced. Even as she said it, she breathed a prayer that Archie Rhodes would not recognize the difference between the African word for "I don't understand" and whatever the Indian word might be.

"Ach!" Archie spat. "Stupid nabob!"

Archie shoved Grace aside and turned his attention to the man behind her.

Quickly—gratefully—Grace followed the line of men along the deck—some fresh and curious, others weather-beaten and worn. One by one they hauled themselves down the ladder to the dark hold. Belowdecks, with the overhead so low Grace couldn't even stand upright, each man claimed a spot for himself by hanging his hammock from hooks attached overhead and stowing his small sea chest. Grace eased in between a young sandy-haired boy who looked as though he might burst into tears at any moment and a tall, pox-scarred fellow of fourteen or fifteen who greatly overdid his self-confident swagger.

The sandy-haired boy stared at Grace. "You be the bloke from India?"

"Yes," said Grace. "Ashok Iravan. I am . . . Ashok."

"I be Jackie Watson," the boy said with the trace of a sniffle. "I never been on a ship before, and I wish I wasn't 'ere now."

"Yes," Grace murmured.

"Can we stick close by, you and me? 'Elp each other out a bit?"

Grace nodded. It would actually be good to have a friend . . . if she were very careful.

"Up to the main deck wi' ye, mates." A seasoned sailor barked the order down into the hold. "Now. Capt'n says so."

Grace followed the others to the ladder, but, mumbling an excuse about something forgotten, she hurried back to her hammock. Quickly she glanced around her. She saw no one, so she slipped the tunic off over her head. She pulled on the sailor blouse and stuffed the Indian shirt into her sea chest. But when she turned back toward the ladder, she ran headlong into Jackie, who gaped at her, his mouth open wide.

"Why is you bandaged up that way?" he blurted.

"I . . . it was . . . a beating," Grace stammered. She kept her eyes carefully averted from the boy's face. "My Indian master. He beat me."

"'E got you somethin' good."

Too flustered to answer, Grace hurried past the boy and on up to the main deck.

May God be gracious to you.

Ashok Iravan might not have been the experienced sailor Sir Geoffrey Phillips had portrayed to Captain Hallam, but Grace did in fact know a good deal more about sailing ships and life at sea than many of the other crewmen. The mid-sized ship *Ocean Steed* was brig-rigged, same as the *Willow*, the ship that had brought her from Africa to London barely a year before. She immediately recognized the distinctive two-masted square-rigging. Already familiar with such a ship, she jumped to and tried her best to help the sailors who were setting sails.

"'Tis an excitin' adventure wot awaits us," Jackie said to Grace afterward, his admiration bubbling over at his new friend's familiarity with a sailing ship.

Before Grace could answer, a sudden commotion echoed up from below. She gasped and shrank back.

"A'feared of horses, is you?" Jackie asked.

"Horses!" Grace exclaimed. "That isn't African slaves?"

Jackie laughed out loud. "There be no slaves on a English merchant ship, not African or any other kind!"

No slaves? From the moment Charlotte first whispered to Grace that she would sail on a ship headed for America, Grace had assumed it would be packed with slaves, just like the ship that had carried her Cabeto away. What other cargo would be carried to such a country?

Just about everything, as a matter of fact. For although American artisans were fine for repair work and one-of-a-kind items, even average men and women in the States preferred to buy most of their manufactured goods from England and Scotland. It was true that slave ships aplenty came into the harbor at South Carolina, but those ships arrived from Africa, not from England. No, the *Ocean Steed*'s hold was filled with fine-tooled furniture and English-bred riding horses, all specially ordered by wealthy Carolina aristocrats.

That night, as Grace adjusted her exhausted body into her hammock, she did her best to remember again the details of Cabeto's face. So much had flooded her since she last traced his picture in her mind. . . .

"You be well enough to sleep?" Jackie whispered.

"What?" Grace asked with a start. "Oh, yes. Just weary, is all."

"I means, the beatin'. Is you well enough from that?"

"Oh! Yes, of course. I'm used to it."

In all things, at all times, be a man.

11

"For a civilized country to continue as such, when a charge is rightly considered and a judgment properly passed, that judgment absolutely must be duly carried out," Lord Reginald Witherham stated through clenched teeth.

It was only with great effort that he managed to control his voice. Even so, the vein on his forehead throbbed, and he laced and unlaced his fingers obsessively.

Lady Charlotte made note of her husband's simmering fury. With measured calm, she replied, "In a civilized country, Husband, one's own handkerchief is not used against one to prove a preposterous charge of thievery in order to elicit a vengeful death sentence."

There was a time, not long past, when Lady Charlotte feared her husband. She no longer did.

"In all matters, a wife should support her husband," pronounced Lord Reginald.

"And your actions, Reginald?" responded Lady Charlotte. "Do you truly believe they deserve my support?"

Suddenly overcome with exhaustion, Lady Charlotte waved off her husband's sputtering response. "I have no doubt but that I did the right thing," she said as she turned toward the stairs and the refuge of her private chambers.

Lord Reginald waited until Lady Charlotte was halfway up the stairs before he called out, "Do join me for tea, my love. A guest will also be in attendance."

Charlotte did not pause in her ascent.

"You will not want to miss him," Lord Reginald insisted. "The guest brings word from your father."

Lady Charlotte stopped.

Lord Reginald smiled. He prided himself on his ability to use a well-timed statement to his advantage.

Lady Charlotte swung around to face her husband. "What of my father?" she demanded.

"Until tea, then?"

A flush of victory refreshed Lord Reginald's stressed features. As his wife hesitated, he turned his back on her and walked away.

*

The parlor clock rang out its fourth chime as Lady Charlotte stepped into the room. Tea had already been laid out on the tea table, and three chairs placed around it. Lord Reginald leaned back in his chair, a smile pasted on his face.

"Sit, my dear," he invited without standing to his feet. "Our guest should join us shortly."

"Who is it?" Lady Charlotte asked.

"Your tea," Lord Reginald said as he handed her a cup.

Fear gnawed at Lady Charlotte and crowded her mind with suspicions. "What have you done to Father, Reginald?" she demanded.

"Done to him? Why, whatever do you mean?" Lord Reginald replied in the cloyingly placid voice that drove his wife mad. "Now that your father is my employee, his success is my success."

Rustin, the butler, appeared at the door and announced, "Your guest has arrived, my lord."

"Excellent, excellent!" Lord Reginald exclaimed. This time he did stand up. "Show him in at once."

Jasper Hathaway stepped into the room.

"You!" Lady Charlotte hissed.

"Did I fail to tell you?" Lord Reginald said breezily. "Mister Hathaway has once again agreed to enter my employ. While he no longer wishes to make the arduous trips to and from the African coast himself, he is a perfect liaison between me and those who labor in so demanding and thankless a clime. As one who intimately knows both Africa and our people involved there, I can think of no one in a better position to keep me adequately informed than he."

Mr. Hathaway, plumped up with a new sense of self-importance, bowed as low as his corpulence would allow. He kept one hand over his mouth, however, to make certain his artificial teeth stayed in place.

"You did well to report to me immediately after Joseph Winslow made contact with you," Lord Reginald said to Mister Hathaway. "Such a one as he must be made to pay for his actions, and because you so promptly—"

"What of my father?" Lady Charlotte demanded.

"Do forgive me, my dear," Lord Reginald said in his taunting voice. "Have my manners left me entirely?" To Hathaway he said, "Please, sir, the letters you received. I, too, am most eager to hear their contents."

With an air of great importance, Jasper Hathaway laid out his leather case, rummaging through it until he located a fistful of papers. These he pulled out and consulted at some length.

"A merchant ship that arrived in port late last week had fortuitously stopped some months ago on the Gold Coast of Africa to load cargo—fine African wood, I believe it was. The captain himself delivered these letters to me. One is from Princess Lingongo and the other from our man, Benjamin Stevens."

Lady Charlotte shifted impatiently in her chair. Mister Hathaway, however, was enjoying his place of attention far too much to hurry along.

"Princess Lingongo raised several items that concerned the renewed operation at Zulina fortress, and she had nothing but praise for Mister Stevens's eager participation in the work. Her exact words—" Hathaway scanned the page. "Yes, yes, here they are. She says, 'As a slaver, Mister Stevens is far superior to Joseph Winslow. He continues to improve with each day that passes.'"

"The words do encourage one, although such a statement cannot necessarily be considered a glowing compliment, can it? I mean, being compared to so run-down and desperate a man as Winslow," Lord Reginald said with a laugh.

"Quite right, my lord," Hathaway agreed. "I should say, almost anyone could do a better job than he."

"Does the princess elaborate?" Lord Reginald asked.

"She does comment on Stevens's increased aggressiveness against the villagers. She also discusses at some length his growing interest in his personal collection of gold jewelry and molded figures of gold—animals and such, I assume. It seems he sets great store by these artifacts."

"That cannot be true!" Lady Charlotte protested. "The person you describe is not my father!"

Ignoring her comments, Lord Reginald inquired of Mister Hathaway, "And what of the letter from Mister Stevens?"

"Facts and figures mostly," said Jasper Hathaway. "He was most eager to share the results of the slave parties he sent out. As a matter of fact, he expressed general pride over the various successes of his partnership with the princess Lingongo."

"What?" Lady Charlotte gasped. "He is in *partnership* with her?"

"His summation reads thusly: 'I am quite certain that your profits from this round of slaves will be the greatest in the history of Zulina slave fortress. I might add that my own wealth is such that I could return to England and live out my days in the most comfortable of circumstances, should I choose to do so. However, I must say, the thrill of success has proven heady indeed. Already I have begun construction on a new house here in Africa, and here I intend to live out my days.'"

Lady Charlotte burst into tears. She bolted from her chair and ran from the room.

With a calm and steady hand, Lord Reginald reached for another cup of tea. The anxiety had smoothed completely from his face. He balanced the teacup on his knee and leaned back in his chair, a satisfied smile on his face.

12

You, you, you, you, and you . . . All of you in first watch," Archie Rhodes ordered as he made his way down the line of men alongside the deck rail. "You too, India Boy. And you and you . . ."

Young Jackie was in the first watch, and Collie Steele, the pock-scarred boy whose hammock hung on the other side of Grace's, too. Starting with the wrinkled thirty-eight-year-old seaman beyond Collie, the rest of the line was in second watch.

Grace understood the routine. It was the same as on the *Willow*. The ship's work was divided into six four-hour watches, each measured by half-hourly rings of the ship's bell. One bell marked the start of a watch, then each thirty minutes another bell was added until eight bells sounded the last watch segment. Half an hour after that, one bell signaled the start of the next watch.

While half the crew worked, the other half was free to sleep or do whatever they wanted. On Captain Hallam's orders, each night first one watch and then the other would stand two consecutive watches. That meant many hours of work with no rest for half the crew, but it also meant that on alternating nights, the men would have a chance for a fair night's sleep.

Each watch had an officer whose job it was to assign duties and to oversee the men under him. No complaints, no arguments. At least, none that reached the officers' ears. James Talbot was the officer assigned to the first watch.

"You! Get yourself to the galley," Mister Talbot ordered Jackie.

Jackie set to work under the cook, a tough old seaman by the name of Paddy Clemmons. Paddy wielded his metal serving spoon like a weapon. It was Jackie's responsibility to see that the livestock was fed and their cages kept clean. He also scrubbed the pots and mopped the galley deck. Actually, Jackie was to do anything the cook ordered him to do.

"India Boy! You work with Bart."

James Talbot motioned Grace toward a short, thick Scotsman who oversaw the ship's maintenance.

"T'will make a man o' ye, young laddie," Bart said to Grace as he administered a sharp slap to her painfully bound back.

Grace's first job was to work alongside a crew of half a dozen men who hauled lines.

Pile up ropes strewn across the deck? Grace thought. *I can do that!*

The job took hours. The entire time, Grace stood in a line with the others and heaved the heavy ropes in time to a rhymed cadence Bart roared out. Before the job was half done, the muscles in her arms and shoulders screamed with pain.

"Ashok! Put yer lazy shoulder to the work!" Bart scolded.

Grace tried with all her might, but she could not keep up with the others.

"Half yer finger be missin'," Bart called. "Hold tight to that line or ye'll lose the next one, too!"

What did Bart know of Tungo's knife? What *could* he know of what she had suffered at Zulina fortress? What could any of them know? How Grace wished she were at work in the galley with Jackie! Mop floors and scrub pans—those things she understood very well.

When at long last the final line was tightly coiled and stacked in place, Grace slumped down on the deck. Several other sailors also groaned in relief.

"Is it a long journey to America?" Grace asked no one in particular.

"Why? Ye gots somewhere's else to be, does ye?" retorted a sailor with only two visible teeth.

"Could be five weeks," said a tall black-haired man called Abner. "If God smiles on us."

"Five weeks!" Grace exclaimed in happy surprise. "It took twice as long to come from Af . . . from India."

"The trade winds is why," said Abner. "We takes the Southern Crossing to the Canaries and catches the trade winds. From there we can sail downhill all the way to the Caribbean."

"Pshaw! Rubbish, that, nothin' but pure rubbish!" growled the sailor with two teeth. "Superstition of the sea is wot it be."

Abner laughed. "Except that it works. And you can't deny it, either, Mickey. Go east, and it be five weeks between London and Charleston. Go west, and it takes half again that long. No trade winds, eh? Well then, you explain the difference to me."

"Luck," mumbled Mickey. "Dumb luck is all it be. Jist dumb luck and nothin' more."

"Men of the sea don't take easy to new ideas," Abner told Grace with a conspiratorial chuckle.

By the end of the first day, it was clear which men were real sailors and which were new recruits. Experienced sailors worked quickly and efficiently, and their muscles stood out on their sun-darkened arms and legs like knotted ropes. Unfortunately for Captain Hallam, experienced sailors numbered few on his crew. Most of his men stumbled and fumbled and groaned under the workload. Pale and malnourished, their scrawny limbs quivered and strained. Even worse, many a man was of a mind to avoid work whenever and however possible. It was up to Mister Talbot to see that those in the first watch were not afforded that luxury.

At the sound of eight bells, eager anticipation swept through the weary men of the first watch. Half an hour later, when one bell sounded the watch change, James Talbot ordered, "To the galley with you!"

Following the lead of those ahead of her, Grace headed for the galley, where she picked up a small wooden plank and spoon, and a tin cup. She settled herself on a bench between Collie and a red-haired man she hadn't noticed before. Paddy Clemmons toted a heavy pot between the benches. He plopped a ladleful of stew with vegetables and a bit of meat on each outstretched plank. Jackie followed close behind the cook and put a biscuit on each man's plate.

"Enjoy the stew!" Abner called out. "Won't be many meals like this one comin' yer way!"

One ravenous sailor after another scooped up his portion of stew and scraped his plank clean. When the men could scrape no more, they picked up their planks and licked off the last of the juices.

Grace thought back to her days on the *Willow*, to the endless meals of porridge made of dried peas, always accompanied by biscuits dried hard as rocks.

"Indian, is ye?" the red-haired sailor demanded of Grace.

"Yes," Grace replied. She did her best to emphasize her accent. "Ashok. That's my name."

"What's a Indian doin' in England?" asked the red-haired sailor.

"Well . . . I—" Grace swallowed hard.

"Goin' to America to find your family, is you?"

"Yes," Grace said eagerly. But since she couldn't very well explain that her husband had been forced aboard a slave ship in Africa, she added, "My . . . my brother. To find my brother."

"You surely be needin' God's help for that task," the red-haired sailor remarked. "That country be filled with Indians, so I hears tell. Some livin' in tents. Some waitin' to slice the scalp off a white man's head."

Grace stared. "Indians? In America?"

"It be the truth," the red-haired sailor said. "And they not the onliest barbarians in that country, neither. Africans, too. Hundreds and thousands of them. But the Africans all be slaves, so they be busy lookin' for a way to kill their masters and get to England."

"You been to America before, has you, Lucas?" Abner asked.

"No, but I hear tell the stories. America be a wild wilderness of a country, that's for sure."

"Best wait to see for yerself before you spread your tales," Abner advised.

"Some things I don't need to see in order to know," Lucas insisted. "Indians be Indians. Africans be Africans. All of 'em be wild people. That much I know."

Grace got up and stumbled away from the others. What she saw before her was not a crew of sailors refreshing themselves from a day's work. What she saw was wretched white men beating her people . . . slavers dashing her child against the rocks. . . . Cabeto locked in chains and forced onto a slave ship. What she saw was an awful reminder of the horrors of Zulina slave fortress.

Who are the wild people? she wanted to scream at the laughing men who licked their dinner planks clean. *"You tell me. Which ones are they?"*

With its sails full to the wind, the *Ocean Steed* glided across the smooth, open sea.

Grace moved to the ladder and climbed down to the crew berth deck below. She ducked her head and made her way through the maze of swaying hammocks until she found her own. As she climbed onto it, she became aware of stifled sobs from the hammock next to her.

"Jackie?" she said softly. "What is it?"

Immediately the crying stopped.

"Jackie?"

The boy turned his back to her. So Grace lay down on her own hammock and cried beside him.

13

*M*uco!" Benjamin Stevens called.

He paused at the door, but only long enough to stomp the African dust off his boots. The sun was low in the sky, yet still no supper fragrance bubbled from the outdoor kitchen behind the house. In fact, only the thinnest wisp of smoke puffed up from where a cook fire should be burning strong.

Benjamin grunted his annoyance and threw the front door open. Inside, all was quiet—silent and severe. The same as it had been every other day since he first came to Africa nigh unto twenty-five years earlier.

Benjamin had built this house with his own two hands. He had made it sturdy and practical, large enough to shelter a family. Those were the days when his heart was still light and his head still filled with dreams of endless possibilities. Back before it occurred to him that his wife, Henrietta, and daughter, Charlotte, might choose to stay in England rather than live with him in Africa. In those bygone days, he never could have imagined that his family would consider themselves generous to grant him one obligatory month of their time every other year, and even that would be cause for weary sighs and complaints.

Now both Henrietta and Charlotte were lost to him forever. Benjamin Stevens was alone.

"Hello? Muco?" Benjamin called, his impatience growing. "Muco! Where do you hide yourself?"

Benjamin sighed with disgust. What was the use of having a house slave if she was not available to tend to his needs? What was the use of owning her if she were not around to keep his house and possessions safe from prowlers and thieves?

His possessions! Gripped by a sudden rush of apprehension, Benjamin hurried through the house to the back room, where he kept his collection of finely crafted gold jewelry and golden images of animals. He almost wept with relief when he saw that the padlock was still on the door, completely undisturbed.

Well, and why shouldn't it be? He kept the only key on a leather lace around his neck.

As Benjamin reached for the key, from the corner of his eye he caught sight of the slave. She seemed to have appeared out of nowhere. Or had she stood in the shadows and watched him the entire time? How he hated the way she crept about on those silent feet of hers! How he hated calling his slave by an African name.

"Bow your head when you stand before me, slave!" Benjamin Stevens snapped.

Muco did not. Her expression remained distant and remote, her back straight and unbent.

The house slave, Muco, had been a gift to him from Princess Lingongo. "You deserve her," Lingongo had told him in beautiful tones that seemed to extend a great compliment. "A slave to keep your kitchen fire hot and your clothes clean. A slave to serve you when you are at home and keep your house secure when you are away."

The gift had pleased Benjamin enormously. Imagine! The great Princess Lingongo had made a gift to him from her own household staff! And yet, with every day that passed, the gift of Muco weighed more heavily on Benjamin's mind. The slave simply would not respect him. And her silent defiance rankled him no end.

"Where is my supper?" Benjamin Stevens demanded of his slave.

"Letters arrived for you . . . sir," Muco said. "Lingongo's man carried them here today. Should I bring them to you?"

"Of course bring them to me!" Benjamin responded in exasperation. "How else shall I read what they say?"

Muco shuffled away in silence and returned with a leather packet, which she handed to Benjamin.

"Your name is no longer Muco," Benjamin informed his slave. "All my slaves carry names from the Bible, and you will be no different. From now on you will be Rhoda."

Without even glancing his way, the slave moved on outside to stoke up the fire.

Benjamin Stevens took the packet to the corner of the great room that he called his office and sat down at his writing table. From the drawer he took the magnifying glass he now needed in order to read and eagerly removed a stack of half a dozen letters from the packet.

The first letter was from the London hospital where his wife was confined with consumption. Her condition continued to deteriorate more rapidly than expected, the letter stated. On the advice of her doctor, it was strongly recommended that Benjamin make all due haste to be by her side one last time.

Poor Henrietta. She had always made it her business to take care of everything and everybody, whether they wanted her care or not. Now there was no one to care for her. Things could have been so different. If she had only come to Africa with him. . . . Of course, there was illness everywhere. Certainly Africa was rife with disease. If she were here, though, Benjamin would be at her side. But in London? No. Not in London.

With a sigh, Benjamin carefully laid the letter aside and set his beautifully carved gold tortoise on top of it.

That tortoise was the most prized item in his gold collection. While the other pieces remained locked away, this one he kept on display for all to see. Princess Lingongo had selected it from the royal collection and had given it to him to seal their business partnership. Certainly he had gold pieces of more value. But this gold tortoise marked his move to a life of prestige and wealth. Whenever he pined over what he'd had to give up to get here, he need only look at the gold tortoise to remember all he had gained.

Benjamin Stevens shuffled through the remainder of the stack of mail: Notices from vendors . . . Statements from several slave ships . . . Invoices for business purchases. Nothing from Charlotte, though. Nothing from his daughter.

Slowly, Benjamin unfolded the final document, a letter of several pages written in the familiar, overly pretentious hand of Jasper Hathaway. As usual, Mister Hathaway began with business matters: accounting issues that concerned the administration of Zulina slave house ("I must demand fiscal restraint of you, my good man! Restraint, that is the watchword!"), questions of exchange ("Do encourage the natives there to accept payment in beads and bolts of cloth rather than insisting on muskets and gunpowder. I am certain you understand that we must strive to retain control of the weapons"), matters that pertained to slave requirements ("Encourage the ship captains to accept more young women of breeding age, for those are sorely needed in the islands. Women can work the fields almost as well as men, but they can also be used to produce a new crop of captive-born slaves for us").

With business matters addressed, Mister Hathaway moved with relish to the gossip of the day. It must have brought Jasper Hathaway immense pleasure to compose the letter's gossip, for it all circled around Grace Winslow:

"His Lordship skillfully crafted evidence against Grace Winslow, and he would have succeeded in his goal of seeing her hanged as a thief from the gallows had it not been for your own daughter, who had the audacity to approach His Lordship the Judge himself and so to prevail against her own husband. His Lordship Reginald Witherham is most displeased with Lady Charlotte, as you can well imagine. Most extremely displeased, I should say. I must alert you, good sir, of your own precarious position, you being her father. For on Lady Charlotte's behalf, Lord Reginald is not at all pleased with you, either. You may thank God Almighty that you are far away from London or I should not want to vouch for your safety."

Benjamin Stevens slammed the letter down on his writing table. He kicked his way out of the chair and clear through to the cooking oven out back.

"When will my dinner be ready?" he demanded.

The slave looked up and studied the sky. "Not before dark," she replied.

Benjamin headed back through the house and out the front door. He walked clear down to the ocean, where he could linger alone along the quiet shore. Where he could watch the sun hang low over the water and listen to the waves lap at the shore as the seabirds called to one another. The sights and sounds of Africa as it settled down for the night, that was what soothed his irritated mind.

While Benjamin worried much about the safety of the gold pieces he so energetically collected, he worried not at all about the security of his private correspondence. That, he assured himself, was the positive side of having no one about but one foolish old slave woman. He could lock up his valuables and keep them away from her. The slave's own dull mind would lock out all else.

But there was much Benjamin Stevens did not comprehend about his house slave. He did not understand how deeply she loved Grace Winslow, and had ever since Grace was a small child. He did not recognize that whatever he called her, she would always be Grace's Mama Muco, and she would risk anything for news of her Grace. And Benjamin Steven never imagined that long ago Grace had taught this slave how to read.

As soon as the front door closed, Muco hurried in through the back door and headed straight for Benjamin Stevens's writing table in the corner of the great room. She settled herself in her master's chair just as though she herself was mistress of the house, and she snatched up the letter from Mister Hathaway. Slowly and carefully she read every word out loud.

When she finished reading, Mama Muco cried out, "Lord, God, hold on to my Grace. Please, Jesus, keep her safe!"

Benjamin Stevens arrived back home to the fragrance of his supper bubbling on the outside fire and the sight of his house slave on her knees beside his desk.

"If I didn't know you to be a heathen, I would swear you were praying to God," Benjamin said. "I never will understand you, old woman. Now get yourself up and set out my supper."

14

"Ashok, you fool! Git yerse'f off this deck!" shouted Abner.

Pounding rain plastered Abner's black hair slick against his head as he and the Scotsman, Bart, tugged at the knotted rigging.

Grace struggled to obey, but she slipped on the water-slick deck and fell to her knees. Just as she found her footing, another wave pounded against the ship and upended two crates of chickens. They tumbled toward her, chickens clucking frantically. Grace dodged the rolling crates only to slip again and fall flat.

"On yer feet, laddy!" Bart ordered. "Grab a bailin' bucket and get yourself belowdecks!"

Old Quin, his arm wrapped around the rail, held a bucket out to her. Grace managed to grab it as she lurched toward the ladder. She was about to descend down the first step when Collie Steele bounded up from below.

"Belowdecks with the both of ye!" Bart bawled. "Mister Talbot done said you lads was to bail water, so git below and set to bailin'!"

"Not me!" Collie shot back. "I will help you secure the sails up here!"

"Git below!" old Quin shouted from the rail. "That be a direct order!"

"I've had me fill of them bailin' buckets," Collie said. "I'll work topside, like a real sailor, same as you."

As he struggled to keep his balance, Collie inched his way forward across the rocking deck.

One huge wave after another surged and smashed against the ship. The pilot strained at the wheel, turning the ship hard to starboard to meet wave after wave, head-on. As the ship rolled to the side, both Abner and Bart grabbed for the shrouds. Old Quin dropped the buckets and wrapped both his arms around the rail. Collie, perplexed, stopped still in the middle of the deck.

The ship lurched to the side, then it lunged forward. With blinding strength, a tremendous wave smashed across the deck.

And Collie was gone.

Grace's voice rose in a shrieking scream. But her cries were lost in the howl of the wind and the crash of the sea.

"Below! You, Ashok!"

Abner and Bart and Quin all bellowed together.

"Git yerse'f below! Now!"

By late afternoon, the crash of the waves had quieted to heaving billows. By dusk, the sea was nothing more than rolling surges. By nightfall, a fair wind filled the sails of the *Ocean Steed*, and the ship cut swiftly through the water.

Grace sank down onto a barrel flipped upside down next to the rail and stared overboard at the black water. She shivered uncontrollably in her soaked clothes. Collie Steele lay down there in the deep darkness. Swept away right in front of her eyes, he was. One moment he stood in the middle of the deck, and the next moment he was gone.

"It could have been me," Grace whispered.

"Sure, and it could. Could be you tomorrow," said old Quin, who had come up behind her. He looked from the choppy water up to the sails that strained in the wind. "Could be me. Could be any one of us. Or all of us."

Old Quin stood next to Grace and stared out over the sea. For a long time, he said nothing.

"Nature fights agin' us at the very same time it helps us, don't y'see," he said at last. "We never kin know when it will grab hold of a ship and have its way with us."

Grace turned and looked up at Quin's deeply furrowed face, weathered and brown. He always wore a cap pulled down tight over his mop of bushy gray curls. Quin continued to stare out to the endless expanse of ocean.

"Do you believe in God?" Grace asked in a quiet voice.

"I believes in ever'thin'," Quin said. "An' I believes in nothin'. That way I won't be disappointed."

Grace finally found the strength to make her way down the ladder. Where Collie's hammock had hung beside hers was now a gaping, empty space.

The next morning, Captain Hallam summoned the entire crew to the main deck. The men stood in unaccustomed orderly rows. They pulled off their hats—except for Grace who left her red rumal wrapped around her head. With uncommon discomfort, the captain stood before the silent men.

Grace, up at the front, heard the navigator, Marcus Slade, whisper to Captain Hallam, "You must say something, sir."

"'They that go down to the sea in ships, that do business in great waters; these see the works of the LORD and his wonders in the deep,'" Captain Hallam intoned. "Our mate . . . ah . . ."

"Collie Steele, sir," Marcus Slade hissed. "His name was Collie Steele!"

"Our mate, Collie Steele—" Captain Hallam said. He shook his head. "I'm sorry. I am not a religious man."

Mister Slade handed the captain an opened Bible. With the men's eyes hard on him, Captain Hallam read, " 'The LORD is my shepherd; I shall not want; He maketh me to lie down in green pastures: he leadeth me beside the still waters. He restoreth my soul; he leadeth me in the paths of righteousness for his name's sake. Yea, though I walk through the valley of the shadow of death, I will fear no evil: for thou art with me; thy rod and thy staff they comfort me. Thou preparest a table before me in the presence of mine enemies; thou anointest my head with oil; my cup runneth over. Surely goodness and mercy shall follow me all the days of my life: and I will dwell in the house of the LORD for ever.' Psalm 23. "

Captain Hallam shut the Bible.

"Collie Steele, into the deep sea and the presence of God we commend your spirit," he said. "Sleep in peace, lad."

✒

As one endless day stretched into another, as her slender arms grew strong and her face baked to a richer shade of brown, as the biscuits Jackie served with cook's endless pease porridge hardened into rocks, and weevils chewed passageways through them, Grace's respect for her father grew. When she was young, Joseph Winslow was sometimes away from home for many months at a time. He always retuned to the African coast strong and sunburned and laden down with wonderful gifts—dresses of silk and lace, and leather-bound books, sometimes with pictures. Always he returned to Africa with tales to tell of exciting adventures and places about which Grace could only dream. In her mind, the life of a sailor was a life of freedom and adventure and excitement and fun. How could she ever have imagined the truth of life at sea? It was incredibly hard work. It was constant danger. It was terrible food and worse water. It was endless days and nights of either raging heat or shivering cold. It was a life of crammed-together loneliness.

"There, now, a thief is what you be! A thief and nothin' more!"

Grace heard the yells long before she saw anything. She was at work sanding out the corner portion of the deck most damaged in the storm, a job she mumbled (but only to herself) must surely be the most loathsome on earth. Her calloused fingers split and bled as the noonday sun beat relentlessly on her back. The men around her had stripped to almost nothing, but of course she had not the luxury to do the same. Instead, she made a great show of how much she enjoyed the heat.

"We will see what capt'n has to say over the likes of you, that we will! And I won't abide no tellin' of lies, neither! That I tell's you straight away!"

Just up ahead, cook Paddy Clemmons dragged Jackie Watson into view. Paddy had him by the ear, and Jackie squalled out his protests loud and long.

"No use to argue with me! I seen you with me own two eyes!" Paddy scolded. "Not hardtack or pieces of fish, neither. No, you has to go fer the captain's own special sausage, you does!"

The very thought of sausage set Grace's mouth to watering. Grace's and everyone else's, too. Good food had grown scarce, which was precisely why stealing it was such an assault on the entire ship.

"What will happen to him?" Grace asked Abner.

"Nothin' good, that's a certainty," Abner said. "Captain won't tolerate thievin' from the galley."

"Specially not thievin' of his own food," Quin added.

At the sound of three bells, Archie led Jackie to the main deck and chained him to the rail. With the full crew ordered to attend, Captain Hallam, his face hard with anger, decreed, "No water for two days, then half rations for one week. No food for three days, then half rations for one week."

Jackie let out a howl.

"May that serve as fair warning to any among you who might be tempted to follow the lead of this young scoundrel," Captain Hallam pronounced. "Thievery will not be tolerated on this ship. The next thief will receive double this punishment. And should anyone be fool enough to attempt it a third time, double again, though it means his very life."

No one dared look Captain Hallam in the face.

"And should anyone have a mind to bring water or food to the prisoner," the captain continued, "the same punishment awaits him."

That night, Grace lay in her hammock as it swung gently with the soft roll of the ship. On one side hung an empty hammock where Jackie should have been asleep, and on the other, an empty space where Collie's hammock had been. Gasping in the heavy air, she panted for breath. Her clothes were looser on her body, yet the bindings around her chest felt more crushing each day. Tonight she feared they would squeeze the life right out of her.

Cabeto! Cabeto! Grace struggled to grasp hold of his image and trace it in her mind. Piercing black eyes that could see clear through to her soul . . . broad nose that flared when he was angry . . . a serious mouth that knew well how to laugh . . . hands strong enough to tear limbs from a tree, yet gentle enough to cradle a child . . .

But Grace's mind continued to return to the young boy on the deck above, chained fast to the rail. All afternoon he had stood in the hot sun and stared out at the wide expanse of water, but with not one drop to moisten his parched lips. All night he would remain chained there through the cold darkness, and tomorrow and tomorrow night, too. How frightened Jackie must be! And how terribly miserable with thirst!

"Yes, *Cabeto*," Grace mouthed silently. "*I know what you would do.*"

Quietly Grace slipped from her hammock and crept up the ladder to the main deck. She slid into the shadows, where she moved soundlessly along the bulkhead to a spot just behind where Jackie was chained. In the light of the half moon, she could see the outline of the boy. He had crumpled down onto the deck. The guard Captain Hallam had posted over him lay in a circle of lines, his head thrown back, snoring.

Soundlessly Grace moved further down the deck to the water barrel. Carefully she picked up the ladle.

Should anyone have a mind to bring water or food to the prisoner, the same punishment awaits him. The captain's words rang clear in her mind. *Awaits* her. *The same punishment especially awaits* her.

Slowly, carefully, Grace lowered the dipper into the water barrel. It made the tiniest plink of a noise. Just as carefully she drew it out again. Grace tucked herself back into the shadows and eased her way over to the boy.

"Jackie," Grace breathed.

"Ashok!" Jackie gasped in surprise.

The guard shifted in his sleep and readjusted his position.

"Shhh!" Grace cautioned, breathing her words. "I brought you water. Quickly now!"

She held the dipper to the boy's sun-burnt lips. Jackie gulped ravenously.

The guard stirred and stretched himself.

Grace dropped to her knees and pressed against a stack of barrels.

"Is that you, boy?" the guard asked.

"Y . . . yes," Jackie stammered. "I's . . . I's just lickin' me dry lips."

"Lick 'em more quiet," the guard said. He stretched again and readjusted himself to a more comfortable position on the lines.

Grace sank back into the shadows. She edged to the water barrel, where she carefully slid the dipper back into place. Moving to the ladder, she slipped down to the berth deck below.

"What is you doin', coolie?" a voice growled at her in the darkness.

"Jus . . . taking in a breath of fresh air, is all," Grace said. She pushed her way through the rows of hammocks until she found her own.

Grace's hammock swayed with the rhythm of the ocean swells—back and forth, back and forth, back and forth. This time Cabeto's face readily came to her. This time it lay gentle in her mind.

The LORD is my shepherd, I shall not want . . .

The Good Shepherd. Yes, even now He carried Cabeto high upon His shoulders. Surely, in that lofty position, Cabeto was safe and protected.

Grace believed that.

She must believe it.

Yea, though I walk through the valley of the shadow of death, I will fear no evil: for thou art with me . . .

"Good Shepherd," Grace prayed, "carry me, too. Oh, please . . . carry me, too!"

15

*C*aleb watched Juba remove his white man shoes and carefully lay them on the edge of the rice field before he stepped onto the sodden ground. With his first step, Juba sank clean up to his bare ankles in mud.

Dat man has somethin' important on his mind, Caleb thought.

Caleb forced his hoe back into the muck. But out of the corner of his eye, he watched Juba pick his way through the field toward him.

Kit, in the next rice field, also saw the driver. He, too, knew something important was about to happen. So Kit also began to work his way over in Caleb's direction. Nonchalantly, of course, but steadily.

"Massa wants to talk wit' you," Juba called out to Caleb. "Get yourse'f outta de mud and cleaned up."

Massa! Kit thought. *What has dat darkie Caleb gone an' done? Somethin' awful good, or somethin' just plain awful!*

Either way, Kit's tongue already itched to spread the news. But his gossip would have to wait. Juba said nothing more than that, and Caleb asked him no questions. Caleb simply tossed his hoe over his shoulder and followed the driver out of the field. He waited as Juba put his shoes back on and silently followed him toward Massa's big house.

✍

Macon Waymon leaned back comfortably in a white wooden chair on the sprawling porch of the White Jasmine plantation house. Since he would only have occasion to deal with slaves that spring morning, he decided there was no reason to encumber himself with anything more formal and uncomfortable than his "smallclothes." Though, to be truthful, he did feel a bit embarrassed to be outside the house so casually outfitted. It simply was not his gentlemanly nature to meet with others, regardless of their social status, attired in nothing but a linen shirt, a waistcoat, and trousers covered with no coat at all. Not even on a warm day.

Caleb stood awkwardly before his seated master and kept his eyes fixed on his own mud-splattered bare feet. He had not been this close to Massa Macon since the day the master bought him out of certain death in Massa Silas's swamp.

"I'll come directly to the point," Macon said, looking up at his slave. "What do you know about cotton?"

Caleb stared harder at his muddy toes. How could he answer such a question from the white man? The truth was, he knew absolutely nothing about cotton. Except that it was a crop slaves hated to hoe, and hated even more to pluck out of its razor-sharp hulls.

Macon Waymon let out a short burst of laughter. "Never mind. It doesn't matter in the least. My new overseer knows everything there is to know about how to grow cotton. What do you know about machinery?"

" 'Chinery? I don't know nothin' about dat, Massa," Caleb mumbled.

Macon raised his bushy eyebrows. "No?" he said. "That's not what Juba tells me. Juba tells me you can make a purse from a sow's ear."

Caleb looked up at Macon Waymon in genuine puzzle-ment. "No, sir," he said. "Not me. I never made nothin' from a sow's ear."

Macon barked out a loud guffaw. "Well, never you mind, boy. It is no sow's ear that causes me concern. It is a cotton engine. A cotton gin."

If there was one thing on which Macon prided himself, it was the civilized way he dealt with his slaves. A *different kind of slaveholder* is the way he referred to himself. He was a rea-sonable, rational man, and endlessly kind to his slaves. Why, he allotted each adult an entire peck of corn every week for a food allowance, and a pound of pork each month, as well. Never mind that it was the pig's feet and ears and stomach they got, and that plenty of fat was squeezed into their allot-ment. Meat was meat.

Every one of his slaves had a blanket to wrap up in against the cold, since they all slept on the drafty floor of the slave huts. Macon made certain they had the tools necessary for their work assignments. Good workers like Caleb and Juba, he rewarded with special privileges: they could hunt turtles and muskrats in the swamp as well as any other wild game they could find, they could fish in the rivers, they could grow vegetables in garden plots.

Oh, and each Christmas, Macon's wife Luleen called all the slaves together in front of the big house. There she generously handed candy around to all the slave children, chickens to the women so they could cook Christmas dinner, and a fresh item of clothing to each slave on the plantation. (Not shoes, of course. Shoes were an extra special reward for a chosen few.)

Macon Waymon said, "An enormous amount of money waits to be made in cotton." Excitement bubbled up in his voice. He still talked to Caleb, but his eyes had drifted past the slave and out toward the cypress swamps.

It was to Macon Waymon's great benefit that Eli Whitney had delayed his decision to make application for a patent for his cotton gin. Fortuitous, indeed, that Whitney and his partner, Phineas Miller, decided it would be far more advantageous for them to first install their own machines at plantations rather than make them available for sale. That way, the two men figured, they could collect up to half the growers' profits as payment for the use of the machine and they themselves would benefit greatly before the invention ever went on the market. The patent could come later.

Back when Macon had nothing but rice fields, with not a boll of cotton to gin, he had readily agreed to Eli Whitney's terms. Even at that time, they had seemed exorbitant and profit-taking, and that had infuriated Macon from the beginning. Yet he had still agreed because he felt he had no choice. His entire plan rested on access to the cotton gin.

With Samuel Shaw's money, Macon Waymon purchased five struggling plantations—all of them already planted in short-staple cotton, as it turned out—and registered them in the name of Mister Samuel Shaw.

Overjoyed, Mister Shaw was immediately eligible to run in the next South Carolina election.

Overjoyed, Macon Waymon discovered a warehouse filled with newly harvested cotton on each plantation. He was assured that he should be able to quickly clean it all with the help of the wondrous new cotton gin—if he had the right person at the wheel, that is.

Macon Waymon stood up and adjusted his crisp shirt, then smoothed his white linen waistcoat over it. "A new day is coming," he announced to Caleb. "And you, boy, will be a part of it!"

"Yes, Massa," Caleb said. He stepped back uncertainly and shifted his weight to his good leg.

"No more mucking through rice fields for you," Macon said jovially. "And no cotton picking, neither. I want you to be my man on the gin. You think you can manage that? You think you can run my cotton engine for me?"

"Yes, Massa," Caleb said, although he had not the faintest idea what a cotton engine might be.

"Fine, fine!" Macon exclaimed. "Tomorrow I will move you upland to the biggest of the cotton plantations. You and Juba and a wagonload of my best slaves will go along with me. I chose every one of you special."

Macon sat down again and leaned back in the porch chair. He folded his hands across his stomach and heaved a satisfied sigh.

"Be proud you are among the chosen, boy," he said.

Proud? Caleb, his jaw set and fire burning in his soul, fixed his dark eyes on the grinning white man.

My massa, he dares call hisself, Caleb thought. *Ruler over me. My owner. Dat's what he thinks, but he don't know nothin'.*

☙

"Dat Juba be leavin' here. We can all be happy 'bout dat!" Kit crowed to the slaves gathered around Tempy's bubbling pot of pork fat and mustard greens. "Soon that traitor be gone away from us!"

News spread fast through the slave compound. Caleb wasn't even back from the big house, yet already everyone knew that Massa Macon would soon move a wagonload of slaves away from the rice fields. And they knew the driver would be included. Juba was not popular with the slaves. Too many backs bore scars from his whip. Certainly Kit's back did.

"Juba be just de same as a white man," Kit said bitterly. His face twisted at the driver's name.

In truth, Juba's whip wasn't the only reason for Kit's resentment, or even the greatest reason. Kit was jealous. The driver got to carry a whip, and he got to bark out commands to the other slaves. Sometimes he was even allowed to carry a gun— officially it was to shoot at the swarming flocks of rice birds, though it wasn't beyond Juba to use it to force obedience from the most resistant slaves.

"I wants to be a slave dat wears white man shoes, too!" Kit muttered under his breath.

By the time Caleb limped into the slave quarters and dished himself up a steaming bowl of mustard greens and pork fat, the talk had turned to the well-worn argument between those who thought it wisest to do the master's bidding and those who held to the dignity of resistance at all cost.

"It be easier on us to let massa think he be the massa," said Kit. "We knows how to make him pay."

"Dat be coward talk," Mose snarled.

"No, it ain't!" said Kit. "We breaks his hoe so we can't work. We steals what he has and makes it our own. We goes to de job, den we takes it nice and easy. Fight with a soft white hand, dat be what we do. An' we keeps our black iron hands clenched behind our backs."

"You mean, keep our black hands helpless in chains," Mose said in a voice hard as steel. "What we should do is burn down de massa's barns. Dat would show him our power!"

Isum, a hulk of a man who sat uncomfortably on a too-small tree stump, finished off his third bowl of greens and fat and wiped his mouth with the back of his calloused hand. He stretched out his long legs, first one and then the other. Mose had just launched into a descriptive story of the fiery destruction of massa's barn when Isum stood up.

In a voice that rumbled deep, Isum said, "Kill de white man."

All talk stopped. Mouths fell open and terrified eyes stared at him.

"We be de children of Africa," said Isum. "We knows how to poison a white ghost of a man."

Quiet enveloped the slave yard. Even Mose found that words had left him.

"Take a cassava from Caleb's garden patch," said Isum. "Fry it crisp and light. Just a short time over de fire, not enough to kill de poison in it. Prudy works in de kitchen at de big house. She can lay de cassava on de white man's dinner plate beside de meat and pour it all over with gravy. By de time . . ."

"No!" said Caleb. "Run if you wants to, Isum. Join a rebellion if you wants. But we do not murder. We are not white men!"

Mose, his face twisted with blind hatred, turned on Caleb. "You be no different den dat traitor, Juba," he spat. "Now de white man got hold of you too!"

"Caleb be right," said Tempy. "We not be killers. Our bodies be weary, but our souls—dey be clean."

Isum spat on the ground. "I will not live under de white man's whip," he announced. "I know de swamp. Tonight, I will run from dis place."

Caleb stared at Isum. How much that proud African man reminded him of his own brother, Sunba. The master wouldn't let Caleb call his brother by his real name anymore, though. He had to call him Samson. The white man took his brother away and shot him dead. A fury Caleb hadn't even known existed in him boiled up and blinded him in rage.

"I will go with you, my brother," Caleb said to Isum. "I will run, too."

❧

But Caleb didn't run. Just before the appointed hour, as the moon rose over the cypress swamps, Juba called Caleb away and told him to prepare the wagons for the next day's move to the cotton plantations. So Isum ran alone.

The next morning, when Macon Waymon should have been loading his best slaves into the wagon to begin the trek up to his new cotton fields, he was forced to hire slave catchers with their fearsome dogs to track down one single slave who had dared betray him at the worst possible time.

When he should have finally begun to earn back some of the money that conniving Eli Whitney demanded for his cotton-engine invention, Macon instead followed the howl of the slave catcher's dogs as he insisted on joining the search for an expensive worker he had considered to be a prize, but who turned out to be nothing but a treacherous rebel.

When he should have been smiling over plans for his new successful cotton venture, he simmered in humiliation over the defection of a slave he had trusted.

Yes, that was it. He *trusted* his slaves. And well he should, since he was so good a master to them. Other slave owners worried about slave insurrection, but not Macon Waymon. He unabashedly congratulated himself on the contentment and loyalty of his slaves. They respected him. They loved him!

Isum's freedom was short-lived. The sun was still high in the sky when a slave catcher rode into the slave quarters pulling the runaway behind him. Isum, his hands bound and tied with a rope to the back of the catcher's saddle, was forced to stumble and run along in an effort to keep from being dragged by the trotting horse.

Macon Waymon, who should have been settling his slaves in their new quarters at the cotton plantation, put on his coat and rode out to the slave quarters to meet the slave catcher. Juba hung back behind Macon, his eyes on the ground.

"Tie the runaway to the post," Macon ordered Juba. His jaw was hard and his eyes flashed with fire.

Juba didn't move.

"Now!" Macon ordered. Fury rose in his face.

Juba glanced uneasily at the slaves gathered around. Every one of them glowered at him. But Juba also saw his master's face—angry and resolute.

Macon Waymon stepped toward Juba and snapped his whip.

"Now, boy!" he ordered.

Still Juba hesitated.

In a flash, Macon's whip slashed across Juba's arm. Blood ran through his sliced sleeve and down his hand, splattering red on his white man's shoes.

Juba edged up to Isum. With shaking fingers he untied the slave from the horse. He kept his eyes averted from the run-away's face as he bound him to the whipping post. Juba looked at no one, but the fiery hatred around him seared through to his heart.

"Out of my way," Master Macon ordered, and Juba fell back.

Macon wielded the whip with an awkward hand. A kindly master such as he was used to leaving matters of discipline in the hands of others.

One lash . . . two lashes . . . three lashes . . .

The whip sliced across Isum's back again and again. After twenty excruciating lashes, Macon stopped.

"I am a merciful man," Macon said. "Plead for mercy."

Isum twisted his head around so that he could see the white man with the whip. Macon stepped in closer in order to hear the wretched man's plea. Isum spat in his face.

Macon, shaking with rage, jerked his whip up and thrashed wildly across Isum's bloody back.

At thirty lashes, Macon stopped again.

"I am known to be a compassionate man," Macon said in an icy voice. "Now, slave, beg me to show compassion to you!"

Isum, his body ravaged but his eyes still fiery with defiance, uttered naught but a wild growl.

Macon roared with fury. He raised his whip and brought it down again and again and again, beating Isum with savage ferocity. The slaves shrieked and begged for massa to stop, but Macon didn't even hear their pleas. Juba fell to his knees and pleaded with his master to quit the whip. Macon didn't hear him, either.

Finally, his whip already poised for another lash, Macon seemed to suddenly recover himself. He dropped his arm and stared at Isum, slumped at the post. In puzzlement, Macon looked down at his own blood-splattered clothes. Almost against his will, he forced his eyes back to the man who sagged on the whipping post, his back in shreds.

Pity pierced Macon's heart. Isum was, after all, a strong and valuable slave.

Pity, yes, but not remorse. The slave had given him no choice. Even the best of slave owners were required to discipline troublesome slaves. Indeed, when a slave owner was able to dispassionately do whatever must be done in order to maintain control, it merely proved his excellence of position.

Suddenly Isum forced himself upright.

Macon caught his breath and jumped back.

Slowly the slave turned his tortured face until he stared straight into Macon's eyes. In a low rumble of a voice Isum said, "Ever' night when you close your eyes, know it might be de last time. Know dat might be de night your slaves rise up an' kill you all."

Macon blinked back his shock. He looked around at the assembly of slaves he knew and trusted. Not one of them moved. Not one of them spoke. Those slaves should love him. He had been so certain they did. Yet now they stared at him with blank eyes. His wife gave candy to their children at Christmas, yet not one said a word on his behalf. The worst of it was that he knew perfectly well he could not run the cotton plantations without them. He *must* make them respect him! He *must* make them obey!

With a sudden bellow, Macon Waymon lashed out wildly with his whip at the entire lot of terrifyingly ungrateful slaves. The whip caught Caleb in the leg. It got Mose across the shoulder. Macon knocked Old Tempy flat before the slave catcher managed to pull the whip away from him.

The slave catcher aimed his gun at the huddled slaves and ordered them all to their cabins. As they hurried away, they could hear Juba behind them screaming, "No, no! Massa, no!"

When the commotion died down outside, Caleb opened the cabin door. Juba was no longer in the yard. Macon Waymon and the slave hunter were on their horses, riding away toward the Big House, the two dogs loping along beside them.

Caleb stepped outside into the silent courtyard. The cooking pot lay upside down, the last of the collard greens spilled out on the ground.

That's when Caleb saw Isum. His battered body hung from a branch of the oak tree.

16

As morning crept over the horizon, Monsieur Pierre Dulcet rode out to survey his vast new field. Already it was thick with slaves at work planting tobacco seedlings. He looked singularly out of place dressed in a fine silk shirt, coat, and white hose, a lavish plumed hat set on his head at a cocky tilt.

Monsieur Dulcet, a Frenchman of exceptionally fine breeding, was not one to notice individual slaves. But he did take note of Samson.

Samson, like so many Africans reloaded onto slave ships in the islands of the West Indies and sent on to the United States, was less than a perfect specimen. But as a slave, he was no slacker. To compensate for his twisted left shoulder, Samson had contrived a box which he hung around his neck with a strip of fabric torn from his blanket and angled toward his left side. This contraption enabled him to reach for a tobacco seedling with his weakened arm and hold it at the ready. At the same time he dipped low, and with his right hand made a hole in the soft dirt. With amazing accuracy, he dropped the seedling to the ground and in one swift move, secured it in the earth.

The Frenchman smiled at such ingenuity in a slave. Tobacco growing did, after all, depend on patient labor, skilled eyes, and steady hands.

Monsieur Dulcet rode to the edge of the field and called out to the slave, "Samson! Wash yourself. The overseer will give you clean clothes to wear and shoes for your feet. This day you shall accompany me to the city."

In Charleston, Samson followed behind his master, his head lowered as Monsieur Dulcet greeted friends and strangers alike with a charming *"Bonjour."* This was accompanied by a deep and courtly bow and a flourish of Monsieur's feathered hat. Whenever Monsieur Dulcet entered an establishment, Samson stood outside the door and waited for him. Should the errand involve a purchase, Samson hefted the package up onto his head and hurried it over to his master's carriage.

When the sun reached its zenith, Monsieur Dulcet motioned Samson up front beside the carriage driver. *"Le Coton Manoir,"* he ordered.

The carriage driver turned the horses away from the city and down a country lane. They passed vast fields filled with slaves busy laying in cotton seedlings, and a few fields being planted in tobacco. The carriage driver turned up an avenue of oaks that led to a majestic brick Big House lavishly decorated with white painted wood.

A rotund man of indeterminate age, his thin moustache meticulously trimmed, stepped out as the carriage approached. When it stopped, he called, *"Bonjour, Pierre! Comment allez-vous?"*

"*Bien, merci!*" Pierre Dulcet responded as he stepped from the carriage. He made a deep bow. "I am most well, Jean-Claude. And you, too, I pray?"

Before Jean-Claude could answer, Pierre turned his attention to Samson, who still sat on the carriage seat. "I shall be occupied for the entire afternoon," he said. He motioned toward a clutch of Negroes who lounged in the shade of an oak grove off to the side of the house. "You are to remain here until I return."

Monsieur Dulcet dashed up the steps to the *Coton Manoir* and followed Jean-Claude inside.

✐

As Samson approached the oak grove, the others turned their eyes on him and fell silent. Samson stopped off to the side and sat on the ground. He waited in silence for the others to inspect him to their full satisfaction.

"Where you from?" a stocky man with a light brown face asked.

"Africa," Samson said, his voice tinged with the slightest note of defiance.

"Why you here?" the stocky man persisted.

"I come with my master," Samson said.

After a moment of silent consideration, a slight man with crossed eyes demanded, "Why?"

Samson shrugged. "Same reason I do everythin', every day of my life. Because Massa tell me to."

The stocky man laughed out loud. "You be a slave, den, sure enough."

✐

Pierre Dulcet had never been particularly homesick for France, but if he had, the cure would have been the *Coton Manoir*. There, he could feel right at home. The décor, the repasts, the ambience—all were pure Parisian. He greeted two other Frenchmen, who were already seated and comfortable. Off to one side, a trio of musicians played softly on stringed instruments.

Jean-Claude noticed that Pierre watched the musicians, and he said with pride, "They are from the symphony orchestra. Charleston has the French to thank for making such a musical treat a possibility."

"*Magnifique!*" Pierre exclaimed.

"Indeed, Charleston has many reasons to be grateful for our presence," Jean-Claude continued. "My own dear wife, Simone, rejoiced when the first of the French dressmakers finally brought fashion to this fair city."

"Have you seen the most recent contribution of the French?" asked a droll fellow by the name of Gaston. He handed Pierre Dulcet a fresh-off-the-press copy of the French newspaper, *Le Patriote Français*.

Pierre glanced at the pages and said with a smile, "I see you still write about Monsieur L'Enfant, even though President Washington dismissed him from his appointment to develop the area around the proposed Capitol and White House on Pennsylvania Avenue."

After a few embarrassed harrumphs, Jean-Claude moved the subject away from the unpopular Frenchman. "Read about the homeland, Pierre. Who can say what will become of France? The revolution, it goes badly."

"*Oui.* And who is this new officer from Corsica?" Pierre asked, pointing to a short item in the newspaper. "This Napoleon Bonaparte?"

"No one of interest, most likely," said Gaston with a sigh. "And yet, with the officer class in France so completely decimated, even this one must be worthy of some notation, however slight."

"Come, come!" Jean-Claude interrupted. "Let us speak of relevant matters. Have you begun to plant the tobacco crop in your fields, Pierre?"

"*Oui, oui,*" said Pierre. "It brings me great pleasure to gaze out across my land and watch my slaves at work in the fields. And I tell you, it will not be long before the land is carpeted in a healthy new growth."

"Well, with revolutionary France officially at war with England, and with America claiming neutrality, the tobacco market should at long last open up for you," said Alain. He always had been a pragmatic soul. "As each of us well knows, every Frenchman is eager for American-grown tobacco."

"*Oui,*" said Pierre Dulcet with a sigh. "But it does crush my heart to hear you speak of revolutionary France."

For a Frenchman of Monsieur Dulcet's aristocratic background, life was far safer in the United States of America than in his homeland, where no one could be quite certain anymore who was friend and who was foe.

"You are aware that King Louis XVI went to the guillotine, are you not?" said Gaston. He shook his head sadly. "Paraded through the streets, he was, the drums rolling. Yet he never lost his courage."

"*Épouvantable!*" said Pierre. "Dreadful! And yet I would beg to disagree with you on one point. I believe that King Louis most certainly did lose his courage . . . step by step. It was his decision that the Constitutional Assembly should abolish slavery in France last year, was it not?"

"Well, I for one say *vive la Republique!*" announced Alain. "The royalty lived in far too opulent a manner . . . bread was much too expensive, and so the masses starved. Half the population had no work and no pay, and the king brought that ridiculous queen over from that ridiculous country. To my mind, all of France has lost its sensibilities."

*

"Your massa be French?" asked the light-brown, stocky man.

"Why you care 'bout dat, Dutch?" demanded Brister, which was the name of the small man with crossed eyes.

"Because dat king of France just got his head lopped off is why," said Dutch. "Dem French peoples wants liberty, like in dis country here. Dey wants freedom like folks in dis place has got."

"Liberty!" Brister spat. "De white man loves to say dat word!"

"Loves to say it for hisself is what you means," rumbled a large man speaking for the first time. His voice was sharp and angry. "De white man don't love to say it for us."

"No," said Samson. "Not for us."

"Not unless we lops off de white mans' heads and takes his freedom for ourself," said the angry man. "Not unless we does dat."

*

"It is good to be in this country that was established on the principles of freedom," said Jean-Claude. He lifted the crystal wine glass to his lips and sipped appreciatively. "This country is not like France. It is not like Europe at all. America is a shining land of equality and opportunity, an example to the entire world."

"Not everyone would agree with that sentiment," Gaston said. "It is true that no titled nobility dominates American society. It is also true that no pauperized underclass threatens it from below. But to the claim of freedom for all . . . well, one must acknowledge the notorious exception of slavery."

"That is an unfortunate economic necessity of our times," Alain interjected. "Do you not agree, Pierre? Surely you could not conduct your own business of producing quality tobacco without the assistance of—what?—one hundred slaves?"

"You are entirely correct," said Pierre. "The number has now reached well over one hundred. And while I treat my slaves well, I do not make pets of them. They are *outils*. Tools. The same as plows and plow horses. I could not operate my plantation without them, yet it is essential that they know their place and keep to it."

"Even the great American patriot Thomas Jefferson would agree with that sentiment," said Alain. "He looked at the bloody horrors of the slave revolt in Saint Domingue, and he proclaimed it a perfect example of what happens when Negroes are allowed to govern themselves."

"Ah, yes," said Jean-Claude. He clucked his tongue and shook his head slowly. "And a horrific example it is, too!"

☙

"I begged for mercy, but de whip kept fallin' on my back," Brister said. His voice was soft, his eyes half closed. "I thought I would die under dat accursed brute's whip. Even now, to remember it pulls de breath from my body, and I likes to die all over again. After dat whuppin', I lay on de floor two whole days afore I could get meself up again. De pain has not left me yet. No, not to dis very day."

Samson said, "'Take him to de field and shoot him.' Dat's what my first massa told Albo to do with me. De massa, he said Albo should dig a hole and bury me after I was shot through. I tried to fight, but Albo had a whip, and he had dat gun, too. He would have killed me for sure, except dat Massa Dulcet come along den, and he was needin' a cheap slave. So he bought me for de price of a jug of whiskey."

One by one, the slaves spoke the horrors they had seen and felt and hidden deep in their souls:

"Branded our arms and our legs with hot irons, dey did, just like we was animals dat belonged to dem."

"Crop down our ears with a knife. Dey never even heard our screamin' cries."

"If dey be a runner, massa chop off his foot. Or if dey be one who tells a lie, massa says slice his tongue away. If he steals, it be his fingers dat gets cut off. Even though de white man run us here far from our homes, and lies to us ever' day we lives, and steals our lives away from us."

"Dey clamped iron collars on our necks and bound us up with chains so we could hardly move."

"De slave box. Dat is de worst place to ever be. Locked away in dat cramped-up place with only a few holes poked in for air. Dey calls it rightful punishment. We calls it a place to die."

ℒ♥

"I have been hesitant to print too many details about the horrifying rebellion at Saint Domingue because it is all too repugnant for refined eyes," said Gaston with a shiver. "Thousands of plantations burned and hundreds of white families killed, their bodies mutilated beyond imagination. The stories that came across on the boats with those who actually witnessed the awfulness are nothing short of terrifying. They are, quite simply, too horrific to be expressed in civilized words!"

"Ah, *oui!*" echoed Alain. "No more are we able to soothe ourselves with the assurance that slave insurrections never succeed."

"But they are not successful here," Pierre corrected. "Not in Charleston."

"No?" challenged Alain. "And how can you be so certain that is so, Monsieur Dulcet? Because local officials diligently search vessels that come to this harbor from Saint Domingue in order to prevent angry slaves from stepping onto these shores? *Pfth!* They are already here!"

"Of course insurrection is possible here," said Gaston. "We have only to look around us to see that it is entirely possible here."

"A slave insurrection in Louisiana was almost successful two years ago," Pierre pointed out. "It was suppressed, that much is true. And yet twenty-three slaves were hanged in the aftermath and three white sympathizers deported."

"Many more Negro slaves live in Charleston than white men," Gaston said. "And I ask you, which of us really knows who of our slaves we can trust with our lives? Or with the lives of our families?"

"*Mon Dieu!*" Jean-Claude exclaimed. "I can only give thanks to God that my Simone is not here to hear this wretched talk! It would throw her into an absolute panic!"

"I say the answer is to require that each slave owner remain in complete control of his own slaves," said Pierre Dulcet. "As for those who belong to me, I can happily report that they are every one the picture of docility, contentment, and loyalty. I cannot speak for my neighbors, but I treat my own slaves well. They reward me with respect and, I dare say, with whatever affection they are capable of extending. I sleep soundly at night because I know I have not one thing to fear from my slaves."

⚜

"I know what happened on de French slave island," rumbled the angry man. "I heard de stories of murder and flames from those who were dere to see it with dey own eyes. I heard all about it from de ones dat fought against de white man and won."

"If slaves done it dere, slaves can do it here, too," said Dutch.

His voice dripped with such hatred that it sent a cold shiver through Samson.

"Dere be fightin' here, too, and soon," said the angry man. "Overseers and drivers—dey be de first to die. Den be de white masters. Dem Big Houses will roar with flames, and de fields will burn around dem. Den we run to freedom."

"But we will not hurt de Quakers," said Brister. "De Quakers won't die. Dey be friends of liberty."

"We will fight every way," the angry man hissed. "White massas think we have no power, but we will fight against dem every way we can. What does it matter if dey kills us? Dey be doin' dat already, anyway."

Samson sat back on his heels. "It sure would be somethin' to be boss of mysef," he said. "Dat sure would be somethin'. First thing I do is find my brother Cabeto. Next thing I do is get me a boat and go back home to Africa."

17

We head due south to the Canary Islands," Marcus Slade, the ship's navigator, said in answer to another one of Grace's endless questions. "There the westerly currents will give us a downhill run all the way to the Caribbean. From there we head up to Florida and on to South Carolina."

Grace's eyes glistened at the sight of the map Mister Slade had spread out before him over a barrel top. How many times she had seen her father sit at his desk in the London house at their compound in Africa and pore over just such a map. Never once had she asked him if she could look at one of his maps, though. She did regret that.

Marcus Slade laughed at the earnest look on the dark young face before him. "A Folger's map. That's what this is called, Ashok," he said. "All these markings are words and directions. Perhaps one day you will learn to read. Then you will be able to decipher such a map for yourself."

"Yes," said Grace, careful to lay on her thickest Indian-sounding accent. "Perhaps one day I will."

"I got this map in America the last time I was there," the navigator said. "In Philadelphia. That's the city where it was printed. By an American, name of Benjamin Franklin, in fact. He was a man who took great interest in the Gulf Stream. He studied it when he crossed the Atlantic Ocean by carefully noting the latitude and longitude of the ship's position several times every day. He would lower a thermometer over the side to measure the temperature of the water. When the water grew warmer, he knew he was in the Gulf Stream. I consider that rather ingenious. Do you not agree?"

"Well, sir, I—"

Grace's answer was interrupted by another commotion on the deck. Once again it was young Jackie, and once again Paddy Clemmons was after him.

"You clumsy excuse for a cook's boy!" Paddy bellowed.

He caught Jackie by the ear, and Jackie let out a shriek. Paddy raised his metal ladle and struck the boy across the face.

"Here, now, Clemmons!" exclaimed Mister Slade. "What has the boy done to deserve such treatment?"

"What *more* has he done, ye means!" roared Paddy. "Jist ruined me whole pot of porridge, is all!"

Paddy raised the ladle to give Jackie another whack, but Grace stepped between the boy and the furious cook.

"Outta me way, ye fool of a nabob!" Paddy ordered. "Or I'll blister yer black hide, too!"

"Stop the insolence this minute!"

The command came from Captain Hallam, who had hurried over in response to the commotion.

"Stop now! That is an order!"

The captain looked with disgust from Jackie to Ashok and back to Jackie. "I should have known it would be the likes of you two! Any more trouble from either of you and I will have you both locked in chains and secured belowdecks. Now, out of my sight!"

Had Captain Hallam been anything like Captain Ross of the *Willow*, Grace might have unwound the red rumal from her head and taken the risk to confide her secret to him. But Captain Hallam was nothing like Captain Ross. Captain Hallam was arrogant, proud, and bigoted. He was especially hard on Jackie, because Jackie was inept and prone to mishaps. And the captain was hard on Grace because he did not like having a crewman with dark skin.

"What happened?" Grace asked Jackie as the two of them lay side by side in their hammocks in the berth deck below.

"I hate working in the galley," Jackie sulked.

"You said that to the cook?"

"Of course I didn't! I'm not so great a fool as that. Cook told me to stand over the hot fire and stir the porridge, but when I did, it splattered on me and burned me hand. I didn't see as how the pot had to be stirred all the time, anyway, so I sat back and took me rest. It was cook's fault the porridge burned to a crisp, not mine. He was the one wot stoked the fire too hot. But it's me wot gets the blame now, ain't it? Always, it's me wot gets the blame."

Grace was quiet for a moment. "You and me," she said.

"Yes," said Jackie. "You and me. We has to stick together, you and me. We has to help each other so long as we be on this ship."

Long spans of nothing but ocean stretched the days at sea out to an endless expanse of time. When the sailors weren't at work or asleep, they made dice from bone and gambled away their meager possessions. Or they stole rum and entertained each other with drinking games and drunken songs. Or they told and retold tales, which grew more wild and exaggerated each time they were repeated. The sailors especially enjoyed any tale that would frighten Jackie and send him into a panic.

"Don't listen to them," Grace would say. But once a tale was begun, Jackie seemed unable to pull himself away.

One hot day, in the sun glare from the glassy ocean, a clutch of men sat together, deeply engrossed in something. Jackie crept closer to watch. Old Quin scraped at the top of Lucas's foot with the sharp end of a long needle. Carefully he dipped the needle into a blue concoction and poked at the lesion with it. Then he tipped the needle into a red concoction and stabbed some more at the fiery-looking wound on Lucas' foot.

"What you be doin'?" Jackie asked.

"Makin' a tattoo," said Mickey.

Jackie's curiosity grew, and he moved in closer in order to get a better view. A definite picture had begun to take shape on Lucas's foot, although Jackie couldn't tell what it was supposed to be.

Finally his curiosity got the better of him. "Mickey," Jackie blurted out, "what's Old Quin drawin' on Lucas's foot?"

"A rooster, of course," Mickey whistled through his two teeth.

The sailors exchanged quick glances and mischief danced in their eyes.

"Ye doesn't know?" Abner asked.

"Know what?" said Jackie.

"About the rooster and the pig," said Abner.

A warning tugged inside Jackie. He glanced around for Ashok, but he was nowhere to be found. Unlike Jackie, Ashok was careful to keep his distance from the other sailors.

"That be too bad," said Mickey. "Because wot ye doesn't know just might drag ye down to the bottom of the sea. Like it did to poor Collie."

An all-too-familiar panic began to rise up inside Jackie. The seamen could see it in his face.

"If'n the ship should sink in a storm, them animals in their crates would float on top of the water. Pigs and roosters and all," said Mickey, his eyes dancing with delight. "But not you. Oh, no, not you. You would sink in that ocean like a big rock."

Jackie opened his mouth, but fear strangled his words into a strained squawk.

"Now, Lucas here, he wouldn't sink. Not with that rooster Old Quin be stainin' on his one foot and the pig on the other. The spirits of them animals would keep Lucas floatin' on top of the water right along beside them animals in their crates."

"Really?" Jackie croaked.

"Ever' true sailor knows as much," said Abner. He pulled up his pantaloons and displayed the tattoos that decorated his own calves. "See? A rooster on the one side and a pig on the other."

"All done," Quin said to Lucas.

Lucas smiled and reached out his foot for all to admire. There it was, a crudely drawn but recognizable rooster.

"Come, boy, put out your feet for your own rooster and pig," Old Quin said.

Quin laid the needle aside and took out his knife.

Jackie gasped and pulled back.

"We hates to be floatin' in safety on the water and watch you alone sink in front of us," said Mickey. "Like poor Collie did."

"A little pain now or a watery grave tomorrow?" Abner said.

Jackie, near tears, gasped, "But why yer knife? Can't you use that needle on me, same as on Lucas?"

"Oh, no," said Quin. "See, Lucas here can swim some, so he don't need so much pertection. But, you . . . Can you swim, boy?"

"No," Jackie admitted.

"That's why I needs to carve the rooster and the pig deeper into you," said Quin. "'Tis yer only hope to make it back to land alive."

Abner and Mickey grabbed Jackie and held him down. Lucas slapped his hand over the boy's mouth to muffle his screams.

When Quin finished his work, Jackie had a crudely drawn blue rooster carved into one foot with the knife tip and a red pig carved into the other. The sailors sat back and laughed as the sniffling boy wiped the blood from his feet and hobbled belowdecks.

"Why, Jackie?" Grace demanded when she saw what the men had done to him.

"Because I was afraid," he said.

Jackie wept through his evening chores in the kitchen, and he tossed in his hammock throughout the night from the pain. The next day was even worse, and the day after that his feet were fiery hot and swollen. Jackie lay helpless in his hammock crying with pain. Grace begged for the ship's surgeon to come and see to Jackie's wounds, but the surgeon refused. A new cabin boy was easy enough to pick up at the next port, he said. So Grace bathed the boy's feet as best she could, and she brought him food and drink.

"No one on this ship is as miserable as me," Jackie moaned to Grace. "No one is so tortured and alone."

Grace wiped Jackie's feverish face with a wet cloth and thought about her own life. Her despair in her parents' compound, especially at the prospect of marriage to Jasper Hathaway. Her anguish in the wretched dungeon at Zulina fortress. Her helplessness as the slave ship carried her Cabeto away. Her loneliness without little Kwate . . . without Mama Muco . . . without Cabeto.

And now, her terror at the unknown path that lay ahead.

"Jackie," she whispered, "you are not the only one."

She closed her mouth and said no more.

18

The action brazenly taken by that pitiful association of people who so pretentiously call themselves an abolition group was a personal affront on you, Your Lordship," Lord Reginald Witherham impassioned to Lord Judge Aaron North. "It is the reputation of the Crown that causes me so grave a concern. When such a one as your esteemed self passes a sentence on a criminal, no person—indeed, no group of persons—should be allowed to follow along behind and overturn the ruling of the Crown. With Grace Winslow on her way out of the country, I fear that you have been shown such great disrespect that the citizens of London shall henceforth hold you up to ridicule. This situation should not, and must not, be tolerated, Your Lordship!"

Lord Judge Aaron North extracted a handkerchief from the pocket of his waistcoat and mopped it across his squat face. He sighed wearily. While he appreciated so great a concern for himself and the Crown, he told Lord Reginald, he most assuredly avowed his supreme confidence that both could manage quite well without any further assistance.

Lord Reginald opened his mouth to plead further, but Lord Judge North had heard quite enough. He rose to his feet and hurried out of his own chambers.

⌇

"England, as you well know, is a country of laws," Lord Reginald informed Simon Johnson when he finally managed to corner him outside the House of Commons. "It is a country of justice. As a member of Parliament, you are most assuredly particularly aware of this fact. It must not be permissible for individuals to circumvent the law simply to satisfy their own personal sentiments. While Sir Geoffrey Phillips remains a friend of both yours and mine, and while he most definitely has a right to subject himself to his own conscience—however misguided that conscience may be—I am certain you will agree that he does not have the right to overturn rulings of the Crown."

Simon Johnson drew a watch from his pocket and checked the time. "My, but you do go on, Witherham," he said. A pressing engagement awaited him, he insisted, and he really must be on his way.

Lord Reginald had more to say, so he positioned himself directly in front of his old friend and opened his mouth. But Simon Johnson stepped deftly around him and was off before the next word was out.

⌇

"It does not please me to be so blunt, but the fact is that Grace Winslow made a complete fool of you," Lord Reginald pointed out to Jasper Hathaway, who had made the mistake of accepting an invitation to take tea at Larkspur Estate. "Can it be that you are not aware that all of London knows you were tossed aside by a *slave*? Can it be that you truly do not understand what a laughingstock she made of you? Of all people, Jasper, I would think you would want to see her brought to justice. Oh, Grace Winslow is a clever one, I will give you that. But we must see that she is not allowed to escape her rightful fate. You and I, Jasper . . . we must see to that. And that is why we must pursue the demand for justice."

In a gesture now automatic, Jasper Hathaway held his hand over his mouth.

"Make a demand for justice, my lord?" he asked. "Perhaps that would not be so wise. Perhaps too many questions would be asked. Perhaps a demand for justice would exact a most unwelcome toll from all of us."

"You forget yourself, Mister Hathaway," Lord Reginald said, a most disagreeable edge to his voice. "I am a person of extreme power and influence."

"Past is past," Jasper Hathaway said. "Perhaps the wiser course would be to let it rest."

✐❧

"I shall not punish you, Charlotte, because I am a most patient man," Lord Reginald said to his wife. "I understand that you are but a woman. And taking that frailty into full consideration, I regret deeply that you were ever thrust into a position that required you to determine a point of law and justice. I only ask that you acknowledge your lapse in judgment. You need not ask my forgiveness, for I willingly and generously extend it to you. But Sir Geoffrey Phillips is most likely so humiliated by having been led astray by your show of female emotion that he has not the least idea how to begin to mend the damage he has caused. It is to him I would have you go. Let him know you have repented of your actions, and urge him to do the same."

Lady Charlotte stared at her husband. Could it be that even now he understood so little about her? She had no desire to explain herself to him yet again. She had no time, either. The others were waiting for her at Heath and Rebekah Patterson's barn.

✒

"As I stated in my message when I sent my carriage around, Mister Winslow, I believe I can be of great assistance to you," Lord Reginald said.

Joseph Winslow sat uneasily on the edge of the Queen Anne chair, his hat in his hands, and eyed Lord Reginald with suspicion.

"I am truly sorry that your daughter turned out to be the criminal sort. It must have been difficult for one in your position to raise a child properly. I have brought you here as an act of Christian charity, and—"

Joseph Winslow leapt to his feet. "I 'as seen yer Christian charity, and I wants none of it!" he said.

"That is to say, I have brought you to here to offer you a chance to set things to right," Lord Reginald said with coddling patience.

Joseph spat on the marble floor. He turned his back on Lord Reginald and walked out of his house.

✒

"I will not forget!" Lord Reginald Witherham vowed through clenched teeth. This he said to no one in particular, for no one was left to help him chase down Grace.

19

The night was fresh, and a warm breeze rustled through the palm fronds overhead. Grace smiled in the twilight of her sleep. She nestled against the softness of little Kwate, who breathed sleeping-baby breaths in the crook of her arm. Oh, that sweet child-smell. Love and happiness filled Grace's heart to bursting. She bent her head to press her lips against the tender face of her little one . . .

Grace's eyes opened with a start. There was no fresh air, no warm breeze, no rustling palm fronds. No soft toddler lay waiting to be kissed.

Tears filled Grace's eyes and rolled down her cheeks. She tugged at the bindings that seemed to squeeze ever more tightly around her, like an African snake crushing the life out of its prey. Gasping in the airless mustiness of the below deck, Grace stumbled from her hammock and silently made her way between the rows of snoring men, up the ladder and out onto the darkened deck.

The night was incredibly black. No moon shone and not one star broke through the thick layer of clouds. Struggling to breathe, Grace stumbled to the rail and stared over the side.

In the darkness, she couldn't even make out the water below. With a desperate gasp, she yanked the sailor shirt over her head. She grabbed hold of the ends of the tight cloth that bound her chest and pulled free.

The strips hung loose, away from her soft figure. Just for a few minutes. Just so she could breathe.

For a long moment, Grace gulped in the night air. Actually, for many long moments, because she was suddenly startled to see faint rays of light at the edges of the horizon. Quickly Grace tugged the binding back around her chest and pulled the sailor shirt over her head. She wiped the tears from her cheeks and turned away from the rail.

"Who *is* you?"

Grace froze. It was Jackie's voice, flat and hard. She stared, but she couldn't see him.

"Who *is* you!" This time it was not a question so much as a command.

"Jackie . . . It's me," Grace stammered. "Ashok. Your best mate."

A glorious sunrise began to splash majestic hues across the horizon, and in the budding light of dawn, Grace saw Jackie in the shadow of the bulkhead.

"Please, Jackie, I have something to explain to you," Grace began.

But as she stepped toward the boy, Jackie stepped back.

"Who *is* you!" he demanded again. This time his voice was icy.

Grace sagged. She could hardly stay on her feet.

"No one else has to know, Jackie," she pleaded. "I only want to go to South Carolina. All I ask is a chance to find my Cabeto."

"A slave!" Jackie spat. "A Negro slave, that's what you is! You lied to me. I trusted you, and you tricked me!"

"I couldn't tell you the truth. I couldn't tell anyone."

Jackie said nothing.

"You don't have to help me," Grace said. "I won't ask you to do that. I only ask you to let me be. Let me continue to work on the ship. Please, Jackie. Give me a chance."

Jackie stared at her in silence. Then he turned and walked away.

As the ship's bell sounded the change of the watch, Jackie trotted toward the galley and Grace hurried to her post on the deck. Her crew had already finished sanding, and the timbers felt smooth as polish.

"Today you be paintin' the first finish," Bart commanded. "Straight and even, that's what it's to be."

A steaming pot of foul-smelling liquid had been lugged up to the deck and the work was ready to begin when Captain Hallam and first mate Archie Rhodes strolled up. The two stopped directly in front of Grace.

"Is it true that Indian faces cannot grow beards?" Captain Hallam asked Archie.

"No, sir, it is not," replied Archie. A grin nudged at the corners of his mouth.

"Are you certain of that, Mister Rhodes?" asked the captain.

"Yes, sir," replied Archie. "With me own two eyes, I once saw an Indian wearin' a great bushy mustache, and a full beard, too."

"That is interesting, indeed," replied Captain Hallam.

The blood drained from Grace's face and a cold terror crept up her back. She could see Bart staring at her, and several of the other seamen, as well. Others simply cast puzzled looks from one to another.

"But if that be the case, Mister Rhodes," continued the captain, "how is it that Mister Ashok Iravan, who tells us he is from India, has not so much as the bare beginnings of either a mustache or a beard?"

"I cannot say, sir," replied Archie. "Unless it be that he is not really from India, after all."

"Or, perhaps, that he is not really a he?" replied the captain.

Curiosity drove even the best of the seamen from their duties. Men had already begun to drift away from their posts and join the crowd that gathered to gawk. Now, with this new revelation, their eyes popped and their mouths fell open.

Grace laid her polishing rags aside. She stood straight and unapologetic before Captain Hallam and looked him in the eye. "You and Mister Rhodes are both right, sir," she said. "I am not from India and I am not a he."

In a sudden fury, Captain Hallam grabbed Grace by the arm and yanked the red rumal turban off her head. Her hair fell around her shoulders in auburn coils. The captain grabbed her shirt and tried to pull it off her, but Grace kicked at him and scratched.

"Stop!" Marcus Slade ordered.

Captain Hallam stared at him.

"Captain, sir! We must not forget ourselves," Mister Slade said. "We are civilized men, after all. Should we not allow him . . . her . . . to explain herself?"

As Captain Hallam regained control of himself, he loosened his grip on Grace. "By all means, do explain," he ordered.

So Grace poured out the story of her capture in Africa, of her husband's enslavement, of the injustices she had suffered in London.

When she finished, Captain Hallam said, "You must be a sorry lot to warrant a sentence of transportation. So you are a convicted thief? Maybe, in truth, something far worse?"

"Lord Witherham invented the accusations," Grace insisted. "None of them were true, sir. I have a sealed letter from Sir Geoffrey explaining—."

"Pshaw," sneered the captain. "Every convict claims innocence. And a goodly number have letters or documents to back up their claims."

"As you well know, sir, many convicts are indeed the unfortunate victims of circumstance," Marcus Slade pointed out.

"Mister Slade, are you a navigator or are you a barrister?" asked Captain Hallam.

"Sir, the English penal code is chock-full of capital crimes," the navigator insisted. "It is a well-known fact that many men with influence have used it unfairly to dispose of those they find inconvenient. You, sir, are more aware than I of the fact that of the thousands of convicts dumped in the colonies by London authorities, more than a few were convicted unjustly."

"Is you English or is you African?" Archie Rhodes demanded of Grace. "Is you colored or is you white?"

Without the slightest pause, Grace answered, "I, sir, am African."

"You are a slave!" said Captain Hallam.

"No, sir," Grace replied. "I am not a slave."

"You will be when you get to America," said James Talbot. "In America, that's what Africans are."

"Till then, you be our gal," chortled Mickey.

A whole new look spread over the captain's countenance. "Not one man will lay a hand on her unless I give the word," he said. "This ship is still under my command. I order you to stay clear of her, under pain of fifty hard lashes."

Tucked away in his cabin, Captain Hallam had a box with a pink silk frock folded inside. He had bought the dress in port with the intention of making it a gift to his wife.

"Fetch a large pitcher of water and a cloth," Captain Hallam said to Archie. "And bring it to my quarters."

That's where the captain took Grace. He pulled out his wife's dress and handed it to Grace. "Wash yourself first," he told her. "Your hair, too. Put on this frock and show yourself to me."

Grace stretched out her preparations so they would last as long as possible. The dress was too large and hung on her, but the silk flowed nicely and was soft and smooth against her skin. She ran her fingers through her wet hair and allowed it to curl down her shoulders.

"I am so sorry, Cabeto!" Grace whispered. "If only I were dressing up for you!"

A sharp knock startled her just before the door flew open. Captain Hallam stood in the doorway and stared. The dirty brown-skinned boy from India was no more. In his place was a lovely young woman of the most unique coloring and features. Captain Hallam could not believe that he had been so easily fooled. Was it the oversized shirt and baggy pantaloons? The rumal-wrapped hair and head? Or was it simply that Abraham Hallam had never actually looked at the boy from India who sailed on his ship?

Captain Hallam's eyes shone in a whole new way, but the glint was not one of desire. No, it was the gleam of greed.

Once the ship arrived in Charleston harbor, the load of horses and fine furniture in the hold would be unloaded for the pleasure of the wealthy men in that city. Captain Hallam would collect his pay as usual, of course, but that would be that. He would not get so much more as a "Thank you, sir." But if he also had a comely wench to sell—one as desirable as this silky mixed breed with all the refinements of an English girl—well, the profit he could garner from such a one could be substantial. And it would be his alone.

"Very good," Captain Hallam said to Grace. "You will, I think, do very well for me on the slave auction block."

⁂

That night, when the officers of the *Ocean Steed* gathered for dinner, Captain Hallam informed them of his decision in regards to Grace.

"She is my personal property, and she carries a great value," the captain said bluntly. "She is not to be touched by anyone, neither officer nor seaman. She will remain under my protection in my quarters both day and night. I will see that she is fattened up and softened."

As though he forgot the others were still there, he added quietly, "It is not likely that another slave like her will ever again be available to me."

The other officers focused their attention on the soup and chicken.

Except Marcus Slade.

Mister Slade ventured his opinion that slavery was a most cruel system, and the sooner America was free of it, the better everyone would be. Why, even their own president, George Washington—a slave owner himself—had said as much.

"You would do well to keep your opinions to yourself," Captain Hallam snapped. "Just as I do well to keep the slave girl to myself."

⁂

Jackie lay in his hammock, swaying with the rock of the ship and glowering into the dark. It had taken every bit of courage he could muster, but he had done it. He knew something important, he had told Archie Rhodes, something no one knew but him. He would tell his secret, Jackie had said, but only for a price. Mister Rhodes must first promise to see that Jackie was moved out of the galley and into a different job. A much better job.

"I want to be a real sailor," Jackie said. "I want to go aloft in the rigging and the shrouds. I want to go to the top of the mast, to be the lookout in the crow's nest."

"Oh, yes," Archie Rhodes had promised. "I kin make that deal with you."

But it didn't happen that way. Archie listened to Jackie's secret. But before he headed for the captain's cabin, he ordered Jackie right back to the galley. Right back to the same job he hated.

"It ain't fair," Jackie mumbled into the dark. "No more Ashok by me side, and I didn't even git the job Mister Rhodes promised to me!"

⚓

Still wearing the over-sized silk dress, Grace lay down on the cot in the corner of the captain's cabin. If only she had not been so foolhardy! If only she had never gone out onto the deck in the first place. If only she had not so readily confessed everything to Jackie. If only . . . if only . . . If only she were not all alone.

But she was *not* all alone, was she?

Grace closed her eyes. Silently her lips began to move: "The LORD is my shepherd; I shall not want. He maketh me to lie down in green pastures: he leadeth me beside the still waters. He restoreth my soul: he leadeth me in the paths of righteousness for his name's sake. Yea, though I walk through the valley of the shadow of death, I will fear no evil: for thou art with me; thy rod and thy staff they comfort me. Thou preparest a table before me in the presence of mine enemies. thou anointest my head with oil; my cup runneth over. Surely goodness and mercy shall follow me all the days of my life: and I will dwell in the house of the LORD for ever."

20

*Y*ou have met Judge Thomas Heyward, have you not?"
Macon Waymon's business partner, Samuel Shaw, asked
Macon.

"No, sir, I have not had the pleasure," Macon replied.
"And I must say, it is extremely good of you to include me in
your visit to his house. From what I hear, his estate truly is a
marvel."

"Politics is hardly a field for shrinking violets, now, is
it?" Samuel laughed. "As I am determined to engage in a
concerted effort to make my name well-known among the
voting public, I consider it essential that I befriend men such
as Thomas."

Macon opened his mouth, but before he could utter a word,
Samuel dismissed him with a wave of his hand.

"Yes, yes, I know what you will say, Macon. You will point
out that Thomas Heyward is a sitting judge and no longer
a congressional representative of our fair state. That is certainly true, of course. But nevertheless, he was a signer of the
United States Declaration of Independence, and therefore he
remains a personage of great importance. He was also the man

chosen to host President George Washington on his singular visit to Charleston. So, whether a sitting representative or not, such a man cannot help but be an asset to my forthcoming campaign."

As Macon had intended to say no such thing, he simply smiled and nodded to his enthusiastic friend.

Samuel could scarcely hide his excitement as he anticipated the coming evening at Thomas Heyward's house. He adjusted and readjusted his stylish velvet frock coat. The garment reached to his knees and was richly decorated with elaborate buttons and embroidery. Corresponding breeches fastened tightly at his knees, and around his neck he wore one of the puffy ties for which he was known. A stylish ensemble, perhaps, but in the opinion of Macon Waymon, a silly set of clothing on a man as stout as Samuel Shaw.

"All is well with the cotton engine?" Samuel asked.

"Extremely well," Macon assured him. "That lame slave I purchased for so cheap a price from Silas Leland runs the operation. After one month with him at the gin, the storage houses on all five cotton plantations are now empty of cotton and swept clean. In just one single month! Why, before the cotton gin, it would have taken a slave ten hours of painstaking work just to separate one pint of cotton lint from three pounds of seeds!"

Sam raised his eyebrows. "The storage houses are swept clean, you say? But the new cotton crops will not be ready for harvest for six more months."

"Yes, yes," said Macon, "but we nevertheless continue to fill our pockets with money. Not through the sale of our own cotton, to be sure. No, no. Rather, by ginning cotton for all the neighboring farmers. And we are able to charge them a pretty penny for the favor, I might add!"

Samuel Shaw laughed out loud. "You have turned out to be a fine businessman, Macon. Indeed you have!"

Macon's man, Wiatt, had not yet announced the arrival of the carriage, although Samuel could see that it already waited outside. He had just picked up his hand-carved walking stick with the brass trim and was about to head for the door, Macon close behind him, when Wiatt hurried to Macon with an urgent message.

"It be Juba, Master," Wiatt said to Macon.

"Not now, Wiatt," Macon said as he waved him off.

"Juba say it be urgent," Wiatt insisted.

Samuel heaved an irritated sigh. "Really, Macon, can you not talk with your slave at a more appropriate time? It would be an extremely poor show to arrive late at the Heyward party."

Macon nodded and moved toward the waiting carriage. Wiatt, however, was most insistent.

"Just a short word with him, Master," Wiatt said. "Juba says that's all he asks of you."

Macon groaned in resignation and tossed his hat onto the table.

"One word, then. Tell Juba I will see him. But tell him I am in a hurry. Just one word and no more!"

The one word Juba had for Macon was "broken." And a most terrible word it was, too. For the cotton gin, it seemed, no longer worked. At the most unfortunate of times, too. With the last of the oceangoing vessels of the season jammed into Charleston Harbor, and already competing for the last freight runs of cotton to England, Macon Waymon was all too aware of the race against time. Every moment's delay in getting the last of the past harvest's cotton ginned, baled, and loaded onto ships meant dollars lost.

"You go ahead to Heyward's house, Samuel," Macon said. "I will deal with this matter. It is much more important that you be at the party than I."

✒

Macon Waymon followed Juba out to the cotton shed. Caleb had secured the gin on a waist-high wooden platform, though he was careful to leave the crank handle fully accessible. Fluffs of cotton, freed from their bolls, lay strewn about the floor. Behind the cotton engine, a line of half a dozen slaves waited for a turn at the gin, huge baskets of raw cotton balanced on their heads or tied to their backs.

"Caleb, I got de massa for you," Juba announced. "Tell him about de problem you has here."

"It be dis gin," Caleb said. "It don't work."

"But what exactly is the problem?" Macon insisted.

"De wire teeth on dis side here," Caleb said as he pointed inside the cotton gin. "Dey be all twisted up . . . Comes from so much turning 'em, I s'pose."

"Can you fix them?" Macon asked.

"I be tryin' to do dat, Massa," Caleb said. "But the base of dem teeth, it be too weak. Dey just can't pull de lint outta de seeds no more."

Macon shook his head in exasperation. Perhaps he could get another machine from Eli Whitney. But even if that were possible, it would never arrive in time to take advantage of the last weeks of this season's cotton shipping. Besides, Mister Whitney was certain to see Macon's desperation, and he would raise the price on his engine. What good was the machine if he and Shaw couldn't earn a profit from their business?

"I been studyin' how I could maybe makes you a whole new cotton machine," Caleb said.

Macon Waymon stared at his slave.

"What?" he demanded. "What did you say?"

"I didn't mean nothin' wrong, Massa," Caleb said quickly.

"No, no, nothing is wrong," Macon said. "Did you say you could make me a new cotton gin?"

"All I needs do is hammer wire teeth into a wood post dat can go round and round and catch all de little cotton lints like dis here," Caleb said. He pointed out the appropriate parts on Eli Whitney's cotton gin. "Dey pulls de lint through de little holes in a grate like dis. See, de cotton seeds be too big to pass through dese holes here, so de lint, it be pulled away. I could make a machine dat would do de same job for you, Massa, but it would be some different. I can't make one exactly de same as dis one be."

"How long would it take you to make another one?" Macon said. It took everything in him to control his excitement. "That is, to make a new machine that works?"

Caleb scratched his head. "If I gets de pieces I need . . . If I works all through de night . . . If I can bend de wire teeth from dis engine back so's dat I can use dem over again . . . maybe by tomorrow in de afternoon."

"If you do that for me, Caleb, I will have Prudie wring the neck on a plump hen and I will have her roast the whole thing just for you!" Macon cried. "And I will have her make the sweetest cake you ever tasted that you can eat after you finish the chicken!"

Macon was out the door hollering for Wiatt to get the carriage ready immediately. As soon as it was brought around, Macon jumped inside.

"To the Heyward House!" he called to the carriage driver. "As fast as your horses can go!"

Charleston's elite was a wealthy group. They had grown so in trade and by making money loans and in crop plantations and with slaves. They all knew each other—indeed, most were intertwined by birth and marriage—and they were united in values as well. Macon Waymon did not really fit in. Actually, Samuel Shaw didn't, either. But both expected to do so very soon.

"Macon!" Samuel Shaw exclaimed as his friend and partner was ushered over to his side. "I did not expect to see you tonight."

"Samuel, I must meet Thomas Heyward," Macon said. "Right away, if you please. It really is quite important."

"I only just met him myself," Samuel said. "I cannot—"

"It is a matter of utmost urgency," Macon insisted. "Please. Surely you can introduce me to him!"

Samuel gestured in the direction of a rather plain-looking gentleman with a long face and no wig on his brown hair. He leaned against a most opulent mantelpiece, and was deeply engrossed in conversation with a tall man with a thick shock of red hair dressed in a fine evening suit.

Macon Waymon placed a smile on his face and headed toward the evening's host.

"Stop!" Samuel insisted. "You cannot just walk up unannounced to a man of such wealth and standing! It would be in the worst possible of tastes."

Macon paid him no mind.

"Macon, please," Samuel pleaded. "Tonight is an important evening for me. Do not make a fool of yourself. I beg of you—"

But Macon had already pushed his way past the other guests. He stepped right up to the mantle.

". . . and I do thank you for taking my humble request into account," the red-haired man said. "To own a copy of our country's Declaration of Independence, especially with your signature at the bottom, would be an indescribable honor for me."

"Not at all, Mister Williamson," Thomas Heyward said. "It shall be my gift to you."

"Mister Heyward?" Macon said as courteously as he could manage. He bowed first to Heyward and then to Williamson. "I do apologize for interjecting myself into your personal conversation, but I have a most pressing matter I wish to discuss with you. Would this be an appropriate time to do so?"

Pace Williamson thanked Thomas Heyward once again for his graciousness and generosity, and promptly excused himself.

"Do forgive me, sir," Macon said, "but may I be so bold as to impose upon you a somewhat delicate question of the law? Here is the situation that confronts me . . ."

When Samuel saw that Macon's interruption did not cause a complete social disaster, he did his best to make his way over and join in on the conversation. But people stopped him to talk, and he felt he must not be rude. More people blocked the way, and he felt he must not be overly aggressive toward them. Still others had questions for him, and he felt he most certainly could not allow those questions to go unanswered.

When Macon Waymon at last looked Mister Shaw's way, he called out, "Samuel! Do come and join us!"

Thomas Heyward smiled politely and congratulated Samuel on his willingness to participate in public service.

But Macon cut their courteous comments short.

"Our troubles are over, and it is all due to the diligent efforts of Judge Heyward," he announced to Samuel. "My slave Caleb is right now at work on his own version of Eli Whitney's cotton gin. It will not be exactly the same as Whitney's, however, and due to that happy circumstance, it will qualify as a 'new' invention. We will owe Mister Whitney not one penny for its use."

"Surely Eli Whitney will sue us!" Samuel exclaimed.

"Surely he will," said Macon. "But it makes not the least bit of difference. Because, according to Judge Heyward, the way the new patent act passed just this year is worded, Mister Whitney cannot win such a suit."

"Is that true?" Samuel asked Thomas Heyward.

"It is," said Mister Heyward.

"By tomorrow morning, we will have our own cotton gin," Macon said. "And we will own it free and clear!"

21

*F*or almost two weeks, Benjamin Stevens had started and ended each day standing watch on the rise outside Zulina fortress. From there he could stare down the road toward the villages. Every day he had waited and watched. Every day he had squinted his dimming blue eyes into the relentless African sun. And every day he saw the same thing—an empty road stretched out before him.

"This infernal delay is Lingongo's fault!" Benjamin fretted. "A conniving witch, that's what she is."

Despite the delay, Benjamin had made up his mind that under no circumstances would he agree to Lingongo's proposed changes in the terms of their trade agreement. Why should he? No other slave trader would offer her and her brother, King Obei, so favorable a market for their African captives. Captain John Conant, whose ship lay at anchor in the harbor, would simply have to wait.

Yet, as the days wore on, Benjamin's resolve began to weaken.

It was Jonah, Benjamin's head slave, who finally caught sight of the human train as it wound up the road. Jonah whooped at the sight and ran to find Benjamin to shout out the news.

"They be comin', Master," Jonah hollered, "The new slaves right now be comin' along the road!"

Benjamin Stevens rushed out to meet the human train. But his elation was short-lived.

Many scores of prime men and women, all from villages hitherto untouched by slavers. That's what Princess Lingongo had promised him. Hundreds of captives, and all top quality. But what Benjamin saw dragging into the compound was something else entirely—a coffle of no more than a dozen skinny, worn-out men and women barely able to stand on their feet, and a sprinkling of exhausted children. The bedraggled captives—metal collars around their necks by which they were all chained together—could barely stand up.

Benjamin ran his hand through his tousled gray hair and shook with fury.

"Go fetch Princess Lingongo!" he ordered Jonah.

"Yes, Master," the slave said, and he took off at a run.

One English slave ship waited in the harbor. One single ship. Yet that ship could hold over three hundred slaves if they were tight packed. The problem was, Captain Conant had reached the end of his patience. He had long since outfitted his ship for a full load of slaves, and it was fully supplied. Since the ship had actually been designed to transport goods rather than people, and because two legs of the triangular slave trade involved crates of textiles and bales of cotton and barrels of molasses, he'd had to carefully plan and refit in order to accomplish this, but it was done.

By the time Princess Lingongo arrived at Zulina, the captives had all been securely chained to posts outside.

"So few of them!" Benjamin accused. He pointed his finger to one after the other after the other. "Why so few? And what took them so long to get here?"

The princess, resplendent in one of the royal kente robes in which she always bedecked herself, gazed haughtily at Benjamin.

"Why so few?" she asked back. "Why so long? Because the white man has already taken so many of our people away from the coastland, that is why. Our warriors must go deeper and deeper into the jungles to search out villages that have not already been ripped apart. Perhaps you do not realize that African villagers do not give up their freedom willingly. They fight back, and they fight hard. So they are wounded. Our warriors fasten them in chains. The captives must march from their home all the way to the coast—a long and difficult walk. If you doubt that, you may accompany the warriors on the next raid. You will see that the trail is marked with the bones of those who did not survive. Perhaps then you will understand why so few and why so long."

Benjamin Stevens's face hardened. "I know the process," he said. "I also know that I need four hundred good captives. Just as you promised me."

"We can only give you what we ourselves can get," Princess Lingongo replied. "Just as you can only give us what you can get."

Benjamin understood her perfectly. The first day of their alliance, Princess Lingongo had informed him that she and her brother would only accept guns and gunpowder in exchange for their captives. They would no longer take bolts of cloth or beads or whiskey, which were common for such trades. They would not even accept iron bars. Guns and gunpowder. Nothing else. Because only guns and gunpowder had the capability to bestow power on their people.

Of course, Benjamin was no fool. He was well aware that too many guns and too much gunpowder in the hands of an African king could well be a threat to him. So with each purchase, he forced the Africans to accept less firepower and more cloth, or iron bars, or whiskey. When the princess challenged him, Benjamin had told her: "I can only give you what I can get."

Benjamin Stevens glared straight into Princess Lingongo's dark eyes. "Perhaps other African kings and warlords will be able to give me what I want," he said.

Princess Lingongo stared back just as hard. "Perhaps they will," she replied.

Benjamin waited for Princess Lingongo's eyes to pull away from his, but they did not. Nor did so much as a tiny flinch crease her beautiful face.

*

"Children!" Captain Conant sneered. "You assured me I would have a ship filled with top-grade slaves, Stevens. For a fortnight now I have waited here to receive what you promised, and now you offer me half-dead children!"

"I see plenty of strong men here, John," Benjamin answered with a wave of his hand. "And supple young women, too. You will get your money's worth. That I can guarantee you."

"Where is the rest of my shipload?" the captain demanded. "Can you guarantee me that?"

"More captives are on the way," Benjamin assured him. "By the time this batch is securely chained in your ship's hold, the others will be ready."

With a grumble and a grunt, Captain Conant spat out an offer for the pitiful group. Although it was disappointingly low, and although Benjamin Stevens had no idea where he would get the extra bodies to fill the ship, he shook Captain Conant's hand in agreement.

✐

"Rhoda!" Benjamin Stevens bellowed as he stomped back into his house. "Rhoda, where are you?"

When no answer came, Benjamin went in search of his house slave. He found her out back, building up the kitchen fire.

"Did you not hear me calling out to you?" Benjamin demanded.

"I heard you," the slave said.

"When I call your name, I expect an immediate answer from you!"

"My name is not Rhoda," said the slave. "It is Muco."

In spite of himself, Benjamin trembled with fury.

"You are my slave, so you will be called whatever I determine to call you."

"My name is Muco."

"I informed you that henceforth you would be called Rhoda. When I call you Rhoda, you will answer me!"

The slave stared defiantly into Benjamin's eyes. "Call me what you want to call me," she said. "I will answer to my name, which is Muco."

Benjamin's face flushed hot and his hands clenched into tight fists. But when he saw the loathing in his slave's black eyes, he breathed deeply and stepped back.

In every circumstance, however it might challenge him, Benjamin Stevens congratulated himself on his ability to think clearly and act with purpose. How was it that everything suddenly seemed to be slipping from his grasp?

No villages left where slave catchers could find decent captives? Impossible! Benjamin Stevens needed Captain Conant's slave payment, in fine British gold crowns, in order to complete his new house, and he would not get it without the slaves. Now his slave chose this moment to stand against him. He could have her whipped for such impertinence, and no civilized man would blame him. He could even have her killed! Surely she knew that, and yet this slave woman dared stand against him over something as ridiculous as the choice of her name!

Unfair! Exceedingly unfair! everything inside Benjamin screamed. *I am the master of Zulina! My word is law!*

Yet, because he was a temperate man, even in his fury he took a deep breath and turned away from his slave's glower.

"I shall take my supper in my study," he said. "Rhoda."

✐

"Today is the day I throw your wretched Africans off my ship and into the sea," Captain Conant informed Benjamin. "I have wasted two weeks of fair skies and calm seas, yet still I see no evidence of the young men with muscles or beautiful young wenches you promised me."

That very same day Princess Lingongo approached Benjamin. "My brother the king sent our warriors deep into the heart of Africa, to distant villages many days' journey from the coast. He sent them to places not yet spoiled by slavers, where the people do not know to run away. The talking drums say their caravan is vast and rich with captives, and that it is but one day away. My brother the king requires assurance that you are prepared to pay for the slaves in guns and gunpowder alone."

Benjamin Stevens clenched his jaw and said yes, he was prepared to meet the king's terms. The princess's terms.

What does it matter? Benjamin asked himself. *Captain Conant will pay me a handsome price for the slaves. So what does it matter if I must bow to Lingongo? Once again?*

The sun sank low over the savanna. The rainy season had come early, but the rainfall was discouragingly light. Benjamin Stevens mopped his face with his handkerchief and longed for the fog of London. After almost a quarter of a century in Africa, he was weary of being hot and weary. He was exhausted and exasperated with his efforts to pretend to cooperate with Lingongo and her fool of a brother.

"Rhoda!" Benjamin called as he opened the door. "Bring me my dinner."

No answer.

Rage rose up in him like a blaze of fire. Benjamin slammed the door and bolted through to the back of the house. He kicked a straight-backed chair aside and grabbed up his horse whip.

"Rhoda!" Benjamin bellowed as he thundered out behind the house. When he saw the slave, he roared, "You *will* answer me when I call for you!"

"My name is Muco," she said, her voice flat and her face expressionless.

"You are my slave and I say your name is Rhoda!"

Benjamin brought the whip slashing down across her back.

"What is your name?" Benjamin demanded.

"Muco," said the slave.

The whip ripped through the air and slashed across her cheek and down her arms. The calabash shell in her hand crashed to the ground.

"What is your name, slave?"

The slave struggled to her feet. She wiped the blood from her mouth and, as best she could, said, "Muco."

Benjamin screamed out his fury. He raised the whip again and again.

"What is your name?" he demanded.

The slave tried to rise, but instead she fell flat. She tried again and succeeded in pushing herself up to her knees. She fixed her eyes on Benjamin and said, "Muco. My name is Muco."

Benjamin's blinding fury faded just enough for him to see the cold hard revulsion in the eyes of the black woman on her knees before him. Her bloody jaw was clamped tight, and her eyes never wavered from his.

Benjamin gasped and shrank back. The slave's blind strength of will forced him back to that horrible day at Zulina fortress. He had seen the same look in the eyes of the rebels who would not quit.

Muco struggled to her feet. She wiped the blood from her face with her apron. She pushed past Benjamin and stumbled to the storeroom where she slept between the piles of yams and cassavas. With determined abandon, she spread a cloth out on the floor and threw her few belongings onto it—her second dress, three head scarves, the missionary's Holy Bible she had saved. She plucked up the corners of the cloth and tied them together and hoisted the load onto her head. Muco turned her back on Benjamin Stevens and his house, and she limped her way down the road.

Benjamin Stevens watched her go. He dropped his whip to the ground, walked back into the house, and sank into a chair. He dropped his head into his hands and wept.

Once upon a time, I was a good and moral Christian man, Benjamin groaned. *Once upon a time, I vowed I would remain honest and true, however rich and powerful I might become.*

Once upon a time . . .

22

As the *Ocean Steed* sailed into Charleston harbor, four men rowed up alongside the ship in a longboat.

"Any slaves set for auction today?" Captain Abraham Hallam called out jovially.

"Why do you ask?" one man hollered back. "You got slaves for sale?"

"That I do," Captain Hallam replied in a hearty voice. "One slave, that is. And a fine one she is, too."

Before the captain knew what was happening, the ship was surrounded by four more longboats. They all joined together to force his ship away from the harbor despite Captain Hallam's bellowed objections.

"You may not enter the harbor!" a yellow-haired man in the lead boat shouted to him. "Proceed to Sullivan's Island and drop anchor there!"

Captain Hallam roared and raged, but the boats blocked his way. He had no choice but to sail on to Sullivan, one of the barrier isles that protected Charleston Harbor from the Atlantic Ocean.

After weeks of anticipation, Captain Abraham Hallam did not enjoy the afternoon one bit. Although it was a fresh late-spring day and mild ocean breezes ruffled through the palmetto trees atop the dunes, he paid them no mind. Nor did he unload his cargo as he had expected to do. Instead, he escorted Grace off the ship, led her around behind the beach, and signed her in to the repugnant "pest house."

"Yellow fever quarantine!" he fumed. "This is an outrage! An absolute outrage! We sailed here from London. Where would we get yellow fever, I ask you?"

When his protestations did him no good, the captain demanded of every person he saw, "Who is in charge in this place? I insist that you direct me to the man in charge!"

Captain Hallam was still hollering when the guard opened the padlocked door and shoved Grace into the filthy pest house. She huddled down in a corner. Up at the top of the cage were two large openings, so at least some air managed to get inside.

One week in the cage, the guard had said. An entire week! If she was not burning with fever by that time, and if her eyes and skin had not turned yellow, the captain would be allowed to take her on to Charleston and sell her at auction.

All night Grace waited alone in the cell. But as the first rays of sun cast their light through the openings overhead, she heard a key slip into the padlock and the door swing open.

"Come on out."

It was Marcus Slade, the ship's navigator. His voice was gentle.

"You are free. The captain says you are to be prepared for auction."

Grace stared in surprise. "I did not expect you," she said.

"No, I don't suppose you did," said Mister Slade. "I am truly sorry that I cannot do much to help you. But whatever I can do, I shall."

Mister Slade unlocked the chain around Grace's wrists and ordered a bucket of water and a sliver of soap be brought so that Grace could wash herself.

"Clean your dress, too," he said. "And do as thorough a job of it as you possibly can. Else, the captain will do it himself."

Grace washed her hair and wrung out her mass of curls. She scrubbed her face, and, turning away from Mister Slade, reached under the baggy dress to scrub the rest of her body. After that, she did her best to wash the dirty spots out of the dress, and to smooth away as many of the signs of having lived in it for two weeks as she could manage.

"What is it like to be a slave in South Carolina?" Grace asked Marcus Slade.

But Mister Slade turned away in silence.

All through the wash and cleanup, Marcus Slade never once looked directly at Grace. He also kept his eyes averted as he led her to Captain Hallam. Silently he took his leave.

When Captain Hallam inspected Grace, he smiled his approval.

And the yellow-haired American from the longboat rode away on a new horse fresh from the hold of the *Ocean Steed*.

✐

Off East Bay Street, next to Charleston's waterfront, it was slave auction day. Sellers clustered together, impatient to display their wares. A nimble colored man was the first one in line.

"Stand up there!" the seller ordered. He pointed to a table set up next to the street. After he allowed the gathering of prospective buyers time to look at the slave, he instructed the colored man to turn around slowly so the crowd could appraise him.

"A skilled carpenter, he is," the seller called out. "I brought samples of his work for you to consider."

Someone made a bid for two hundred dollars. Another raised it to three hundred. In the end, the carpenter slave sold for seven hundred fifty American dollars.

Most of the slaves offered were only field workers, though. Sellers forced the captives' mouths open to show off their teeth. They yanked the shirts off their backs to show how few scars they had for troublesome behavior . . . or else they did their best to keep the scars covered up. The fieldworkers sold for six hundred dollars . . . or five hundred . . . or, if they were older or badly scarred, for three hundred fifty.

Last of all, it was Grace's turn. Captain Hallam ordered her up onto the table.

"A unique slave this one is," the captain called out. "A house slave that would make even the most cultured master proud. Her name is Grace, and she speaks perfect English. She is from the Gold Coast of Africa, of mixed race. Of greatly preferred breeding, too. That I can assure you."

Captain Hallam jumped up on the table beside her. "Turn around," he said to Grace. "Slowly."

"She ever been in a seasoning camp?" one man called out.

"Certainly not! No need for that," Captain Hallam answered. "Grace was born broken in."

"Why's her finger partly lopped off?" another called out. "She a thief?"

"No, no, my good man!" the captain insisted. "A kitchen accident, that is all. And she misses the small bit not in the least."

"Three hundred dollars," a man in the back called out.

"Please!" Captain Hallam chided. "This is not a cheap, shiny-black cornfield slave I'm offering you here. Grace is a light-colored darky, already trained for house service. She has the manners of a white lady. Born and raised broken in. And none of them worthless American dollars. I will only accept English shillings."

After a good bit of murmuring, a man called out, "Ten shillings."

Captain Hallam forced Grace's mouth open. "Excellent teeth, as you can see." He jerked her head down and yanked back her hair. "Look behind her ears and you can see her true color. Pull up her dress if you desire and see the creamy skin untouched by the sun."

Grace caught her breath and fought back tears.

Captain Hallam hissed at her, "Don't look distraught. If you make the price go low, I will whip the life out of you!"

A tall man with a long, straight nose and a shock of red hair stepped forward. "I, sir, am prepared to offer you thirty shillings."

Captain Hallam caught his breath. His eyes glistened. No one else said a word.

"Sold!" the captain shouted.

He ordered Grace off the table and bound her hands with a rope, which he gripped securely until the tall man counted out the money and placed it in the captain's hand.

"I thank you, sir," said the captain.

Abraham Hallam handed the rope, and Grace, over to Pace Williamson.

⚜

Pace Williamson led Grace down a street paved with sand. A bloated man with a yellow face and two women, equally ill-complexioned, lay sprawled along the side. Mister Williamson covered his nose and mouth with a handkerchief and crossed to the other side of the road.

"Asa!" he called.

A slave dressed in a rough-woven shirt and short trousers ran up to him. "Yes, Massa," he said.

"Take charge of this new house slave. Her name is Grace."

"Yes, Massa."

"Keep her away from any with the yellow fever."

Pace Williamson handed the rope over to his slave. He shook his head and muttered, "What has happened to this city? Throw people out to die on the streets? We would do well to throw out the island French that bring the sickness!"

For over an hour, Asa led Grace along the road in silence. As they passed a large field with many slaves at work, Asa suddenly said, "City girl, is you?"

"What?" Grace asked.

"All dressed fancy the way you is," Asa said. "Does you think you on yer way to a big ball? Does you think you be a honored guest at a white man's party?"

Grace said nothing.

Up ahead Grace got her first glimpse of her new master's Big House, an enormous white mansion set back in a forest of tall trees, shaped to form a lovely arch over a long flowered walkway. Grace and Asa didn't walk down that path, of course. They walked around behind the house—past many bushes covered with pink flowers, past a tree with huge white blossoms and the sweetest fragrance Grace had ever smelled—all the way to the back door.

A colored man worked with a hoe around the beds of flowers, and when Grace passed by, he stopped to stare. As Grace and Asa walked up the back stairs, a Negro woman who reminded Grace of a light-colored Mama Muco opened the door. Several other slaves pushed up behind her, and they also stared.

"Come see what we has here!" Asa called in a mocking voice. "A city girl! A spoiled city slave girl."

"That be enough outta you, Asa," said the Mama Muco woman. "She be a slave just like you be a slave and I be a slave. All us slaves should be pullin' on the same end of the rope."

The Mama Muco slave took the fetter from Asa and untied Grace's hands.

***

Pace Williamson and his substantial wife, Eva, took great pride in the high caste of their house servants. Although they had nearly one hundred slaves at work in their ever-expanding plantation, they kept to a small household staff of just eight. All were light-skinned and all well mannered. But when Eva Williamson came to the kitchen to inspect the new slave her husband had purchased, and to bring one of her castoff dresses for the girl to wear, Eva immediately raised her eyebrows.

"Goodness me!" she said, and in a not-altogether-pleased manner.

Grace was everything Pace had assured Eva she would be—refined and creamy-skinned and well-spoken. But while all that was true, it did present Eva with something of a dilemma. Her son, Timothy, was at the awkward age of sixteen, when he looked with favor on attractive girls. He had been known to wantonly pursue just such slave girls as Grace. Such a situation would never do. No, no, it would never do!

So Eva went straight to her husband's study and announced, "We shall arrange a marriage for Grace with one of the field hands. And the sooner she is with child, the better for everyone."

"Oh?" Pace asked as he looked up from his papers. "Which slave hand did you have in mind, my dear?"

"I have no idea," Eva said. "Nor do I see that it makes a difference. We all know slaves don't have family feelings the way we do. The important thing is that I want this new slave married and in a family way as soon as possible."

Honeysuckle—that was the slave who reminded Grace of a pale Mama Muco—gave Grace instructions about the house and the jobs she would be expected to perform. Grace paid her scarcely half a mind. As soon as she could manage to get in a question, she asked, "Do you happen to know of an African man by the name Cabeto?"

Honeysuckle stared at her. "There be many slaves here," she said.

"You would remember him," Grace said. "Cabeto was in a terrible accident, and he is lame in his left leg. His brother Sunba is with him, and Sunba has a badly injured shoulder. They are both very big and very strong."

"Those sound to be African names," Honeysuckle said. "African names gets stripped off slaves here. What be their slave names?"

No longer Cabeto and Sunba? Grace had never considered such a notion.

"They probably be dead, anyway," Honeysuckle said with a shrug. "Forget Africa, Grace. Forget everyone from before."

But Grace would not forget. She could not.

When Grace went to the quarters reserved for the house slaves, before she lay down on her cot and pulled the blanket over herself, she asked the other slaves, "Does anyone know a large, strong slave with a lame left leg? His African name is Cabeto, but I don't know his slave name. He is with his brother, whose African name is Sunba. Sunba has an injured shoulder. Does anyone know them?"

Only Tucker, the man she had first seen in the flower beds with his hoe, bothered to answer her. "Walk out to the fields and you find fifty big, strong slaves, lame and injured. If you wants a man, take you'sef one of them."

Grace did not sleep that night. For the first time since the slavers dragged Cabeto onto the slave ship in chains, she slept close to the same place he slept. She could almost hear his heart beating next to hers . . . Almost feel his strong arms around her . . . Almost feel his breath on her cheek.

Almost.

23

*Y*ou always stands up when white folks is around,"
Honeysuckle instructed Grace. "No matter if your back be
breakin' and your body be achin', you stands up just the same.
If you doesn't, you gets the whip."

The jobs assigned to Grace included helping Melly out
with the kitchen cleanup, making certain the dust and dirt
stayed outside the house, and keeping the furniture and floors
clean and polished. One day while Grace was on her knees in
the parlor polishing the carved wooden chair legs, she started
to giggle. How Mama Muco had hated to dust furniture! Such
useless work, she had insisted. Why waste so much time and
effort wiping away dust that would just settle back in the very
same place tomorrow?

What would Mama think if she could see me now? Grace
wondered.

Grace sat back on her heels and looked around the plantation parlor. A dark red humpbacked sofa pushed against the
far wall with two large windows filled up most of the width of
the room. A straight-backed chair fitted in on either side of it.

Dusting and polishing those two chairs had already taken up much of her time.

The furniture was not nearly so fine as what her father had brought to Africa by ship to furnish the London House. Those furnishings had ornate cushions and pillows, intricate carvings, and inset wood.

What would these white folks think if they saw my library in Africa? Grace thought. *Rows of bound books. Some with pictures . . .*

A wonderfully colorful rug, intricately woven in a pattern of birds and flowers, covered most of the floor. To the side of the sofa was a stunning marble fireplace that encompassed a goodly portion of the adjoining wall. Brass andirons gleamed in the fireplace—or at least they would gleam after she polished them. Over the mantle hung a painting of two yellow-haired children—a young boy in a blue suit with white blouse and stockings, and a girl, somewhat younger, in a white dress with ruffles and lace, and blue ribbons in her hair. The children were seated together on a tiny horse.

All morning, Grace worked in the parlor. She scrubbed, polished, washed, and waxed. She still had not finished when Melly called to her to come to the kitchen and help clean up after luncheon.

Actually, kitchen work quite appealed to Grace. Perhaps she would get something to eat. She'd had very little since she left Sullivan's Island for the auction block. Just some bread and cheese, and when she awoke at dawn, a bowl of porridge.

"Phiba done fetched and heated the water," Melly said. She pointed Grace toward the stone sink with a pile of dirty dishes and pots on the table beside it. "Now you get to work. And take care with them plates and glasses, too. Break one and Missus will whip us both."

"Nobody goin' to break nothin' in this kitchen," Honeysuckle said with an air of finality. She picked up a stack of soiled laundry and tossed it toward the back door.

Grace wiped her sleeve across her face. Even though the fire was dying down in the fireplace, the bake oven still glowed hot. The kitchen was stifling. Without looking at her, Honeysuckle said, "You gets used to it."

Gingerly Grace picked up a plate from the top of the stack and sighed. Every plate looked as though it had already been licked clean.

"If you woulda' come here sooner, you coulda' had some of the mutton scraps off the white folks' plates," said Melly.

"Is there anything else I can eat?" Grace asked as she poured warm water over the plate.

"Ever'thin' be gone," Melly said. "You shoulda' come sooner."

Carefully, Grace laid the plate aside and picked up another. She poured warm water over it, set that one aside, too, and picked up a third plate. Then a fourth one and a fifth. When no plates were left in the stack, and when all the fine glasses were washed, Grace cleaned up the pewter spoons and knives and set them aside, too. After that she went to work scrubbing the pots. When the entire stack of dirty things had been washed, Grace wiped the table clean.

Only then did Honeysuckle say, "Here be somethin' for you."

She laid out a thick slice of still-warm bread, a chunk of cheese, and a portion of mutton.

"Oh, thank you most kindly!" Grace said.

"Melly speaks true," said Honeysuckle. "You has to come before the master and mistress finish eatin' if you wants to get a share of their leavin's."

"Insufferably lazy, every last one of you darkies!" Eva Williamson huffed. She was in the midst of one of her regular inspections of the kitchen. "Why, any white lady alive would have had this kitchen clean as a pin hours ago! Do I not provide you with the nicest skillets for cooking? Do I not make the best saucepans available, and even a rolling pin for your pie crusts? Do you not have a fine oven right here inside the kitchen to bake the bread, and a spacious fireplace, as well?"

The slaves stood in a line throughout their mistress's rant, their heads lowered respectfully.

"And you!" she said. Here she swung around to point at Grace. "I do believe you are the most incompetent and slovenly of the lot! My husband paid a goodly sum for you, and I expect you to earn back that price!"

Grace looked up and opened her mouth. It had been her intention to ask what it was she had done wrong, but she did not get the chance.

"And no impudence from you, either!" Eva snapped. "You will remember yourself. You are my slave! I do not wish to get my whip, but I shall if you make it necessary."

After a bit more huffing, she turned on Honeysuckle. "The house is your responsibility," Eva said.

"Yes'm," Honeysuckle replied. "We has everythin' we needs, ma'am, and we do thank you for it, too."

It amazed Grace to hear the head slave's cheerful voice after the sound and unfair scolding they had just endured.

"That you most certainly do," said Eva. "And in return for my generosity, I expect a well-run house."

"Yes'm," Honeysuckle said with a pleasant smile.

After the mistress left, Honeysuckle said to Grace, "White folks likes to see us slaves cheerful and content. It don't matter to them if our lives is nothin' but work and work and work. It make no difference what we thinks or how we feels. Cheerful and content, that's all that matters."

"*Pshaw!*" Melly spat.

But Grace knew perfectly well how to act cheerful and content on command. She had learned that skill at her mother's knee. Lingongo had taught her daughter how advantageous it was to obey the white man when necessary, but when his back was turned, how easy to do exactly as she pleased.

Cheerful and content, Grace could do. And she did.

Which was why Eva Williamson, demanding though she was, quickly decided that she liked Grace, after all. Grace didn't complain, and she was always pleasant. Furthermore, Eva could understand every word she said, a most delightful trait in a house slave.

Eva often hit Phiba as punishment for mumbling or for bumbling or just for "unpleasantness." Melly sometimes got slapped, too, especially if Eva didn't like something about the food served her. But Grace never did. In fact, within weeks Eva started to reward Grace with extra privileges.

$\mathcal{L}$

"Get the water buckets, Grace!" Melly ordered.

Grace had rushed to the kitchen a bit late because Mistress Eva had kept her in the parlor with endless instructions on how to more effectively polish wood furniture. Now Melly was impatient and tired of the wait. She wanted Grace to wash the luncheon dishes.

"Phiba sent for the water boy from the slave cabins, and he waits outside with the buckets," Melly groused.

A small boy did indeed stand outside the door, a heavy wooden yoke draped over his small black shoulders, balanced by two full buckets of water. He struggled to stand under the weight of the load.

Grace ran to take one of the buckets. But as soon as she did, the unbalanced load tumbled and the other bucket poured out on the ground. The little boy burst into tears. "Now I has to go back to de well and haul dem buckets up all over agin'!" he cried.

Honeysuckle took the bucket from Grace and poured the water into the kettle over the fire. "You stay with your own job," she said to Grace.

"I only wanted to help the boy," Grace said as she fought back tears.

"Don't make no matter what you wanted," Honeysuckle said. "White folks gets to make mistakes. Darkies doesn't. Just do your job right and let other folks do their job any way they can."

That evening, Pace and Eva Williamson sat down to dinner with their yellow-haired children, Timothy and Angel. The young ones had long since outgrown the pony on which they had posed for the picture in the parlor. Now fourteen, Angel was two years younger than her brother. Honeysuckle lit the candles Eva had carefully arranged at the center of the table.

"Beeswax candles, they be," Honeysuckle excitedly reported to the others. "Eight of them all burnin' at once! And in fine brass candlesticks, too. How much money does you s'pose the massa has? Enough to burn up, that's for sure."

"I wants to serve the plates tonight," Phiba said.

"No!" Melly insisted. "You will trip and fall, and spill everythin'."

"I wants to see the table all lit up with eight beeswax candles," Phiba begged.

But it was Grace who was honored to witness that amazing extravagance of beeswax. The mistress herself requested that Grace serve the family their dinner.

"This one time only," Eva told Timothy in private. "I will not let your father know it was your request. And, please, do not ask for Grace again."

❧

All morning Grace worked in the private chambers of Mistress Angel. Her bedclothes were a jumble, and all the girl's fine frocks lay on the floor in front of her wardrobe, heaped together with her shoes and stockings and petticoats.

Honeysuckle was most impatient with the girl. "A woman what acts like a spoiled child," the slave said. "That's all that girl be!"

Yet when Mistress Eva had told the head slave that Angel's chambers were a shambles and in need of a good cleaning, Honeysuckle smiled contentedly and said in her most cheerful voice, "Yes'm. Most certainly, ma'am."

Immediately she had dispatched Grace to do the job.

Actually, Grace didn't find the job so odious. Except for the fact that Angel's skin was white instead of bronze, and her hair yellow instead of dark brown with a blush of auburn, and except that Angel lived in America instead of Africa, there wasn't so great a difference between her and Grace when she was fourteen. Grace, too, had had a wardrobe filled with lovely dresses. And she, too, had cared little for them. She had often left them piled on the floor for her family's slave to pick up. It was true that Angel thought only of herself, but Grace had been much the same at her age.

Oh, how things had changed!

Grace straightened Angel's bed, and she folded up each of her pretty dresses. Then she dusted away the grit that had settled on everything, and washed the floor, and polished the furniture to a high shine.

In her mind, Grace was back in Africa. Back on the savanna in the summer's heat with the wind blowing through her hair. In her mind she was back with Cabeto in the village of thatched-roof huts.

*

"Where do the hundred field slaves live?" Grace asked as she lay down on her cot in the house slaves' cabin. She had been at Pace Williamson's plantation almost a month, but still had not seen any of the field slaves.

"In the slave quarters, down by the fields, of course," Melly said.

"I wish they was closer to us," said Phiba.

"We more luckier than they be," said Melly. "We gets better food and better clothes. This cabin be better, too."

"But they has all of them others," said Phiba. "An' all we has is just us."

Grace lay in silence for several minutes. Finally she said, "I wish I could see them. I would ask if any of them knew about Cabeto."

"Sometimes Massa say I can go down there on Sundays to visit with my family," said Honeysuckle. "Mistress Eva, I heard her tell the massa that she wants you married and with child. I'll ask can I take you to meet the menfolk there."

"Sunday!" Grace exclaimed. She jumped up from her cot. "How many days until Sunday?"

"This day be Friday, and tomorrow be Saturday," said Honeysuckle. "The day after that be Sunday."

"But I won't marry a slave," Grace said, "because I'm already married. And I won't be with child, either."

"You will if massa says you will," said Honeysuckle. "You a slave now, girl."

"Well, I don't care what he says," said Grace. "I only want to go down there to find out about Cabeto."

Honeysuckle looked at Grace and shook her head. "I'll ask Massa Pace can you and me go down to the slave quarters after breakfast is cleaned up."

In answer to Honeysuckle's request, and with matrimony on her mind, Mistress Eva brought an old dress out from Angel's wardrobe and presented it to Grace.

"Make yourself pretty," Mistress Eva said. "Meet all the men in the slave cabins." With a smile and a wink, she added, "Find one that pleases you and I will see that he is yours."

On Saturday night, Grace drew herself a bucket of water and bathed. On Sunday, after the breakfast plates were washed and the saucepans scrubbed clean, she went back to the slave cabin and put on her new dress. It was a blue ruffled frock with a square-cut neckline. The nice thing was that it wasn't loose and baggy like the dress from Mistress Eva. This one fit Grace just fine. Grace fluffed out her curly hair with her fingers and pushed it back off her face.

The field hands' slave quarters were made up of a handful of crudely-framed cabins built from rough-hewn logs chinked with mud. They were positioned in a circle around a bare dirt courtyard. Grace could see small garden plots beside some of the cabins, and a handful of skinny chickens pecked around in the dirt. What looked like a wooden animal trough was pressed over against one side of a cabin. Two little children, with coarsely carved spoons grasped in their hands, scraped at bits of porridge stuck in the corners and cracks.

The field slaves eagerly welcomed the two house slaves, although some could not resist the chance to tease them about their fancy clothes. All the while, the slaves moved over behind the circle of huts to a spot where sitting logs were laid out in rows.

"Come and sit," Honeysuckle said to Grace. "That man in the white shirt is the one they call 'Preacher Man.'"

Grace sat, and Honeysuckle eased herself down beside her.

"Massa don't know about Preacher Man," Honeysuckle said. "Only talk about the other peoples you met here and the crispy chicken feet they give you to suck on and not about the preachin'."

Preacher Man had plenty to say. In fact, he found it difficult to contain his excitement, which periodically bubbled over into shouts. "Let my people go! Dat's what de Lord tol' his man Moses to say to old Pharaoh!"

Grace immediately recognized Preacher Man's story—Moses and the plagues wrought on the stubborn Egyptians, who would not release the slaves. She had read it in Captain Ross's Holy Bible on the ship from Africa to London.

"'Dey will not be your slaves,' Moses tol' Pharaoh," Preacher Man continued. "Let my people go, that we may serve God. Dat's what he said!"

From all sides, men and women called out, "Amen! Amen!"

"King Jesus be our Moses," declared Preacher Man. "He say, 'Let my people go so dat dey can serve me!'"

"He say it to de white man!" a man near Grace called out.

"He say it to every master dat owns slaves," said Preacher Man. "He say it to de debil hisself."

Again, men and women called out, "Amen! Amen!"

Suddenly, Grace was terribly lonely for Mama Muco. Had she been there, she would have been amen-ing louder than anyone, and she wouldn't care what massa said, either! Everything Preacher Man said could have come from Mama's lips.

"But de freedom not be for nothin'," Preacher Man said. "It be so we can serve de Lord."

When Preacher Man finished, the slaves launched into songs. Grace didn't know any of them, but they still made her heart sad.

Then the people prayed to God. They asked that He would make vegetables grow large in their gardens, that their families would not be sold away from them, that the yellow fever would not strike the slave quarters. They prayed that God would touch a child injured in a fall and make her whole again. They asked God to give them what Preacher Man called the "Fruits of the Spirit": love, joy, peace, long-suffering, gentleness, goodness, faith, meekness, and temperance. And they ended with this request: "Please, Lord God, let our people go! Let us go so's we kin serve you."

When Preacher Man at last sat down, everyone's eyes turned once again to Grace.

"Is you one of us, den?" asked Preacher Man.

Grace nodded her head. "Yes," she said. "I am African. I am a slave, just like you."

"We has to get back to the Big House," Honeysuckle said. "Massa don't let us to stay away for too long."

"Wait!" Grace cried. "I have an important question to ask. Does anyone know of a slave with the African name Cabeto? He is a strong, brave man, and he walks with a limp because he was badly injured in a rebellion. His leg was burned."

Everyone stared at Grace, but no one answered.

"I think Cabeto is with his brother, whose African name is Sunba. Sunba was injured, too. He has a bad shoulder."

One head after another shook "no."

"Please . . . are you certain? No one has seen Cabeto?" This time Grace was pleading. "No one?"

Honeysuckle stood up. "Come, Grace," she said gently. "The massa will be askin' after us."

Grace did her best to choke back the tears that welled up in her eyes. She had already turned to follow Honeysuckle when a hand brushed against her arm. A stooped woman was close behind her.

"He limps perty bad, does he?" the woman asked. "An' his brother, he can't hardly use his left arm?"

"Yes," said Grace. "Yes!"

"He be dark black?" the woman asked. "And real tall?"

"Yes, yes!" said Grace. "That's him. That's my Cabeto! Do you know where he is?"

The woman turned her eyes away and slowly shook her head. "De other massa who owned me and dem, too—Massa Simon. He didn't like de way dem two work. De broder of your man, he be shot dead. The one you ask about went to work in de swamps and he never come back."

"Did you see it happen?" Grace demanded. "Did you see someone shoot Sunba?"

"I don't want to talk about dat," the woman said. "Massa Simon done sold me here. Dat time be done and past."

Grace grabbed the woman by the arm and pulled at her. But the woman cried out and tried to pull away.

"I saw it," said a stringy man. "The one you call Sunba, he couldn't work no more so Albo took him out to a field. Albo had a gun with him, and he poked it in Sunba's back. When Albo came back, he be all alone. Dat boy Sunba be gone to heaven for sure. But the other one, the one you askin' over

. . . his slave name be Caleb. Slave talk say he be bought away from de swamp. Say he be workin' in another massa's fields now."

"Come, Grace," Honeysuckle said, her voice strained with urgency. "We has to go. Now."

Late afternoon sun cast dark shadows over the leafy carpet that surrounded Master Williamson's Big House. Grace stepped easy and tread lightly, a smile lifting the edges of her mouth.

"You does look cheerful and content," Honeysuckle noted.

"Another man's field," Grace mused. "Do you suppose that field is very far away from here?"

"Maybe not far for a white man's carriage," Honeysuckle said. "But forever away for a darkie slave like you."

24

$\mathcal{L}$ady Charlotte adjusted the three blue bows down the front of her pale pink brocade taffeta gown and straightened the skirt so that only the barest flounce of her petticoat showed beneath the hemline. The sun shone through the window over the front door, but she was not fooled. Even in late May, a cool afternoon wind might decide to blow.

"Fetch my cloak, Owens," Lady Charlotte said to the maid.

As Penny Owens ran to do her mistress' bidding, the butler Rustin stepped inside and announced, "Your carriage is ready, m'lady."

"I say!" Lord Reginald called from the top of the staircase. "Are you going out, Charlotte? To visit your mother, perhaps?"

"I am going out, but not to see Mother," Lady Charlotte answered. "As a matter of fact, I am on my way to Greenway's Coffeehouse."

Lord Reginald's jaw twitched, and he paused for a moment to collect himself.

"Rustin," he said to the butler, "do tell the driver that Lady Charlotte will not be in need of the carriage today, after all." To his wife he said, "Join me in my chambers, my dear. Now, if you please."

Rustin bowed and moved toward the door. He caught Owens as she hurried in with the cloak and gave her a look that clearly meant "tread carefully."

Angry determination settled over Lady Charlotte's pale face and hardened her blue eyes. The look became her.

Lord Reginald took great pains to compose himself. He offered his wife the best chair. As was so often the case, he chose to stand beside the fireplace, his elbow rested against the mantle. He purposefully assumed as nonchalant a pose as he could manage.

"I shall go to the meeting," Lady Charlotte stated before her husband could launch into one of his long speeches.

"I fully appreciate the powerful pull one's emotions have on one," Lord Reginald said in his most magnanimous tone. "And I certainly take into full account the fact that you are but a woman. Yet you are nevertheless an intelligent woman, one I believe capable of understanding what is at stake here. As controller of Zulina fortress, I am in the slavery business. And as the employer of your father, the way in which I conduct that business affects your family as well as it affects mine."

"My father must make his own decisions," said Lady Charlotte. "Just as I must make my own."

"I fear that you do not fully grasp the situation, my dear," Lord Reginald continued. "Slavery was not my invention, nor was it the creation of England. Slavery was established long ago by the decree of Almighty God."

"Oh?" Lady Charlotte asked. "And how is it that you, my husband, are in a position to know the mind of God?"

"Slavery is sanctioned throughout the Bible," Lord Reginald explained with exaggerated patience. "It began in Genesis when God cursed Noah's son Canaan to be the lowest of slaves to his brothers. On the contrary, Noah blessed his sons Shem and Japheth, and he made them masters over Canaan."

"I see," said Lady Charlotte. "What I do not see, however, is how you can use Noah and his sons to justify your own actions at Zulina fortress. Or how you can use that long-ago account from Genesis to keep kidnapped Africans enslaved in the Americas today."

"Noah's son Canaan was a man with black skin," said Lord Reginald. "Everyone knows that."

"Do they, now?" asked Lady Charlotte. "How exactly is that so, when Canaan's father and two brothers were white, and his mother, as well? And where exactly does the Bible say that Canaan's skin was black?"

Lord Reginald cleared his throat and stepped away from the fireplace. He pulled his coat back into place and stood uneasily before his wife.

"The important point for you to understand is that slavery is a natural state," Lord Reginald said. He could feel control slipping away from him, yet he was at a loss to know what to do about it. "It has existed in every age, you see. People of the highest civilizations had slaves. Even those in the most intelligent of nations, I might add."

"Such as ours?" Lady Charlotte asked.

"Yes, exactly," said Lord Reginald. "Ours, and all the rest of Europe. But most certainly ours."

"And did all of these highest civilizations send ships to Africa to exploit the continent for financial gain?" Lady Charlotte asked. "Did all of them do whatever they took into their hearts to do, however atrocious and appalling the deeds might be, in order to achieve their ends? Did they select unrelated verses out of the Bible in order to salve their consciences by maintaining their deeds were sanctioned by God?"

"No, no!" insisted an exasperated Lord Reginald. "You have it all wrong!"

Sir Reginald paced to the far side of the room, turned around, and strode back toward Lady Charlotte's chair.

"Atrocious and appalling behavior is exactly what it is, too," Lady Charlotte said. "I know that to be a fact, Reginald, for I witnessed it with my own eyes. We commit those atrocious and appalling actions, all the while insisting that the wretched slaves accept with contentment the position into which we thrust them."

"And so they should!" exclaimed Lord Reginald.

"Grace did not accept it," said Lady Charlotte. "Nor would I have done."

Lady Charlotte stood up and walked out of the room and down the stairs. "The carriage," she called to Rustin. "It is still ready for me, I presume?"

❧

By the time Lady Charlotte stepped from the Witherham carriage and entered Greenway's Coffeehouse, two tables were already filled with men and a sprinkling of women vying to voice their thoughts on the abolition of slavery. No longer did Ethan Preston and his small group hide away in Heath Patterson's drafty barn. Not since the House of Commons had passed William Wilberforce's second abolition bill. True, the House of Lords had promptly defeated the bill, but even so, the subject was now an acceptable one for discussion, especially in the coffeehouses.

All the regulars sat along the tables, but many others had joined them, as well. Ena was there, and so was Sir Geoffrey Phillips. Joseph Winslow, too, although he sat a bit apart from the others, silent and self-conscious. Lady Charlotte eased herself onto the bench next to Joseph.

". . . and a compromise forged by the good Sir William Dundas provides for gradual abolition by the first day of January in the year of our Lord, 1796," Sir Thomas McClennon was saying. "We have Prime Minister Pitt to thank for that. It came about only at his personal behest."

"Too long!" Jesse snorted. "Three more years of the slave trade! Too long!"

"Yes," agreed Lady Susanna. "Far too much can happen in three years."

"That may well be true," allowed Sir Thomas. "But with the chaos in France absorbing so much of Parliament's attention, it is fortunate that the Houses moved forward on this matter at all."

"Yet there is also the disaster at Saint Domingue," Ethan Preston pointed out. "We cannot allow ourselves to ignore that."

"God in heaven help us!" exclaimed a hefty man Lady Charlotte had never seen before. "Do not tell me we must endure another year without sugar!"

"Who can say?" asked a man with long hair that hung straight over his shoulders. "Once again, we are at war with France. So who is to say what will happen?"

"Pshaw!" spat the hefty man. "France is not even a rightful country any longer. Naught but a lawless disgrace, is what."

"Nevertheless, we are at war with them," said the straight-haired man. "And the talk is that France will soon abolish slavery."

"Nor should we be surprised," said the hefty fellow. "Have they not already abolished or demolished everything else within their grasp?"

"And yet the British public does not speak their objection to the slave trade as openly as they did after William Fox's pamphlets first appeared," Lady Charlotte ventured. "I do find that odd. When it comes to something about which I care deeply, I, for one, cannot remain silent."

"Nor can I," said Jesse, as he bounded to his feet.

Men of African extraction were not an uncommon sight in London, if one looked for them in expected places. Yet they were quite a rarity in genteel establishments such as coffeehouses. And when they did attend, they kept themselves to the corners and the back places where they would not attract undue attention. Certainly they did not jump to their feet and publicly shout out their opinions.

"What of America?" Jesse challenged. "African slaves there can't even hope for freedom. No law protects them for they be nothing but white man's property. Negro babies born to slaves belong to the master, just like the lambs born to his sheep be his. If master takes it to his mind to sell the baby, well and good. Go to the auction block and buy someone else's baby if that's what he desires. Buy another man's wife, too. Anything massa wants be just fine, 'cause the slaves be his."

All other conversations in the coffeehouse stopped. All eyes turned to stare at the railing Negro.

"Scare the slaves good!" Jesse continued. "Whup 'em and beat 'em hard. Hang 'em from the trees. Anything be fine, 'cause they only be property."

Suddenly Jesse looked around him. He hadn't seemed to notice that the entire coffeehouse had fallen silent. His eyes darted around in an effort to assess the mood of the staring faces. Without another word, he sank to his seat and slumped down low.

No one spoke for a moment. It was Lady Charlotte who finally felt compelled to add her thoughts.

"And yet, in Africa, being white did entitle one to great privilege," she said. "And to be able to call oneself Christian pardoned any multitude of transgressions." She looked at Joseph beside her. "Is that not true, Mister Winslow?"

Joseph's blotchy face flushed hot. He said nothing.

"It is not for us to judge others. Nor are we here to condemn individual slaveholders as corrupt or un-Christian," said Sir Geoffrey Phillips. "For if slavery did not already exist amongst them, few slaveholders would choose to introduce it. And as for us, if we were in the place of, say, American plantation owners, would we willingly and instantly give up everything we owned and held dear?"

Oliver Meredith slammed his fist down on the table. "Nevertheless, they are still wrong!"

"Yes, of course they are still wrong," said Sir Geoffrey. "But it is useless to employ a voice of thunder, abhorrence, and condemnation when we speak of them. Are we not all complicit to some degree? Condemnation of them must surely be met with condemnation of ourselves. Abhorrence of them must be met with abhorrence of ourselves."

"You, sir, speak wisdom," said Ethan Preston. "It is true that we are all capable of horrific deeds, yet every one of us is also capable of love and kindness and generosity. Let us calm our voices so that we will be in a better position to reach the hearts of our countrymen, and to help them see the true cost of the slave trade."

"We cannot stop it only 'ere in England, though, can we?" asked Joseph Winslow. "We must also reach acrost the ocean, mustn't we?"

"Yes," said Mister Preston. "Even though that means we must reach more deeply into our own purses."

"God in heaven help us!" the hefty man exclaimed again. "Another year without sugar!"

25

*F*or four days, Melly kept Grace busy scrubbing out the springhouse so it would be ready for the fresh cheeses. When she finished, Melly set her to work with the broom, and for the next two days Grace swept away the last of winter's debris and prepared the kitchen for summer.

"Mmmm, summer," Melly cooed. "Berries and fruits a'plenty. We puts it all out back in de dryin' baskets so's it can dry in de sunshine."

"My Mama Muco used to dry fruit that same way in Africa," said Grace. "Fish, too."

Grace pulled down the last vestiges of the dried herbs that hung in bunches from the kitchen ceiling.

"Soon you will help me gather fresh ones," Melly said.

Melly scrutinized the sprinkling of onions, turnips, and beets that still hung in the far corners of the kitchen. Just after the fall harvest, she had braided their stems together and suspended them from the rafters, but most of the root vegetables had been eaten through the winter.

"A bit withered, they be," she said. "Still, we hasn't any fresh vegetables in the garden yet. We best leave those last ones be."

"Honeysuckle? Honeysuckle!"

It was Mistress Eva's voice. When the head slave didn't immediately answer her call, Mistress Eva headed for the kitchen.

"Honeysuckle!"

Honeysuckle puffed obediently down the stairs and into the kitchen.

"There you are," Mistress Eva said with more than a note of irritation. "Spring is in the air, Honeysuckle. Time for shrimp pie. Master and I have decided that Melly should prepare one for our luncheon today."

"Yes'm," said Honeysuckle with a smile. "That be a fine idea, ma'am."

"Oh, and Honeysuckle," Eva added. "I am not pleased with the condition of the house. It's not scrubbed and polished to my satisfaction. Why do you have Grace at work here in the kitchen with Melly instead of allowing her to keep up with her own duties in the rest of the house?"

"Yes, ma'am," said Honeysuckle, the smile still pasted on her mouth. "I will see to it at once."

Eva sighed in exasperation and swept from the room.

As soon as the door closed behind Mistress Eva, Honeysuckle's smile vanished. She lifted her apron and mopped at her face.

"Call for Tucker, Melly," Honeysuckle said. "Give him your dishpan and send him to the city at once to find the shrimp man. And you, Grace—"

At that moment Dorcas, a scrawny slave who spent her time in the scullery scrubbing the laundry and minding the other dirty work of the house, stuck her head into the kitchen.

"Wot of me? I needs help, too," she whined to Honeysuckle. "I gots soap and candles need makin'. Who's goin' to help me?"

"You take Phiba to stir your soap," Honeysuckle said to Dorcas. "Grace, you best get back to your own work."

Each of the mornings that Grace had spent spring-cleaning the kitchen, Honeysuckle had done her best to keep up Grace's responsibilities in the family's private chambers. But the rest of the work had been set aside for the time. Which meant Grace had much to do. She hurried to begin her rounds.

From one private chamber to another, Grace rushed. She fluffed pillows and made up beds with crisp white sheets. She picked up the clothing strewn across the floor, folded it, and stacked it on wardrobe shelves. She emptied chamber pots and scrubbed them clean. She refilled mantle water pitchers with fresh water. She dusted and she swept.

Mistress Eva's chambers she cleaned first, then Master Pace's. Grace bypassed Master Timothy's—she did her best to enter his chamber only when she knew him to be safely out of the house—and went on to Miss Angel's chamber.

When no one answered Grace's knock at Miss Angel's door, Grace opened it and went in. Miss Angel, dressed in nothing but her boned stays and gauzy pantaloons, sat at her dressing table.

"I'm sorry, miss," Grace gasped. "I will come back later."

"Never mind," said Angel with a wave of her hand. "Just clean up my room."

Grace moved to the rumpled bed. Angel picked up a fluff of cotton wool, dipped it into a dish of flour on her dressing table, and liberally dusted the flour over her pock-scarred face. While Grace made up the bed, she sneaked glances over at the yellow-haired young woman who was applying flour to her face again. When Angel's face was ghostly white, she dipped her finger into a pot of red stain and touched it to her cheekbones, taking care to rub away the color that pooled in the pox scars. Angel bit her lips just enough to bring color to them. She touched her lips with the same red stain as was on her cheeks.

Angel looked around in irritation. "Where is the blue and white dress I laid out on my bed?" she demanded.

"Oh, I am sorry, Miss Angel," Grace said. "I folded it and put it away in the wardrobe."

"Well, get it out for me!" Angel ordered. "I would not have laid it across my bed had I not wanted it, would I?"

"No, ma'am," said Grace.

She hurried to get the dress out of the wardrobe.

"Well?" said Angel.

"Yes, Miss Angel," said Grace.

Grace helped her mistress into the dress just the way Mama Muco used to help Grace into her own dresses. As Grace reached up to adjust the clasps at the neckline, her rich mocha hand brushed against Angel's flour-white face.

"Foolish darkie! Foolish slave!" Angel scolded.

Dark always meant slave. White always meant free. How could it be that for so many years Grace had failed to understand this simple concept?

Grace was at work in the parlor when the clock on the mantle struck two o'clock. Time for her to report to the kitchen and clean up after luncheon. Grace preferred to keep a distance between herself and the dining room during mealtimes, even though it cost her a share of the plate leavings. There, too, Timothy made her extremely uncomfortable, the way he leered at her with half a grin on his pimply face. One time, as Grace passed him, he had actually grabbed at her leg under the table.

Grace put her cleaning rags in the bucket and headed toward the kitchen.

"Mmmmm." Grace breathed in appreciatively at the pungent fragrance that greeted her in the kitchen. "Onions and green peppers."

"Fried in hog fat," said Melly, who smiled proudly. "I puts the shrimps in last of all."

"Phiba ain't back with the water bucket," Honeysuckle said. "So you have time to eat somethin', Grace. I saved you back some scrapin's of the shrimp pie."

❦

With the plates and glasses and pans washed and stacked back in their places, with the worst of the dust wiped from the family rooms, with the master and mistress and Timothy and Angel closed up in their chambers for their afternoon rest, Grace took up her rags and bucket and headed for Master Pace's study. It was not a room she entered often, so everything in it was coated with a thick layer of dust.

Grace paused at the doorway and gazed in delight at the sight of an entire wall of shelves stocked with bound books. She knew she should beat the rug and mop the floor. She knew she should clean and polish the intricate carvings of the chairs and the massive desk legs. She knew she should wash the grime off the windows. But Grace's eyes kept returning to that wall of books.

Do not let anyone know you can read. That's what Captain Ross had warned.

Well, Grace would not let anyone know. But that didn't mean she could not sneak a peek at the wonderful volumes when no one else was around.

A surge of fear mixed with nagging guilt as Grace dusted her way over to the bookshelves that held the bound treasures. She glanced back over her shoulder, then moved closer to the books. The light from the single window was hazy, so Grace was forced to lean in close in order to read the names on the covers. She traced the title on the nearest book with her finger.

Grace's lips moved: *Robinson Crusoe*, by Daniel DeFoe.

She touched the next book, a leather-bound volume. *Hudibras*, by Samuel Butler.

The next book was crisp and new, and gold-leaf letters spelled out the title: *The Critic*, by Richard Brinsley Sheridan.

The one after that had a well-rubbed leather cover: *Gulliver's Travels*, by Jonathan Swift.

At the sound of footsteps on the stair, Grace leapt away from the bookcase. Her heart pounded as she dropped to her knees and rubbed furiously at the leg of the desk.

The footfalls approached the study. Grace shook uncontrollably.

But the steps passed on down the hall.

Careful! Careful! Grace must be oh, so careful!

26

"Come now, Grace, tell me a story," Timothy Williamson insisted in his most teasing voice.

Early that morning a parcel had arrived for Master Pace from Thomas Heyward, and it had absorbed every bit of his and Mistress Eva's excited attention. Timothy had taken advantage of the distraction to set upon Grace with determined bedevilment.

Grace started for the parlor door—Timothy blocked her way. Grace glanced desperately at the window—it was locked tight. She thought about crying out—what would she say? She was naught but a slave, after all, and he was the master's son. There was no way out.

"Tell me about the trickster!" Timothy ordered. "I always did love to hear those stories. Honeysuckle used to tell them to me when I was a little boy."

"You are not a little boy anymore," Grace said.

Grace had been scrubbing the parlor floor before Timothy came in, but she did not dare get back down on her knees. Not with Timothy in so menacing a mood. So Grace hurried over to the fireplace and busied herself with the sheen of the marble.

"You are not Honeysuckle, either," Timothy said. "But I *am* your master. And I *do* order you to tell me a story."

"I have a great deal of work to do," Grace insisted.

"That clever, conniving old rabbit," Timothy said. "Tell me a story about him."

"Mistress Eva was quite clear that this work must be completed today," Grace said. "She will be angry if it is not done."

"Mother has other things on her mind," Timothy laughed. "She has already forgotten about her instructions to you. Tell me about the spider and the tortoise."

"Please, Master Timothy, allow me to do my work," Grace pleaded.

Timothy stepped toward her. The smile faded from his lips. "I command you to tell me a story!"

Grace made a dash for the door, but Timothy caught her by the arm.

"Now!" he said.

Grace tried to pull free, but Timothy's grip was strong. Her mind worked furiously. She looked up and stared into his blue eyes, thinking . . . grasping . . . searching . . .

Finally Grace said, "Lion was hunting. He saw Goat lying on top of a big rock. Goat worked his mouth. He chewed something. Lion crept up to catch Goat. When Lion got close to Goat, he watched him very closely."

Grace paused and again tried to pull away from Timothy.

Timothy tightened his grip. "The story," he ordered.

"Goat kept on chewing," Grace said. "Lion tried to find out what it was that Goat ate, but he didn't see anything except the bare rock which Goat used for his nap. But Goat chewed and chewed and chewed. Lion still couldn't figure out what was going on, so he came close and said, 'Hey! Brother Goat! What is that you eat?' Goat was mighty scared to see Lion right there in front of him, but his heart was gallant and brave. So Goat answered: 'It is this rock that I chew. And if you do not leave me alone, when I finish eating the rock, I will eat you, too.' Lion was so terrified that he ran away."

"That's the story?" Timothy demanded.

Grace nodded.

"What does it mean?"

"It means that a bold person gets out of a troublesome spot, but a cowardly person loses his life," said Grace.

Timothy loosened his grip just a bit.

"How about you?" he asked. "Are you a bold person or a cowardly person?"

"A bold person," Grace said in a steady voice. "If I were not, I should no longer be alive. I am bold like Goat."

Timothy glared at her. "I am your master," he said. "Do not think you can mock me with such a story."

"Mock you?" said Grace. "I am but a slave who obeyed her master's command."

Timothy laughed out loud. "Yes," he said. "I believe you are bold. Still, as you say, you are but a slave."

"Timothy!"

Timothy dropped his grip on Grace's arm and wheeled around to face his mother.

Eva Williamson glared at her son. Timothy's pale face flushed crimson.

Still looking at the boy, Eva spoke to Grace in measured clips. "I believe the upstairs is in need of your immediate attention," she said.

"Yes, ma'am," Grace said gratefully. She grabbed up her cleaning supplies and piled them into the bucket. Pushing past Timothy, she hurried out of the parlor and on up the stairs.

Uncertain as to what was expected of her, Grace set to work rubbing the stairway banister to a sheen. Eva slammed the parlor door closed. At first, all Grace could hear was a background of voices in a subdued argument. But as Eva's voice raised to a shout, it carried through the closed door.

"Why must you persist along so destructive a path?" Eva exclaimed in frustration. "God expects us to maintain the proper order of creation—coloreds are to keep to their own kind, and we are to do the same. That is what the good Lord intended." In tearful exasperation, she exclaimed, "Why must you behave as such a fool, Timothy? Can you not understand that we are the superior race?"

When the parlor door opened, Grace pulled back behind the top stairway landing. But the door quickly closed again, and the house fell silent.

By mid-morning, Angel had departed the house by carriage. Grace had not seen Master Pace since the parcel arrived, though Timothy had told her his father was on his way to see Thomas Heyward. After such a lecture from his mother, Timothy was not likely to be in Grace's vicinity; Eva would not let him out of her sight. All these thoughts crossed Grace's mind when she noticed that the door to Pace Williamson's study was slightly ajar. She looked down the stairs and saw no one. So she picked up her cleaning bucket and eased into the study.

Grace crossed over to Master Pace's desk and gave it a cursory swipe with her polishing rag. The smooth mahogany was richly inlaid with soft leather. To one side stood a fine pewter tray supplied with four holders, each of which contained a finely trimmed turkey feather pen propped upright. Two inkwells off to one side and a pounce pot of fine sand to dry the ink more quickly sat along one side of the tray. On the other side lay a sharkskin case that held Pace Williamson's tools for fashioning quill pens.

It was Grace's intention to take another quick look at the books in Master Pace's library. But her attention was waylaid by a parchment document centered on Master Pace's desk. Across the top, in large, beautiful letters, it read:

In Congress, July 4, 1776

Under that heading were the words:

The Unanimous Declaration of the thirteen United States of America

Carefully, gently, Grace ran her hand across the fine sheet of parchment. She leaned down close so as to better see the opening lines:

When, in the course of human events, it becomes necessary for one people to dissolve the political bonds which have connected them with another, and to assume among the powers of the earth, the separate and equal station to which the laws of nature and of nature's God entitle them, a decent respect to the opinions of mankind requires that they should declare the causes which impel them to the separation.

We hold these truths to be self-evident, that all men are created equal, that they are endowed by their Creator with certain unalienable rights, that among these are life, liberty and the pursuit of happiness . . .

Grace stopped reading. She could not believe the words before her. Could this document, which lay on the desk of the man who owned her and over one hundred other slaves, actually say what she thought it said? Grace picked the parchment up and whispered the words as she reread them:

"We hold these truths to be self-evident, that all men are created equal, that they are endowed by their Creator with certain unalienable rights—"

"What is the meaning of this!"

Grace jumped. The parchment dropped from her hands, onto the desk.

"I was . . . cleaning, Master," Grace stammered. "Cleaning up your desk, sir."

Terror rose up in Grace as she raised her dusting rag for him to see. The rest of her cleaning supplies were all the way across the room, right next to Master Pace's feet.

"You were reading," Master Pace accused. He did not raise his voice, which somehow made the fury that burned in his face even more terrifying.

"I could see the marks and they were so pretty, Master," Grace said. "I just wanted to see them more closely. The pretty marks, that is."

"You . . . were . . . *reading!*" Master Pace exclaimed.

❧

Grace stood in the parlor, in front of her master and mistress. Pace and Eva Williamson sat uncomfortably before her. Timothy stood behind his father.

"Put her in my care, Father," said Timothy. "I can handle a slave who reads."

"You have done quite enough for one day," Pace Williamson said.

"The worst of it is that I *trusted* her!" said Eva. "I say we must make an example of her. Turn her over to Asa and entreat him to apply his whip most liberally."

"And then what?" asked Pace.

"And then nothing," answered Eva. "Asa should whip her to the end of her life."

Pace glared at Grace. "Whip to death a slave for whom I paid thirty shillings? More than eight hundred American dollars? Absolutely not! We shall put her back on the auction block and sell her. Let her be someone else's predicament."

"We cannot pretend to be unaware of this most undesirable flaw," Eva said. "Yet if we let it be known that this slave can read, no one will buy her."

"I paid a goodly sum for Grace," Pace insisted, "and I fully intend to get my money back!"

27

"Ahhhh!" Samuel Shaw sighed. He stretched his arms over his head and leaned back in the comfortable wooden chair next to Macon Waymon on Macon's side porch. Samuel closed his eyes and breathed in the fragrance of the first magnolia blossoms of the season.

"You said our partnership should meet with success, Macon, and so it most certainly shall," Samuel said. "Next week I begin my service with the grand jury. Merely a first step along the road to political success, I realize. Yet a most encouraging first step, would you not agree?"

"That I most definitely would!" said Macon. "I congratulate you on conquering the locked door of our fair city's governmental body."

Samuel laughed out loud. "And what of the cotton gin business?" he asked. "Does that continue to proceed well?"

"Absolutely," said Macon. "That lame slave of mine, name of Caleb, set out to fix the broken gin box. He actually took that cotton engine of Eli Whitney's completely apart. And when he put it back together again, he refigured it just enough to make it stand legally as a new machine. Whitney would be a fool to try to sue us about it. He could never successfully claim it as his own."

"This Caleb, does he crank the machine himself?" Samuel asked.

"Did at first," said Macon. "Worked day and night, that boy. But the baskets of cotton came in too fast for him to do it all alone. Now I have four slaves on the job. They all take their turns on the crank. That machine does not get one moment's rest, day or night!"

Samuel let out a long whistle. "I wouldn't have thought all that reworking possible from a darkie," he said.

"Why not?" asked Macon. "Plenty of plantations make good use of slave craftsmen, Sam. Why, Jonathan Weeks, two places over from here, has him a slave that makes wood furniture nice enough for Jonathan to sell on the open market. Negroes can be taught to do many things."

Macon Waymon leaned back in his porch chair and breathed in the fragrance of his success.

"I knew I had a good slave in that Caleb right from the start," he said. "Soon as I saw how he fixed his broken hoe, I knew it. Soon as I saw him put together a new plow for Juba."

Samuel gazed up at the blue sky. "Just so you don't let that good slave forget himself," he warned.

"Forget himself? Not Caleb! Caleb is a right mild slave, obedient and willing to work hard. Of course, I do reward him with a bit of pocket money and such. And I reserve the best of the garden plots in the slave quarters for him. So don't you worry about Caleb. He is one happy Negro."

A horse-drawn cart turned off the road and onto the carefully manicured sand lane that led up to the house.

"You have company," Samuel said.

Macon squinted at the newcomer. "Looks to be that new preacher man in town," he said. "Wonder what he wants way out here?"

Evidently Preacher Knight caught sight of the men watching him from the porch at about the same time they saw him, because he drove his cart all the way around to the far corner of the drive before he stopped and got out. A tall young man, straight as a pine tree, he unfolded his legs and stretched himself.

"Morning, Preacher," Waymon called out. "Will you join us for sweet apple cider?"

"I will do that," Preacher Knight answered. "Thank you kindly."

Waymon leaned toward the open door and called into the house, "Anniebelle! We have us a guest. Bring apple cider and tend to us!"

Wasn't the day sunny and bright, Preacher Knight commented as he settled himself into a chair on the far side of Macon. Macon allowed that it was, indeed. Preacher Knight asked after the cotton planting. Macon assured him it was progressing exactly as expected.

When Anniebelle brought the apple cider, Preacher Knight thanked her most kindly, just as if it had been Macon's own wife who served him and not just a slave. Macon and Samuel exchanged glances.

"What can I do for you, Preacher?" Waymon asked.

Preacher Knight cleared his throat. "I have made it my mission to visit with each plantation owner in the area, such as yourself," he said. The preacher lifted his cider glass to his lips and took a long drink.

"I am not myself a man who condones the practice of slavery, either as a moral pursuit or as a Christian one," he stated as he set his glass down on the table. "However, I do recognize that slavery is the law of the land. Therefore I can do no more than to ask you to examine yourself through the eyes of God and to judge yourself as He might judge you."

Macon Waymon took a long drink of his cider, wiped his mouth, and set his glass down.

"Surely you do not suggest that I abandon my livelihood, sir," Macon said. "As you yourself said, I am a law-abiding citizen. Samuel Shaw, himself newly appointed to the grand jury, will tell you as much."

"Indeed I will," said Samuel. "A law-abiding citizen he is, as well as an upstanding member of the church."

Preacher Knight afforded Samuel no more than a cursory nod.

"Several of the slave owners around Charleston allow me to hold Christian services for their slaves," the pastor continued to Macon. "I would kindly request your permission to include your slaves in this mission. Perhaps you will allow me to come out here one Sunday afternoon each month. Or I might even—"

"My slaves are already guided toward Christianity, sir," Macon interrupted, a brittle edge to his voice. "I allow them to stop work early on Saturdays in order to get themselves cleaned up and settled into a reverent state of mind. They are permitted to hold their own worship services every Sunday after their own fashion."

"I see," said Pastor Knight. He lifted his glass to his lips and took another long drink. "And do you treat your slaves well, sir? Do you keep at all times in your mind that some among them are your brothers in Christ?"

"Brothers!" Samuel exclaimed, jerking himself bolt upright. "May I remind you, sir, that those slaves are Africans! They are Negroes!"

Macon cast Samuel a warning glance.

"If it is true that they be brothers, Reverend," Macon said, "then they are brothers who are my property. If my slaves desire to pray and sing on this Lord's Day, they have my permission to do so. But they will stop by nightfall. Tomorrow is a work day, which they well know. I am a businessman. I know to keep worship in its place, just as I know to keep slaves in their place."

"I will be most pleased—" Pastor Knight began, but Macon cut him short.

"Most kind of you, I am sure. But I have no need to prevail upon you in this or any other matter."

Pastor Knight sat for a bit longer, but as there was obviously nothing more to say, he soon bade farewell. Other plantations awaited him.

"They are my slaves," Macon said to Samuel. "I do not need a preacher to tell me how to be a good master."

"Nor to tell your slaves how to be dissatisfied with you," said Samuel.

❧

The cooking fire at the slave compound had burned low, but even so the women took care to put the potatoes into the coolest of the coals to bake. They lay the cornpone in to roast alongside the potatoes. Already chicken bubbled in the pot that hung on a crane over the hottest part of the fire.

Posey stopped stirring long enough to dip her long-handled spoon into the pot so she could get herself a taste. "Ummm, mmm!" she exclaimed. "Dere never was no better tastin' somthin' to eat dan dat!"

Usually on a Sunday, Caleb took his dinner alone, over at the far side of the compound next to his garden patch. Many of the slaves looked forward to preaching time after the food was dished out, but all that was awkwardly unfamiliar to Caleb. He didn't trust the white man. Why should he trust the white man's God?

"He isn't really dere God," Jeremiah told Caleb. "De white folks just think he dere God."

Jeremiah acted as preacher for the slaves. Massa Macon had bought him from another plantation, where a white preacher had come every Sunday for years, so Jeremiah knew more about the Bible and its stories than any of the others did. Even though he couldn't read, even though he had never actually seen a Bible, he knew a lot about God and how God did things. "God, and his son, Jesus Christ, dey be freedom for us," Jeremiah said. "Freedom for our souls."

On the slave ship, Caleb had spent hours and days and weeks begging the ancestors for help. But they didn't help him. Now here he was, a slave in a foreign land. Here he was alone, his brother dead and his son dead and his wife gone away from him forever.

"We knowed about the creator when we was in Africa," Jeremiah told Caleb. "We just knowed him by his other name."

But Caleb didn't want to hear what Jeremiah had to say. Mama Muco had trusted this God, and look what had happened. Look what had happened to all of them.

As the women began to gather on the logs closest to the fire, and the men on the logs behind the women, as the children scrambled to get the best places on the ground up in front and Jeremiah took his place, Caleb moved back toward the security of his garden plot.

One voice began a mournful tune, and others picked it up: "*Steal away, steal away, steal away to Jesus . . .*"

It was time for the worship to begin.

Actually, Caleb liked the singing. No drums in the slave complex, of course. Massa wouldn't allow that. But everyone clapped their hands and stomped out the rhythm with their feet.

"It weren't enough dat ol' Daniel have to be a slave!"

Jeremiah had started his sermon. Caleb turned his back and set to work pulling weeds from his garden bed.

"Daniel have to be a slave locked up with a angry lion who had nothin' to eat for too long!"

Daniel in the lion's den. Caleb had heard Jeremiah tell that story before. Not as many times as Moses and the Egyptians, but often enough so that Caleb knew what happened.

"A slave with no way out, dat was old Daniel. No way out but to die!"

Caleb clenched his jaw, grabbed up a handful of weeds, and ripped them out of the garden with a wicked vengeance. No way out but to die! Turn the wheel of the cotton gin every last day of his life. Every last day unless massa lion rip him to pieces first.

"But Daniel didn't die!" Jeremiah announced in triumph. "God saved him from dat lion!"

"Dat's right!" someone yelled.

And someone else cried out, "Praise Jesus!"

Deliverance. That was the message Jeremiah preached. But this time, Jeremiah pressed further. This time he said, "Does we suffer?"

The people cried as one, "Yes, we does!"

"Jesus knows dat we does," Jeremiah said. "He suffered, too. Dat's why he understands. And he promises if we come to him, he will give us his rest."

"Preach de word, brudder!" someone called. From all around, others responded, "Amen! Amen!"

"Didn't my Lord deliver Daniel?" Jeremiah called.

All around, men and women shouted, "Yes, He did! Yes, God!"

"Didn't he shut dat old lion's mouth?" Jeremiah called.

"He did!" the others answered. "Dat's de truth!"

"Den why we cryin'?" Jeremiah called. "Why we mournin'? Why we lettin' our hope fail us? God ain't done with us yet! God liberates his children. God saves dem from de lion's teeth!"

"Yes, yes!" the people shouted. "Praise Jesus!"

And then everyone was singing again. Only now their cadence of despair swept up into a tempo of assurance. Clapping hands and stomping feet beat out a whole new rhythm.

A God who shuts the lion's mouth. A God who leads his people to victory, in this world or the next.

"*Goin' home, goin' home. Goin' home, Sweet Jesus,*" the slaves sang.

Caleb shook off the garden dirt and wiped his hands on his pants. He moved in a bit closer so he could better hear the words of the songs.

"*Jordan River, I's bound to go. Bound to go, bound to go . . .*"

Clap, clap, clap, measured and sweet.

Stomp, stomp, stomp, beat out the rhythm.

"*Brudder, sister, I's bound to go. Bound to go, bound to go . . .*"

"*Carry me, Jesus, I's bound to go.*"

Caleb moved closer until he was just behind the men at the back of the circle. A strange, unknown feeling moved through him. Slaves sobbed now, swaying backward and forward.

"Bless de Lord!" the man just in front of Caleb shouted.

"Yes, God!" echoed another.

Suddenly, Caleb could contain himself no longer. He leapt forward, up in front of the cook fire. He ripped off his shirt and waved his strong arms over his head. And he lurched into the old dance of limping beauty.

The slaves closed into a circle around him, shuffling around and around. They clapped as they sang, one song after another after another. Words of struggle and pain. Words of overcoming and of faith and of hope. Around and around they danced and sang.

Someone shouted out words of praise.

Another raised his voice in prayer.

Many cried out words of burning desire for God.

28

Skin agreeably silky and a creamy shade of pale brown, yet hands rough enough to prove their familiarity with hard work. A body slender and supple, yet surprisingly strong and resilient. Capable of intelligible speech—a particularly attractive feature in a part of the country where so many slaves spoke in the gullah dialect of *de* and *dat*. Sparked with a striking glint of fire through her dark hair.

Oh, yes, Grace showed exceedingly well on the auction block.

Yet, invariably, it all came around to one question: "Why do you wish to sell such a fine specimen of a house slave?"

No matter how delicately Pace Williamson attempted to word his answer, no matter how positive a twist he applied, the response still ended up the same: "She can read." And so each prospective buyer—though he made his decision about Grace with regret—shook his head, replaced his money in his pocket, and walked away.

"Perhaps you are right, my dear," Pace Williamson said to Eva as they took their afternoon tea together in the sunny parlor. "It just may be that there is nothing to it but to turn Grace over to Asa and his whip."

"It would serve as a worthy lesson to the other slaves," Eva said.

"Ah, but a most dear lesson it would be," Pace mourned. "And with a grievous cost to my purse."

"Perhaps it would serve a greater good," Eva said. "After all, someone taught that slave to read. And we can be most certain it was not another slave!"

After the tea setting was cleared away, after Eva retired to her chambers for an afternoon rest, Pace lingered alone in the parlor. He was quite fond of that room, especially on afternoons in the early summer. Wispy trails of wisteria hung down over the open window slats, and the gentle breeze carried sweet nectar inside. Pace stretched out his long legs, tipped back the chair, and let his eyes drift closed.

"Massa," Honeysuckle called from the doorway.

Pace awakened with a start.

"A visitor be here to see you, sir."

Pace hurriedly straightened himself into a more genteel position.

"Who is it?" Pace demanded more irritably than he had intended.

"Name be Mister Hull," Honeysuckle said. "He wants to see you 'bout that slave you be sellin'."

"Grace?" Pace said. Suddenly wide awake, he jumped to his feet. "A man wants to see me about Grace? Well, show him in, Honeysuckle. By all means, show the man in!"

Had Pace Williamson seen John Hull drive up to the plantation house in his deep-sided wagon, thoroughly splattered with mud and pulled by a yoke of lumbering oxen, he might have been less enthusiastic. Or perhaps it would not have made any difference. Being a peaceable man, Pace was not at all eager to see a healthy young slave girl whipped to death on his plantation, even if her beating did serve as a lesson to the others.

Honeysuckle showed John Hull to the sitting room. In one quick glance, Pace took in the rough cut of the stranger's wrinkled coat and trousers, his badly scuffed boots, the mussed look of his untrimmed hair, the two-day stubble on his cheeks. Hull was a slight man, but he was sturdy and well-calloused. A small-time farmer, no doubt.

"Do sit down, sir," Pace Williamson said after John Hull had introduced himself. "You have come to inquire about my slave, Grace?"

"Yes, sir," said John. He started toward a chair, but changed his mind and positioned himself uncomfortably on the edge of the fine red camelback sofa. "I looked in at the slave market in Charleston, but I couldn't find what I wanted. Some fellows there told me I ought to come up here; that you had a slave girl you might sell for a goodly price."

"I do, indeed," Pace said. "And a fine slave she is, too. Fair to the eye and a right good worker as well. Bred to be a house slave, she was, but nevertheless strong and capable enough for fieldwork. She would make a good breeder, too, should that be your desire."

John shifted uncomfortably. He fixed his eyes on his hat, which he shuffled back and forth in his fidgety hands.

"You do have other slaves, do you not?" Pace asked.

"As a matter of fact, no," said John. "I am not actually a slave owner."

"In that case, Grace would be a perfect choice for you, sir," Pace insisted. "Not only can she cook and clean, but she can also keep up your kitchen garden. As for your missus, Grace can most certainly do for her, too."

"Yes, well . . ." John stammered. "Well . . ."

John Hull stopped talking and stared in silence at his hat.

"I see," Pace sighed. He slapped his hands down onto his knees and stood up. "So, you have heard the talk in town. You already know about Grace. Well, you must still have some interest in her, or you would not have come all the way out here, would you? Is it a good price you're after?"

"I am not a man of means," John admitted.

"Yes, that I can clearly see," Pace said. He quickly added, "No offense intended, of course."

Pace walked to the fireplace and paused. When he turned back to John, he said, "Do not think you can take advantage of me because of my business success."

"Oh, no, sir," said John. "I most assuredly do not think that. Fair is fair. It's only that . . . Well, you see . . . the difficulty is that—"

"I am perfectly aware of the difficulty, sir," Pace stated, his words suddenly clipped and short. "Do you think you and I would be meeting here in this fashion were it not for the difficulty?"

John stared at Pace.

"No, sir," John said hesitantly.

John Hull felt as though he had somehow missed a most important part of the conversation, although he was not at all sure where the gap occurred.

"Mister Hull," Pace said, "you have an interest in purchasing my slave. I am most desirous to sell her. I'm certain we can come to an agreement that will satisfy both our needs."

"Is it true that your slave can read?" John Hull asked.

Pace took a deep breath.

"Yes," he said. "Yes, it is true. But let us not dwell on the negative. Other than that one defect, Grace is an excellent slave. May I be candid with you, sir? I paid thirty English shillings for her at auction."

John Hull gasped and paled. But Pace didn't seem to notice.

"That's more than I ever paid for any other slave. And yet I am willing to look favorably at the price you offer me. So, I ask you, what is your price, sir? Three hundred American dollars?"

John, still confused, struggled to collect his thoughts.

"All right!" Pace said. "Two hundred fifty, then?"

John stared at the tall, red-haired aristocrat. He fit so well into this fine mansion of a house. John, on the other hand, was obviously so very out of place.

"Two hundred dollars," said Pace. "But I shall not go one dollar below that price!"

John Hull finally found his tongue. "Yes," he said. "Yes, two hundred dollars. That's a fine price."

"Sold!" Pace stated. "Stand up, my man, and let us shake hands on the deal."

❧

It was Honeysuckle who told Grace she had been sold.

"Sold?" Grace cried. "But I must not leave this place! My Cabeto is close by here. Where will I go, Honeysuckle? Will it be far away?"

Honeysuckle said she had no idea where the new master lived. And it made no difference, either, she said. When the white folks makes a deal, the colored folks goes where they's told.

"It don't do you no good to have a man you cares about," Honeysuckle said to Grace, "'cause if you does, you always gets sold away from him."

Tucker jumped up into the back of Mister Hull's already overloaded wagon. He pushed crates of chickens to one side and stacked them as high as he could. He shoved sacks of seeds and flour and such over toward the opposite side of the wagon bed. Between the two stacks was just enough room for Grace to squeeze in and sit upright.

"Bind her hands and tie her fast to the wagon stays, Tucker," Pace Williamson ordered. "Mister Hull is going all the way to Georgia. He doesn't want his slave to escape before he gets her home."

"Thank you kindly, sir," John Hull said as he climbed up to the wagon seat. He called to the oxen, "Hip, hip!" They pulled together in the wooden yoke and the wagon inched forward. "Haw!" John Hull called, and the oxen turned left and lumbered slowly down the lane.

Grace twisted and pulled at the ropes that bound her to the wagon. She jerked her arms and yanked with all her might. And she kept it up until her wrists were raw and bleeding. But all she accomplished was to upend one crate of chickens and send them into a commotion of wildly flapping wings and loud cackles.

"Cabeto!" Grace moaned in despair. "I am sorry! I'm so, so sorry. Oh, what have I done?"

As the plantation disappeared into the dusty distance, so did Grace's hopes of ever seeing him again.

29

$\mathcal{E}$ight mornings straight Grace awoke, crammed upright in her small space, to the squawk of chickens.

Eight endlessly long days she sat bound fast as John Hull's wagon clattered down cobblestone streets, or—more often—rolled along dusty country roads. Three times each day, John would stop the oxen in some isolated place and untie Grace's hands. "For your necessaries," he told her. "If you don't try to run, you can have your privacy." He offered her a meal of cheese or dried beef and a generous piece of bread. If they were beside a stream, they drank fresh water. If not, they drank weak ale from a cask. Afterward, John retied her hands and they were off again.

Eight evenings Grace watched the sun sink over rolling hills . . . or marshy lakes . . . or long stretches of cotton fields.

Eight nights she slept uneasily on the hard ground for a couple of hours. She couldn't even turn over, for one hand was always tied to a wagon wheel. Long before light, John Hull said, "It's time to go."

For eight entire days and nights, Grace's heart ached with despair.

As dawn broke on the ninth morning, Grace jerked awake from her dreams of swaying in a hammock aboard a ship sailing across the Atlantic Ocean to find that her wagon-prison was surrounded by water. It took her several minutes to realize what was happening. The oxen had pulled the wagon down into a fast-flowing river. Grace gasped and yanked at the ropes that held her. At the very same moment, the wagon lurched sharply to the left. The current grabbed hold and pushed the unwieldy wagon first one way, then tugged it around to the other.

"Put in!" John Hull called to the oxen.

As the beasts regained their footing, the wagon righted itself and the powerful oxen hauled the wagon on to the opposite shore.

On the tenth day, as the wagon lumbered down a country road no different from countless other country roads, as the sun grew warm just as it did every other day, John Hull suddenly called out, "Gee!" As one, the oxen turned to the right in their wooden yoke and headed up a narrow, rutted dirt road. The wagon pitched and jerked past neat, green fields, up to a whitewashed clapboard house.

"Whoa!" John called to the oxen. He climbed stiffly down off the wagon seat and gave his aching body a long, grateful stretch.

"I'm sorry," John said as he climbed into the back. He untied the knots at Grace's wrists one last time. "I truly am sorry."

Grace, every bit as stiff and sore as John, and bruised from the jostling ride besides, struggled to stand upright. John reached out his hand to help her down, but Grace sat on the edge and carefully let her painful body down alone.

"The house is nothing fancy, as you can see," John Hull said to his new slave. "You can cook over the fireplace. And you can wash the clothes in the washtub, of course, and do the garden work."

"You are my master," Grace answered in a voice of flat resignation. "I will do as you say."

"Yes, I suppose I am," said John. "But, please, you need not call me master."

"Yes, sir," Grace said. "As you say . . . sir."

"I see," John said, although he did not see at all. "You would want for a place to put your things, I suppose."

"I have no things," Grace answered.

"Oh. Of course, that is so," John said hurriedly. "No, I can see that you do not. But a place to sleep, then. I have no slave house, you see, for I have no slaves."

"I can make myself a bed beside the fireplace in the kitchen," Grace offered.

John stretched himself again, long and hard.

"Charleston is a long way from Savannah," John said. "I do apologize for your discomfort on the trip."

Grace said nothing. How she longed to stretch out and sleep! But the sun was still high in the sky, so sleep, she knew, would be a long time coming.

"I should be about my work," John said, more to himself than to Grace, in the fashion of one who had lived too long alone. "I must need unpack the wagon and see after the oxen . . ."

"Shall I start the fire, sir? Shall I prepare your dinner?"

"Oh . . . yes, indeed!" John said. "That would be most kind of you. Please. . .let me know what you need."

Grace looked at her new owner with suspicion. She had never before seen a white man like him.

Cooking was not one of Grace's skills. In Africa, she had seldom had a reason to cook, though she had helped Mama Muco often enough. She certainly had not cooked at Missus

Peete's house, nor at the Foundling Hospital. And not on the plantation, either. Which meant Grace was at a bit of a loss in John Hull's sparse kitchen.

She did find a bag of ground corn, however, so she stirred up a pot of porridge the way she had seen Mama do so many times. She went outside to the garden and picked an armload of greens to add to the porridge pot. Other interesting things grew in the garden, so she grabbed several handfuls of this and that to throw into the pot as well. A packet of salt lay on the table. Grace knew salt made everything taste good, so she added a generous amount to the pot and stirred everything together.

When Grace set the bowl of porridge and vegetables before her new master, she said apologetically, "Tomorrow I could kill a chicken and fry some bread for you, sir."

"This porridge looks mighty fine to me," John allowed.

John picked up his pewter spoon and spooned a generous bite into his mouth. A startled look crossed his face. He swallowed hard and coughed. He grabbed for his mug and drank down a long draught.

"The truth is, sir, I am not especially handy in the kitchen," Grace said. "I'm sure I can learn, but it's not something I know well."

"The porridge is fine, Grace," John said gently. "And even if it were not, I have been doing my own cooking all my life and I could keep right on doing it. I can wash my own clothes, too. And, as you can see, I do a goodly job of growing food in my garden. If you can help me out in these endeavors, I will be most grateful to you. But that's not why I purchased you."

Grace stared at him.

"Where is your bowl?" John asked. "Please, sit with me and eat."

"Oh, no, sir," Grace protested.

But John insisted. "Come, Grace. Ladle a bowl of porridge for yourself and sit down. Please."

Because John Hull was her master and he gave her an order, Grace obeyed . . . though hesitantly. She took her bowl to the far end of the table and sat down. She took a bite, and her eyes opened wide. She sputtered over the saltiness of the porridge.

"I am not a rich man," John Hull said as he continued to eat. "I am but a farmer who works alone on a small plot of land. I have chickens—you rode home with them and saw them running about in front. I have the two oxen that pulled the wagon—they also pull my plow in the fields—and I have four goats which I mainly use for milk. I grow hay and corn, and plenty of vegetables—mostly to sell. I would appreciate your work in the house. And if you choose to help me outside, I would appreciate that, too. But, as I said, that is not why I wanted you here."

"Why did you want me?" Grace asked.

"Because you can read."

"What?" Grace exclaimed. "No one wants a slave who can read!"

"I do," said John. "Because I want you to teach me."

Grace stared at him.

"But I have no book," she said. "I cannot teach you to read without a book."

John Hull pushed his chair back from the table and walked over to a rough-hewn wooden chest shoved back against the wall. He opened the top drawer and carefully took out a black leather-bound book.

"Here," he said as he carried it over to Grace. "We can use this."

"The Holy Bible!" Grace exclaimed. "Oh, yes, sir. This will do just fine."

John Hull regulated his days by the hours of daylight. He rose from his bed when the first shards of sun cracked through the darkness, and he didn't stop until it was too dark to see the plowed ground. At least, that had always been his practice. But so eager was he to get to his reading lessons that he groaned especially loudly over his painful back and made a great show of the weariness of the long trip. He allowed as it would do them both good to retire early.

Yet John did not go straight to bed after dinner as was his custom. Instead he stoked up the fire and said to Grace, "Show me the words."

In the beginning, God . . .

Those were the first four words Grace taught John Hull to identify.

In the beginning, God . . .

Grace guided him through the story of creation. Although she did most of the reading, she pointed out more words for him to identify: *the . . . and . . . was . . . Lord . . . it.* She read with him of the serpent in the garden, and the great sin of Adam and Eve. They read the stories of Cain and Abel, and Noah and the flood. With each story, Grace pointed out more words for John to identify.

When the fire burned low, John pulled out a treasured tallow candle. He stood it up in an iron candleholder and said, "More, Grace. Let us read a bit more."

They read of the tower of Babel, and of Abraham and his nephew Lot. They read of the wicked cities of Sodom and Gomorrah.

"And the LORD said, If I find in Sodom fifty righteous within the city, then I will spare all the place for their sakes." (John read all of these words except "righteous" and "Sodom.")

They read the stories of Isaac and of Jacob, and of all Jacob's children. And they read about Joseph—his adoring father, his wonderful coat of many colors, his brothers who hated him.

"Have we not read enough for tonight, sir?" Grace pleaded. "Can we not stop and sleep?"

"Just a bit more," John said. "Just to the end of this story."

So they read on. They read of the two great injustices against Joseph—of his brothers who sold him into slavery and of Potiphar's wife whose false accusations landed him in prison. They read of Joseph's ability to interpret dreams, and of his promotion to a position of great power by Pharaoh. And they read of Joseph's starving brothers who came to beg him for food although they had absolutely no idea who he really was.

"Even so, it was not right," Grace said. "What happened to Joseph, I mean. He got a good position of power, and his brothers got the food they needed, but it was still horrible and unfair."

"Yes," said John Hull. "God did not undo the injustice done to Joseph. But God did use those wrongs to prevent something much worse from happening. Had Joseph not been in Egypt, the entire tribe of his family would have starved to death."

Grace closed her eyes and said, " 'But as for you, ye thought evil against me; but God meant it unto good, to bring to pass, as it is this day, to save much people alive.' "

"Yes, yes!" said John Hull. "That's it! Where does it say that?"

"Not until the very end of Genesis," Grace said. "Not until after Joseph's father Jacob is dead."

"Ah," said John. "It is often so, is it not? We cannot see the purpose in it all until the end."

"Joseph's brothers sold him to be a slave," Grace said softly. "For almost his entire life, he had to live as a slave. Sometimes he was in prison and sometimes he lived well, but always he was still a slave."

"They meant it for evil, but God meant it for good," John said.

Grace set her jaw, and her face grew hard.

"You are thinking that it is easy for me to say such a thing because I am not the slave," John said.

Grace said nothing.

John took a faded red ribbon from inside the Bible cover. Carefully he laid it across the page to mark the place where they had stopped reading, and closed the Bible. He stood up and stretched himself, took the Bible to the wooden chest and replaced it in the drawer.

"Everyone who knows me, knows I cannot read," said John. "So we must be careful to always put the Bible away. It would not do to have our project discovered."

Grace sat in silence.

John hesitated. "It doesn't mean that Joseph's slavery was just or that it was good," he said. "Only that God used it to bring about a good far larger than the wickedness thrust upon Joseph."

Still, Grace held her peace.

"God did not remove the curse from him," John said. "But he did redeem it. God did do that."

Grace stood up, her face still hard.

"Will you need me for anything else tonight, sir? If not, I ask your permission to make myself a bed beside the fireplace."

30

*N*o longer did Monsieur Pierre Dulcet ride out to the tobacco fields to call Samson to accompany him to town. Instead, he sent word to his favorite slave the night before: Be ready at dawn, dressed in your *vêtements*. It meant that Samson was to put on his new white man's clothes—the trousers and jacket and boots Master Pierre had given him. Monsieur did not actually send for him at dawn, of course. Often, not until close to the noon hour. But Samson was to be ready at dawn, nevertheless—ready and waiting.

Sometimes Monsieur Dulcet had errands to attend to that required Samson's good shoulder and strong back. But more and more often he went straightaway to le *Coton Manoir*. Many times, as they rode up in the carriage, Monsieur Dulcet called out a happy "*Bonjour!*" to Jean-Claude, and Samson did not see his master again until late afternoon. Sometimes not even until after dark. On those days, Samson had nothing at all to do but sit and wait with the other slaves, who made themselves comfortable in the shade of the oak grove.

"I would rather work out in de field den lay in dese trees," Samson said.

"Dat be a fool thing to say," said Dutch. "Lay youself back in de cool of de trees . . . Dere, now. Dat much better den workin' de fields, ain't it?"

"It don't feel right to me," said Samson. "Feels like I's doing somethin' wrong and it's goin' to catch me."

Actually, Samson was doing something *right*. He was learning to be a savvy slave. In the shade of the oak trees, he listened as Dutch and Brister and the angry slave, whose name was Ruf, talked about slave rebellions and running away to freedom.

None of the talk seemed all that relevant to Samson until one particular day. The four slaves had all shed their white man's jackets and boots, and had stretched themselves out under the trees. Out of nowhere Brister commented, "My massa says he don't want to pay to use de cotton engine no more. He says he wants one of his own."

No one answered because none of the others knew anything about cotton engines, and none of them cared.

"We takes our cotton to Massa Waymon's plantation," Brister said. "He don't pay for his cotton engine 'cause one of his slaves made one for him."

"You know dat to be true?" Dutch asked.

"Shore enough I do," said Brister. "My massa wants me to make one for him, but I don't rightly know how."

Dutch looked at Brister's crossed eyes and laughed out loud. "Did you tell him you can't even see straight?"

"If Caleb can make one . . ."

Samson didn't hear another word. He sat bolt upright.

"Caleb!" he demanded. "De slave dat done dat is named Caleb?"

"Yes," said Brister. "He be a big, black Negro. Like you."

"Is he lame?"

"Shore enough is," said Brister. "Has a bad leg."

Cabeto! It had to be his brother, Cabeto! And Brister knew where he was.

That was the day Samson stopped thinking of himself as Samson and started to think of himself as Sunba again. From that day on, he watched for his chance, because that was the day he made up his mind to run away.

☙

Samson was ready at dawn, dressed up in his white man's clothes and boots. He sat outside his cabin as he did every time Master Dulcet called for him, and he waited for massa to come. Samson waited throughout the morning. The sun reached its zenith, and he continued to wait.

It was well into the afternoon that Julien, Massa Pierre's white overseer, trotted toward Samson and called out, *"Viens ici!* Come at once!"

Master Dulcet had taken ill, Julien said. Master wanted Samson to walk to *le Coton Manoir* and carry a message to Jean-Claude.

"Best put this inside your shirt," Julien instructed. He gave Samson a folded-over letter, sealed with wax, and stamped with Monsieur Pierre's ring.

Julien looked up at the sun and frowned. "When the Charleston bells toll ten o'clock, all slaves must be off the streets," he said. He gave Samson another slip of paper. "Keep this in a safe place, and don't lose it. It's your written permission to be out after curfew. Master does not want you beaten and thrown into prison."

"Yes, sir," said Samson.

"If it should happen that you are detained in Charleston and it seems too late to start back, master says you are to sleep in Jean-Claude's oak grove and come back tomorrow in the daylight."

"Yes, sir," said Samson.

"Go, now! Take the message!"

"Yes, sir," said Samson. And he set off at a trot.

*

Samson ran with his eyes closed. To run blind and free in the fresh air—it took him back to his days in Africa, back to when he would run along the trails that crisscrossed the flat savanna. Samson continued to run until his breath came in great gasps and pants. He slowed down, but he didn't stop. It frustrated him that he could no longer do what he had done with so little effort in Africa.

The sun was low on the horizon when Samson approached the edges of Massa Jean-Claude's vast cotton fields, so he picked up his pace again.

A rush of gratitude flooded Samson when he finally saw the avenue of oaks that led to Jean-Claude's majestic brick house. Of course, he knew he was not welcome at the front, so he ran on around to the back, past the shade of oak trees where he had spent so many hours with Dutch and Brister and Ruf, waiting for his master. Samson ran straight on up to the back porch.

"*Salut!*" a young slave called out when she saw Samson.

"For your massa," Samson panted as he handed her the message Julien had given him from Monsieur Pierre.

*

A young slave girl brought a bowl of porridge and a large hunk of bread out to the porch for Samson. He told her he would sleep in the grove and leave early on the morrow. He hunkered down in the grove, in the spot usually reserved for Ruf, and ate the porridge. But he wrapped up the bread and tucked it into his shirt. The metal bowl he laid upside down on the ground.

Turn over a pot, Ruf had said. *Dat sanctifies de ground and covers it with extra bravery and good fortune.*

Samson ducked through the trees and sprinted back toward the road.

Massa Waymon's cotton plantation. That's where Brister said Caleb was. No, Samson would not call his brother Caleb. That's where *Cabeto* was. Samson would find him there and the two of them would run together to freedom.

"Stop right there, Negro!"

Samson froze. Two white men walked toward him, guns pointed at his head.

Beware of de slave patrols. That's what else Ruf had said.

"What you doin' out alone in the middle of the night, darkie?" demanded a scruffy white man in dirty trousers and shirt.

Play innocent. Play dumb. That's what Ruf said.

"Jist carryin' a important message for my massa," Samson said.

"Yeah?" said the scruffy white man. "You got a pass that says as much, does you?"

Play dumb.

"Don' know 'bout no pass, massa," said Samson. "Got's me a letter from me massa, is all."

"Gimme that letter," said the other white man, who more growled than talked. "You cain't even read!" He snatched the letter out of the scruffy one's hands and held it up close to his face.

Twenty lashes. That's what Ruf said a slave caught without a proper pass would get. That's the first thing. After that, the slave would be dragged back to his master for still more punishment.

"Massa tell me to hurry, now," Samson said. "He be sick."

"What does the letter say?" Scruffy asked Growly.

Growly shook his head and shrugged.

"Go on," he said to Samson. "But you best get back there right quick."

"Yes, sir," said Samson. "Thank you, sir. I gits right on back to me massa now." And he took off at a run.

✑❧

Because Samson wasn't expected back at the plantation until the following day, because he was so often away from the fields at his master's bidding, because Monsieur Pierre Dulcet was sick in bed with a raging fever, almost three days passed before he was discovered missing. Even then, when Julien took word of his disappearance to Master Dulcet, Pierre simply shook his head.

"Samson is worried about me, I have no doubt," Pierre said. "I suspect he has slipped off into the woods, perhaps to say prayers for my recovery. He will return."

But Samson did not return. And so, although it pained him greatly to do so, Monsieur Dulcet sent for the slave hunters. They arrived on the fifth day of Samson's absence, whips and neck irons and leg irons clanking from their saddles. Their dogs howled and strained at the ropes.

Dem slave hunters. Dey de worstest of de worst. Ruf had actually shuddered when he spoke of their hounds.

Samson traveled by the light of the moon and hid himself in the woods during the day.

The moon was high and he walked fast. He had not yet found his way to Macon Waymon's cotton plantation, but he was certain he was close. That's when he heard the first howl of the slave hunters' dogs. They were down the road behind him. Panic seized Samson. He dove off the road and into a field. The cotton plants, still small, offered him no shelter at all. He dropped to his hands and knees, but the howling came closer. So Samson jumped back up and tried to run through the soggy cotton field.

No matter how fast Samson ran, the howling grew louder . . . and closer. He could hear the clop, clop, clop of horses' hooves as they pounded on the road. His breath came in painful gasps. Then an iron hand reached out and grabbed him.

Samson lashed out with his good arm. He hit and kicked and growled in furious terror.

"Hush up and follow me!" a voice whispered in the dark. "Hurry, now, or it be too late!"

It was a black man that had him by the arm. Another slave, it was. He pulled Samson toward a small cabin and shoved him inside.

"Slave catchers," Samson gasped. "Dey be . . . after me."

"I knows dat," said Juba. "You thinks I don't knows dat? Ever' slave around here be quakin' at de sound of dem howlin' dogs."

Juba slammed his cabin door closed. The lone cabin stood at the far edge of the cotton field, away from the main slave quarters.

"Quick," he said. "Git down here."

Juba shoved his cot aside and kicked a plank out from the floor. He reached down and pulled open a trap door.

"Hide inside 'til de dogs be gone, den follow de tunnel to de outside," he said.

"You ever hear of a slave name of Caleb?" Samson said. "He be my brother."

"Git in de tunnel, or you be no one's brother!" Juba said.

Samson pushed himself into the clammy dirt hole, though it was barely wide enough for him to squeeze through, and Juba slammed the door shut on top of him. Samson wriggled his way down the tunnel until he could poke his hand through the brush and out into the open on the other side. He sank back into the tunnel to wait.

De slave catchers, dey don't never give up.

How long he lay hidden in the underground hideaway, Samson couldn't tell. Hours? Days, even? It felt like weeks! Several times he pushed the brush aside and poked his head out, but each time he heard the baying of the hounds, so he squeezed back in and waited some more.

When the howling at long last died away, Samson blinked out into the sunshine of bright daylight. He couldn't walk during the day, so he ducked back into the hole and waited for dark. Finally when he looked out, all was still and the sky was black. The moon had not yet risen. Ever so cautiously, Samson pushed the brush aside and twisted and pulled his way out of the tunnel. He got up on his knees on the solid ground and squinted out into the night darkness.

Nothing.

That is, he could *see* nothing, but Samson knew the slave catchers were still out there. Somewhere.

Dey don't never give up.

Then he heard the dogs. Samson stumbled through a thicket of trees and underbrush. He could see that he was not far off the road. His foot tangled in a winding vine, and he fell flat. Samson kicked at the tough weed and called down curses from the gods on it.

Samson stopped, grabbed at the vine, and gave it a hard jerk. The moon was just beginning to rise, and by its emerging light he clawed at the vine, following it along the ground. He ripped and pulled at it, until he had freed a long piece of the rope-tough plant.

Quickly, Samson shimmied a ways up a slender tree that grew alongside the road and tied one end of the vine securely around the trunk. He scurried down, ran across the road, and climbed up onto a rail fence on the other side. Tugging the vine taunt, he tied the other end to a low-growing branch of a huge tree that overhung the road. Samson jumped down and faded back into the thicket of trees.

By that time the moon was quite bright. Frighteningly bright, in fact. Samson sank down at the edge of the thicket and listened to the hurried clop, clop, clop of a fast-approaching horse. One of the slave chasers was on the road, apparently hot on Samson's trail.

Samson could see the rider. It was the slave catcher, and he had his gun on his saddle and a whip in his hand, and he was eyeing the ditch beside the road. When his neck hit the vine stretched tightly across the road, he didn't even have time to call out. The catcher hit the ground with a heavy thud, but his horse kept on running. The dogs did, too. Samson snatched up the slave catcher's whip and took off at a run.

The turned-over pot, Samson decided. *It shore enough did sanctify de ground. It shore enough did bestow bravery and good fortune.*

But with the one slave catcher down, the other would be that much more determined to claim the whole reward for himself. Samson knew that. If he made it to his brother now, they would both be chased down. Better to lay low for a while. Better to let the dogs forget his scent.

So Samson turned toward the last place any white man would ever want to go—the dark swamp.

31

*D*awn broke earlier each day, and the sun stayed longer in the sky. The lengthening of days brought joy to John Hull's heart, for it meant more time for his reading lessons. It was important that he accomplish as much as possible before fall brought its endless work of harvest. After that, winter would be back with scarce hours of sunlight.

John grabbed the two-tined hay fork from just inside the barn and set to work. The past fall, he had cut the hay from the fields, and had bound and stacked it to cure. Now the hay was ready for the barn.

Over in the garden, between the barn and the house, Grace was at work. It pleased John to see how much pride she took in the great leafy expanse of collards and chard. She exclaimed over the tiny yellow blossoms on the tomato plants and carefully prodded the peas and beans to climb high on their poles.

Grace was a good slave. She worked hard and she never complained. Each day, she cooked him up a goodly diet—a combination of American food and African—okra and greens and squash, porridge and fatback and fish and chicken, fried bread and boiled eggs. She didn't fuss and she didn't talk back to him. Even more, she was a good and patient reading teacher.

✐

And Joseph died, and all his brethren, and all that generation.

As they moved to the first chapter of the book of Exodus, John stumbled through more words than he was able to recognize.

And the children of Israel were fruitful, and increased abundantly, and multiplied, and waxed exceeding mighty; and the land was filled with them. Now there arose up a new king over Egypt, which knew not Joseph.

Together John and Grace read about the changing attitude of the Egyptians, about how they made slaves of the Israelites who had once been welcome guests in their land. They read of Moses—the baby hidden by his mother in the bulrushes, who grew up to demand that Pharaoh let the slaves go.

Let my people go, that they might serve me.

"This Moses," Grace said, "do you think maybe he was an African?"

"No," said John. "He was Hebrew. He was white."

"Are you certain?" Grace asked.

"Yes," said John. "I am certain."

They read about the plagues God sent when Pharaoh refused to release the slaves. And they read of the blood from the Passover lamb that all Israelite families were instructed to put on their door portal as a signal to the death angel to pass over their house.

For I will pass through the land of Egypt this night, and will smite all the firstborn in the land of Egypt, both man and beast;

and against all the gods of Egypt I will execute judgment; I am the
LORD.

And they read the wonderful story of how Moses led the
people out of slavery and into freedom. The Egyptians chased
after them, of course, but God parted the Red Sea so that the
Israelites could walk across on a pathway of dry land and not
get their feet wet. The Egyptians tried to follow them, but
they could not. They all drowned because the sea closed back
up on them.

"Why does God not do that for us?" Grace asked. "Why
doesn't he open up a path for slaves to walk away from here
and go back home to Africa?"

❧

Sometimes John Hull used a bit of his precious time to help
a neighbor out, and sometimes a neighbor would come by and
help him. Now and then, when the work was done, the men
sat together at the table by the kitchen fireplace and enjoyed
a neighborly talk.

"I wouldn't say all colored folks is depraved," Chase
Ambrose remarked over his dinner plate at John Hull's house
one afternoon. "That one of yor'n, for instance. She don't
seem so bad. Makes you wonder, don't it: If a slave never were
a slave, would they still act like a slave?"

"Hmmm," John said. "That I don't know."

Chase wiped his mouth on his sleeve. "You ever hear of one
Benjamin Banneker?" he asked.

"No," said John. "Can't say that I did."

"Well, that right there is a very smart Negro man," Chase
said. "Old Tom Jefferson himself wrote about him, either last
year or the year before that. He said that colored man was

so good at figuring out mathematics that he just might be as smart as a white man."

"Is that so?" said John. "Well, it could be. It could be."

John glanced up at Grace, who stared straight back at him. He quickly turned his eyes away.

"We should be able to finish the repairs on the barn by this afternoon," John said to his neighbor. "I do thank you kindly for all your help, Chase."

But his attempt to change the subject was not successful.

"Now Alf Stone, there's a savage for you," Chase said. "He is a beast to his slaves. Whips them for any little mistake. Alf lashes his Negroes something terrible."

"Unforgivable behavior," John said, shaking his head. "Utterly unforgivable."

"Alf's brother in Atlanta beat his favorite house slave to death just for mouthin' off to him," said Chase. "Now, I must tell you, no one stands up for such behavior as that."

"I should think not!" said John.

"Excepting Alf, of course," Chase said. "When he told me about it, he was laughing. And laughing hard, too. Thought it was a right funny story, he did."

John said nothing.

"Speaking of Alf Stone," Chase said. "My Lily told me I was to ask if you plan to go to the dance he's holding at his house Saturday week."

"Yes," John said. "I haven't been out of the house since I went to Charleston. It should be a pleasant evening, I believe."

"That it should," said Chase. "Alf always puts on a good party."

$\mathcal{L}$

John and Grace read about the land God promised to the Israelites. But always the people disobeyed. They read about kings that came and kings that went. Some were good and godly, but most were bad and evil.

I made you to go up out of Egypt, and have brought you unto the land which I sware unto your fathers; and I said, I will never break my covenant with you, John Hull stumbled to read in Judges, chapter two, verse one.

"It seems that we have read that same verse so many times before," Grace said. "Why must God continue to remind the people of the same thing over and over? Would they really forget so quickly?"

"Perhaps it is more than just to make certain they remember," John said. "Maybe God wants to tell them to *do* something *because* they remember."

"What do you mean?"

"Perhaps they must first recall what happened and after that they must act differently *because* of what happened."

Grace continued to read with John, but it was clear that her mind was not on what they read. Finally John took out the faded red ribbon to mark their place and closed the Bible. But he did not get up to put it away in the drawer. Instead, he looked into Grace's face and asked, "What is it? What causes you such trouble?"

Grace stared down at her hands and sat in silence.

"I command you to speak!" John Hull said. But he immediately shook his head and wiped his hand across his face. "No, no. I do not command you. I ask you to speak freely. Please, Grace, tell me what is on your mind."

"The white man named Alf Stone," she said. She continued to stare at her hands. "The one who is so cruel to his slaves. The one who laughed when his brother beat his favorite slave to death."

"Yes, yes," said John. "Terrible, terrible business, that!"

"And yet, you accept Alf Stone's invitation to a party at his house. He does such a terrible thing, and you continue to treat him as your friend."

"Well . . . that," John said. "To attend his party is not at all to accept his actions. No, not in the least. You see, I accepted his invitation because I did not wish to offend his wife and daughter."

Grace looked up into her master's face.

"I do not say his actions are right, Grace. In fact, I say they are very wrong. I made that clear to Chase. But, you see, the way things are here . . ."

Grace's huge dark eyes fixed on John's hazel eyes.

"The way things are between colored folks and white folks, that is . . ." John said.

Grace continued to search his face.

"Not that I think it is as it should be," John continued, "but the fact is that down here, slave is slave and free is free."

A sadness crossed Grace's face, but still her eyes remained on her master's eyes.

"We live in a sinful world, Grace. Plenty of people deserve better from life than they get."

"Esther did," Grace said.

"Yes! Absolutely," John said. "That is my point exactly. Esther did deserve better, and so did Joseph. But plenty of people deserve worse than they get, too."

"Like Mister Alf Stone," said Grace.

"Well, yes," John said, although with less enthusiasm.

"I have seen that," Grace said. "Horrible people get rich by selling other people, and innocent children die."

John forced his eyes away from Grace. "I pray that we will see justice in the next world because we see precious little of it in this one," he said.

For many minutes, they both sat in silence. "Was Job a colored man?" Grace asked.

"No," said John Hull. "He was white."

"I think he was a colored man," Grace said. "Too much trouble in his life for a white man. Too much hurt for a white man. I'm certain Job was a colored man."

32

$\mathscr{I}$'m glad I let you live, boy!" Macon Waymon laughed as he watched Caleb turn the crank on the reengineered cotton gin. "I do admit there was a time when I wondered what you were really worth to me. But look at you now. Just look at you!"

"Yes, Massa," Caleb said. Muscles bulged on his powerful arms as he reached for another basket of raw cotton.

"Just look at you!" Macon said again. "Got to get old Silas Leland over here to see what he lost when he sold you to me. Well, keep that gin going, boy. You are a right fine slave. That you are—a right fine slave!"

The expression on Caleb's face stayed flat. His eyes never wavered from his work.

"A right fine slave, is it den?" a woman who toted the basket of cotton asked with a laugh. "Dem be mighty pretty words for a massa to give a slave. What you doing for him to earn his praises?"

"Turning de wheel on his gin," Caleb said. "Just turning his wheel so dat he keeps on makin' money."

One slave after another after another came in bearing a load of cotton. "Get in line," Caleb said to each one.

Caleb kept on turning the crank on the cotton gin until the slave Zekiel finally came to take his place.

"Woo . . . wee," Zeke whistled. "I'll be turnin' dat crank all de long night."

"You can have it," Caleb said. "My arm is close to broke off."

Caleb walked across the bare yard and headed down toward the slave quarters. Suddenly he did a quick spin around, looking up and down and on all sides. When he saw no one, he gave a fat hen in front of him a sound kick. It tumbled to the edge of the yard, then flopped over on its side and lay still. With one fluid motion, Caleb swooped up the hen and tucked it under his shirt.

"Fresh chicken for supper tonight!" Caleb announced as he strolled into the slave quarters.

"Where you get a chicken from?" Prudie asked him.

"Massa gave it to me," Caleb said with a grin.

"Thank you, kind Massa!" Prudie laughed. She took the chicken and hugged it to her.

"Massa say it be time we have us some decent food," said Caleb.

Prudie laughed again, harder this time.

"He say after all de hard work we do down here, he owes us slaves a proper supper," said Caleb.

Now Prudie was laughing so hard she could barely stand up.

"Dat Massa, he a good man!" she laughed.

"Oh, he be dat!" said Caleb. "I'm right glad we let him live. Yes'm! He be a fine white man!"

"Word is, someone stole a big fat hen right from under Massa's nose," Juba said to Caleb.

"Dat so?" Caleb asked.

"Dat's so," said Juba. "And on de very same night dat de slave quarters be simmerin' with chicken stew, too. Now ain't dat a interestin' happenstance?"

"It do seem to be," said Caleb.

"When you going back to work on de gin?" Juba asked.

"Zekiel's finishin' his turn at de crank," Caleb said. "Next be Amos, den Henry, den me again. But I be back up to de gin before dat because I's de one dat has to oversee all de workin's."

"Watch out dat no chickens get in de way of dose big feet of yours," Juba said.

Caleb nodded and asked, "Dat other fat hen . . . Do you reckon I needs worry about dat?"

"No," said Juba. "No, you do not. Just see dat it don't happen too many times."

"Certainly not," Caleb said with a smirk. "I be a right fine slave."

"Listen to me, Caleb," said Juba. "You be a right *valuable* slave is what. Shore, you be worth a lot because of de work you do for Massa. But you even more valuable if'n he puts you up for sale. You know how much white men is willing to pay for a slave dat can make a cotton engine de way you can?"

Caleb shrugged.

"Well, I be tellin' you dis, boy. Don't make no trouble for youself or Massa might take it into his mind to sell you off to de highest bid."

"What do I care?" Caleb said. "When de right day comes along, I'm goin' to run from here, anyway."

"You be a fool!" Juba said. "Massa treats you good. He wants you to live. He wants you with him. Dat de most a slave can ever hope for."

Caleb spat on the ground. "No, it is not," he said. "It's not de most I can hope for. I can hope to walk free."

"Watch de way you talk," Juba said. "Dat talk going to get you whupped."

"What about you, Juba?" Caleb challenged. "You think you're different from me? You think Massa cares about your woman and your children? Dey can't even live in your cabin with you! You think he won't sell dem away from you if it suits him? You know he will!"

"Hush!" Juba hissed. "Don't you be a fool!"

"Once in my life I fought for freedom," Caleb said. "I did it den and I can do it again. What I got to lose?"

"Maybe somethin'," said Juba.

"Yeah? What?" asked Caleb. "My job turnin' de crank on de gin? You can have dat!"

"Somethin' else," Juba said. "One night before de weather turned warm, I helped a runnin' slave get away from de slave catchers. He asked me, did I know a slave name of Caleb."

"Who was he?" Caleb asked.

"Didn't give me his name," Juba said. "But he looked an awful lot like you."

Caleb stared at Juba.

"Had a lame arm, he did."

Caleb caught his breath.

"He said the slave Caleb be his brother."

"Sunba!" Caleb breathed. "Sunba is alive!"

33

Grace lifted the pot of hot water off the edge of the fireplace and toted it over to the table. As soon as she dipped the first bowl in, she cried out, "Ow!" The water was too hot. Even so, Grace went ahead and quickly scrubbed the bowl clean. She plunged the second bowl in without waiting for the water to cool. Grace was eager to finish the housework and get outside in the warm spring air. How different it was from the damp, suffocating smoke of London!

After she wiped her hands dry on her skirt, Grace grabbed up a small sack of dried corn and ran out to the dirt courtyard.

"Click, click, click," Grace called as she tossed out handfuls of corn.

Mother hens, followed by little yellow fluffs of baby chicks, ran over to scratch at the corn kernels in the dirt. John Hull didn't want Grace to give the chickens too much corn, but Grace couldn't resist. They enjoyed it so much!

In addition to the garden, Grace had offered to take over responsibility for the two goats as well as for the chickens.

"You don't have to do all of that," John said as he approached her in the yard.

"I want to," said Grace. "I want to feel the warmth on my face again. I want to breathe in the sunshine."

Indeed, it did please John to see Grace take such pride in the animals and the garden. She caressed the ripening tomatoes with tenderness, and was so eager for the peas and beans that she picked them before they even had a chance to fill out their pods. The pungent onions she cut early, too, and hung them in the corners of the kitchen ceiling.

✒

As the days lengthened, John Hull cut his work hours shorter. He wanted his supper ready as soon as he was in the house and cleaned up. While Grace finished in the kitchen, he opened the Bible and reread the last chapters they had read together.

"I do enjoy the words of the prophets," John said to Grace. "Did I tell you that at one time I wanted to be a preacher?"

"No," Grace said. "Why did you change your mind?"

"It was just the impossible dream of a young boy," John said. "I must say, though, that the idea did please my father. He was not himself a landowner, just an itinerant farmer who worked other men's fields. Still, he was so eager to see his son grow up to be a man who spoke God's message that he did without many things in order to save his pay. It was he who gave me this Bible."

Together, John and Grace read Isaiah, Jeremiah, Ezekiel. They read Daniel, too, about how a young man of royal birth was taken away as a captive into a hostile land, and of the horrors he experienced there. They read how he ignored the Babylonian king's orders to pray only to him, and he kept right on praying to the God of Israel three times every day.

Then the king commanded, and they brought Daniel, and cast him into the den of lions. Now the king spake and said unto Daniel, Thy God whom thou servest continually, he will deliver thee. And a stone was brought, and laid upon the mouth of the den; and the king sealed it with his own signet . . .

"That king! He liked Daniel. And he could have helped him if he really wanted to," Grace insisted.

"It may seem so," John said slowly. "But many times, people cannot accomplish things as easily as would seem possible to those who stand and watch."

Then the king arose very early in the morning, and went in haste unto the den of lions . . . the king spake and said to Daniel, O Daniel, servant of the living God, is thy God, whom thou servest continually, able to deliver thee from the lions? Then said Daniel unto the king . . . My God hath sent his angel, and hath shut the lions' mouths, that they have not hurt me.

"God does answer prayer," John said. "I know that to be true. Ever since my father gave me the gift of this Bible, I have prayed that I would one day learn to read it. God sent you to me as an answer to my prayers."

Grace lifted her eyes to John Hull. She looked hard at her master. At the man who owned her.

"I have prayed, too," she said. "I've prayed and prayed and prayed, but the dead are still dead. The slaves are still slaves."

"Yes," John said. "I see."

They read about Hosea, and his unfaithful wife. Of Joel and Amos, of the horror and the promise. They read Obadiah and Jonah. And they read Micah—the very words that had so touched Grace when she read Captain Ross's Bible.

Wherewith shall I come before the LORD, and bow myself before the high God? shall I come before him with burnt offerings, with calves of a year old? Will the LORD be pleased with thousands of rams, or with ten thousands of rivers of oil? shall I give my firstborn for my transgression, the fruit of my body for the sin of my soul?

John stopped reading, and for several minutes he pondered in silence. "That, right there, is my question," he said. "What can a simple man like me ever do to satisfy the Holy, Almighty God?"

"What could God want from a slave like me?" Grace whispered.

John read the next verse—the one Grace had thrown back at Lord Reginald.

He hath shewed thee, O man, what is good; and what doth the LORD require of thee, but to do justly, and to love mercy, and to walk humbly with thy God?

Chase Ambrose drove his wagon up the rutted road to John Hull's house, his wife Lily anchoring herself on the seat beside him. Even as John hurried over to welcome his neighbors, he shot a warning glance to Grace. She hurried inside the house. Quickly she grabbed up the leather-bound Bible they had left open on the table, put the red ribbon marker in place, and replaced the Bible in the top drawer of the wooden chest.

How careless to leave it out! John had stressed again and again how important it was to keep the reading lessons their secret.

"For your sake and mine," he said. "Besides, it is no one else's business."

Lily Ambrose brought two of her old dresses into the house for Grace. But it was John she gave them to. "I thought it would be good if your slave could have a change of clothes," she said to John. "It would help keep her clean, you know."

"Thank you kindly," John said.

Grace couldn't help but look at Lily Ambrose's full middle and her round, well-padded sides.

"And I brought this for her, too," Lily added. She handed John a large sack. "It's a sleeping mat for her. Your slave can stuff it full with corn husks. It will make for better sleep than a hard floor, I should say. In the daytime she can push it into the corner and out of your way."

"I do thank you," said John. "And so does Grace."

After he bid the Ambroses good-bye, John went out to the back of the house. When he came back, he carried a small chest.

"For you," he said as he handed it to Grace. "Now that you have belongings, you will need a place to keep them."

✿

"The New Testament of Our Lord and Savior Jesus Christ," John read. He looked over at Grace and smiled triumphantly. "'The book of the generation of Jesus Christ, the son of David, the son of Abraham. Abraham begat Isaac; and Isaac begat Jacob; and Jacob begat Judas and his brethren; and Judas begat Ph . . . Phar—'"

John sighed loudly. "I could read this much more easily if people didn't have such terrible names in those days!"

Grace laughed. "You mustn't worry about the names, sir," she said. "Say them any way you want. Who will know?"

Saying the names any way he wanted, John read through Matthew, all the way into chapter eighteen. There he read: "'If a man have an hundred sheep, and one of them be gone astray, doth he not leave the ninety and nine, and goeth into the mountains, and seeketh that which is gone astray?'"

Tears suddenly sprang to Grace's eyes. She tried to stop them, but they spilled over and dripped down her cheeks.

"Grace," John said. "Whatever is the matter?"

Grace shook her head and wiped at her teary face.

"Is it this story, Grace? Is it the Good Shepherd?"

But Grace steadfastly refused to speak about it. When she finally managed to choke back her tears, John continued to read.

When they finished reading through the four Gospels—all the stories of Jesus—Grace asked, "Was Jesus a colored man?"

"No!" John exclaimed. "He most certainly was not! What a thing to say, Grace. Of course Jesus was white."

"Was he an Englishman?" Grace asked.

"Well, no," John said. "He was born in the Arab lands, I do believe."

"And men in the Arab lands, they are white?" Grace persisted.

"Actually, I suppose they are more of a brown shade," John said.

"A brown shade like me?" Grace asked.

John shut the Bible with a thud. "Why do you persist in asking me such ridiculous questions, Grace?" he said. "You are a slave. Please remember that."

❧

Grace had long since given up trying to trace Cabeto's face in her mind. It was too painful to remember. Too hopeless, now that she was an ox wagon ride of ten days away from the plantation that might have been somewhere in the vicinity of the place where he might possibly have been held as a slave. It wasn't that she no longer yearned to see him, to run her hand along his strong arm, to feel his touch on her face. Oh, how she yearned for that. It was just that Cabeto was too long ago and too far away to be truly real to her anymore. Like Mama

Muco . . . and Kwate . . . and everyone and everything else firm and solid in her life.

Grace was just a slave. She must remember that.

⚘

No longer did Grace read to John Hull. As they progressed through the New Testament, he was able to read almost all of the text by himself. He read aloud to Grace, and she helped him when he needed her.

For by one Spirit are we all baptized into one body, whether we be Jews or Gentiles, whether we be bond or free. . . .

"Bond or free?" Grace asked. "That would mean, whether slaves or free men, would it not?"

"I suppose it would," said John.

He continued to read about the body of Christ, about the large parts and the small parts and how all are equally important. About how no part could be looked upon with less honor than any other.

Whether one member suffer, all the members suffer with it; or one member be honored, all the members rejoice with it. Now ye are the body of Christ.

"All of us are parts of the very same body?" Grace asked. "African slaves and free white men?"

"Well . . . I can't say that," John said. "I mean, this speaks about the persons that the Bible was written to . . ."

"Was it written to men in America?" Grace asked.

"Well, no . . ."

"Or in England?"

"No. But . . ."

Grace's dark eyes flashed. "My Mama Muco had a Holy Bible," she said. "Mama said it is not about the God of the white man. She said it is about the true God of all people. Just like the words you read: All together. No one greater and no one less. All equal parts of one body."

"Well, I . . ." John stammered, "Maybe it is not for us to know, you see. Maybe . . . that is, it could be that . . ."

But Grace had stopped listening. She stood up from the table. "I don't want to read any more," she said. "Whip me if you will, but I don't want to read any more."

"Grace—"

"You don't need me to teach you any longer, sir," Grace said. "You have learned well. You can read for yourself."

"Please, Grace," John said. "I still need you to help me."

"No," Grace said. "I will cook and I will clean and I will work in the garden and take care of the animals. I will do whatever you tell me to do, except this one thing. I will not read any more."

John Hull put the faded red ribbon in the page marked "First Corinthians, chapter twelve." He closed the Bible and put it away in the drawer.

"Grace," he said. "I will tell you now what I did not intend to tell you until later. When you finish teaching me, so that I can read the entire Bible for myself . . . then I will no longer keep you as my slave. I will give you your freedom."

34

$\mathcal{W}$hite men didn't go deep into the black swamp, where duckweed covered the murky water like a green carpet. White men didn't, and black men didn't, either. But Samson did. Samson knew that swamp.

That's not to say he had no fear of it. He most assuredly did. The fact was, he feared it all the more because he *did* know it. Snakes with poison in their mouths swam in those waters. Alligators slipped in and made themselves to look like innocent logs of wood as they waited to clamp their jaws down on something fresh and juicy.

"You be my friends," Samson said to the snakes and alligators. "You be my friends because you scare de slave catchers away from me. And you scare away dem dogs dey have with dem, too."

But, as Ruf said, the slave catchers would not give up easily. Especially not after they found one of their own sprawled across the road with his neck broken. And not after Massa Pierre Dulcet raised the reward for Samson's capture to one hundred fifty dollars.

Samson did not dare allow himself to rest. He waded into the swamp water, dodged the snakes and kept his eyes open for logs with alligator eyes. Deeper and deeper into the swamp he pressed.

How long ago was it that Massa Silas had bought him and his brother Cabeto from the slave ship? How long since Massa Silas had forced him to work in that very swamp? Back then, Samson had thought he would surely die there. Certainly that's what Massa Silas intended for him. But Samson did not die. And it just might be that by sending him to work in the swamp, Massa Silas had saved his life this day. Because Samson remembered the swamp. If he went far enough . . .

From the corner of his eye, Samson caught a glimpse of a snake swimming toward him, its nose stuck up out of the water. A narrow wake trailed behind. In a flash, Samson leaped to the side. But his foot hit against a tree stump, and he tripped and fell directly into the snake's path. Samson pushed out in front of him with his lame arm, right in front of the . . . turtle? Yees! It was just a yellow-bellied turtle!

Samson laughed out loud.

That's when he saw what he had been searching for—a small rise, hidden behind a clutch of cypress trees in the water. A tiny island, barely large enough to hold a shelter. Just the right size for a hiding place.

The sun was already low in the sky. For the rest of the afternoon, Samson hauled up dead wood, remains from the swamp's cypress trees. He also grabbed a few large palmetto leaves he found floating on the water. There wasn't much, but enough to piece together a small lean-to. Enough to give him protection from the sun and rain, and also from any potential eyes that might wish to pry.

Samson stood beside his new shelter and gazed out across the swamp. In the moonlight, he could see nothing but ghostly cypress stumps jutting up out of the black water. An owl called from somewhere overhead. Samson shivered in spite of himself.

"Trees, dey be," Samson said to no one, because no one was there except him. "But for all de world dey looks to be hunched-over slave catchers."

✍

Samson stood on the edge of his now familiar swamp home and cast his fish net out into the water. At the beginning of his stay, he had knit the net together from the fronds of a palmetto tree in the same manner as he had seen village men do in Africa. He caught fish and turtles in that net, enough to keep his belly filled. He ate tender young fern shoots, too, and now and then he discovered a duck's nest and had himself a couple of eggs.

"So much water," Samson said out loud. "Everywhere I looks, dere be water. But if it don't rain, dere be no water good enough for me to drink. I's thirsty from de top of my head to de bottom of my feet."

How long had Samson been in the swamp? Weeks? It seemed like months. But he could no longer remember. What he did know was that he was hungry for real food and thirsty for fresh water.

"And I ain't getting nowhere else when I sits here," he said.

Maybe the slave catchers had stopped their search for him. Maybe Massa Dulcet had found another slave to go along with him to Jean-Claude's *Le Coton Manoir*. Maybe someone else sat all day under the oak trees and listened to Dutch and Brister talk, and Ruf plot out a slave rebellion.

Maybe it was time for Samson to leave the swamp and find his brother.

Samson stepped his dripping wet feet out of the black water swamp and onto the dry bank. He gazed up at the pale shaft of moonlight that shone through the trees and moved on toward the road. He took care to stay back so as not to be seen by anyone who might be out at that hour. The brush was not thick there, though. He would need a safer place to hide before the break of day.

At first, Samson stayed well back from the road. But as the night wore on, he hugged it more closely, keeping his eye out for a place to take shelter come daybreak. Or maybe for another slave. Another slave might help him. Or another slave might turn him in. The truth was, he could not afford to trust anyone.

Samson spied a small farmhouse, dark and closed up for the night. What actually caught his eye was a well house over to the side of the main house. His body cried for a long drink of fresh water. Carefully, cautiously, Samson crept up to the well and drew out a full bucket of water. He drank the entire bucketful without stopping to take a breath.

His thirst quenched, Samson suddenly realized how exhausted he was. He looked about for a haystack to hide under, but found none. What he did see was a weathered wooden door, flat against the ground. He grabbed the metal hook and pulled the door open. It led to a root cellar—just a dark hole in the ground scattered with the remains of last season's sprouted potatoes and withered apples. He crept inside and hunkered down, and pulled the door shut behind him. He ate an apple, made himself as comfortable as the hole would allow, and fell asleep.

It's hard to judge the passage of time in a dark hole in the ground, but when Samson awoke, he could hear muffled voices outside. At times, men called out to one another, and at other times, the cadence of slaves sung out a work rhythm. Samson dozed, but awoke again with a start. He listened hard. But nothing seemed to be amiss, so he laid his head back and dozed some more.

Sharp sounds directly over his head reawakened Samson with a start. As the noises began to fade away, the door to his hiding place suddenly jerked open. A shaft of light flooded the cellar and blinded him. Samson leaped to his haunches, like a leopard ready to pounce. Someone gasped, and the door slammed shut.

Samson waited, his heart pounding. He stayed in his ready-to-pounce position as long as he could, but finally his muscles ached so badly he had to relax.

"Who's dere?" Samson growled in the most threatening voice he could manage.

No answer.

Because he had no other choice, Samson sat back down on the dirt and waited.

After what seemed like an interminably long time, the door opened again. This time, no shaft of light came through.

"I brung you somethin' to eat."

The voice was soft. A woman's voice.

"You best leave tonight. If Massa find you, he skin you alive."

"Thank you kindly," Samson said as he reached out for the food. "Can you tell me, is Massa Waymon's plantation nearby?"

"I don't know of no Massa Waymon," the voice said. "Dis be Massa Flume's land. If'n he catches you, he'll whip the hide clean off your back!"

"Thank you for de food," Samson said again. "I's obliged to you."

But the door closed again before he finished talking.

Samson waited another hour, maybe two. He ate another withered apple. Finally he pushed the door open and cautiously climbed out. Before him lay a field almost knee-high in new growth. Samson ducked down low and loped across it toward the road.

What made it especially difficult for Samson was that he had no real plan. Suppose he did find Massa Waymon's plantation. What would he do then? He couldn't simply walk into the slave quarters and ask for his brother.

It could be that he wouldn't even make it that far, that Massa Dulcet's patrols were waiting for him on the road. But even if he did make it, and even if he found Cabeto, how would the two of them get away?

These matters certainly concerned Samson. Still, they didn't concern him as much as doing nothing at all. So, despite his fears, he continued to press on. He ran at night in the general direction Brister had indicated, and as daybreak grew near, he looked for a place to hide.

Early one morning, a sharp hay fork poked Samson out from under a haystack where he had found refuge for the night. He took one look at the astounded white man who wielded the fork and took off at a run.

"I am a Quaker!" the man called after him. "Thou art most welcome to take whatever thou findest here, and may God go with thee!"

Samson did not get far that day. The road was clogged with white men on horses. In desperation, he ran back to the Quaker's house, and for the next three days he slept under his haystack and ate his food.

35

All night, Grace tossed on her corn husk mattress in haunted sleep. Her dreams, harsh remembrances from the past, tangled together with strange things that never were.

Her mother, Lingongo, scolding, scolding, scolding. Then Mama Muco brought Grace's gazelle, Bondo, back to her, alive and well . . .

Her father Joseph, his face blotchy and red, sailing out of the flames of Zulina fortress, shouting curses at her. Then Heath Patterson's barn—Joseph again, this time with Lingongo beside him, their arms wide open, called out to Grace . . .

Lord Reginald Witherham running after her. Then Charlotte and Ena both put out their feet and together blocked his way . . .

Captain Hallam forcing her onto the slave auction block. Then Captain Ross jumped up next to her on the table, his Holy Bible open and in his hand a silk purse bulging with shillings.

Grace awoke with first light. She got up quickly and straightened her rumpled dress. The kitchen was clammy and damp. Outside, rain fell heavily. Grace started the fire in the fireplace.

"Uncommon weather this morning," John Hull said. He stepped up to the fire to warm his hands. "A late rain is fine, but we do not want a flood just as the crops are setting."

Grace fried up bread and pork back fat, and put it on a plate for her master's breakfast.

"The fire is warm and bright," John said. "A good morning to read, I dare say. Whilst you clean the dishes, I will find our place in the Bible."

Grace did not argue. John Hull was still her master. Anyway, the sooner their reading was finished, the sooner he would set her free. Free! After so much anticipation and hope, she hardly knew how to imagine it.

John read the rest of the book of First Corinthians, and then he read Second Corinthians.

"I'll see about the weather," he said. He pushed his chair back and opened the door. "More rain than before!" John called. He came back to the table and sat down. "This is most definitely a day to read."

John read Galatians. When he got to the end of chapter three, he read: "'There is neither Jew nor Greek, there is neither bond nor free, there is neither male nor female: for ye are all one in Christ Jesus.'"

"What?" Grace asked.

John read the verse again: "'There is neither Jew nor Greek, there is neither bond nor free, there is neither male nor female; for ye are all one in Christ Jesus.'"

"Is that true when you go to church on Sundays?" Grace asked.

"Is what true?" John said.

"That everyone is just the same. That slaves are the same as freemen. Women are the same as men."

John stared at her. Every Sunday morning he dressed in his best suit and put on his good shoes and went to the meeting-house to hear the preacher preach. Of course he never took Grace along with him. Not a slave. Such a thing would never be allowed in the white Christian meetinghouse.

"Over at Brampton's barn, maybe five . . . six miles from here, a Reverend Abraham Marshall leads an African Church," John offered. "Baptist, I believe it is. I could take you over there, sometime."

"And you would stay and worship, too?" Grace asked.

"I said it is an African church," John said.

"I do not understand. If it is true what you read . . . If we are all one . . . why are things divided up the way they are?"

"I don't know, Grace," John said. "I do not know." He thought for a minute. "I surely do not know."

*

The rain didn't let up until late in the afternoon, and even then the ground was too water-soaked to allow for any work. So John Hull continued to read the short books of Ephesians, Philippians, and Colossians. He also read all of Thessalonians, First and Second, all of Timothy, First and Second, and the short book of Titus. By then the hour was late and the fire had burned low.

"Philemon," John said. "It's only one page long. Let's read one more page."

As John read the Apostle Paul's letter to his friend Philemon, whose runaway slave he had met and whose case he was pleading, Grace's eyes filled with tears. John read verses 15 and 16: "'For perhaps he therefore departed for a season, that thou shouldest receive him for ever; Not now as a servant, but above a servant, a brother beloved, specially to me, but how much more unto thee, both in the flesh, and in the Lord?'"

Grace burst into tears.

"What is it, Grace?" John said. He laid the Bible down. "Please . . . I insist that you tell me what causes you such distress!"

And so Grace sobbed out her story. She told of her family compound in Africa where she was raised, of Lingongo and Joseph Winslow and Mama Muco. She told about the threatened marriage to Jasper Hathaway, and her escape from her first slavery. And she told of the slave rebellion at Zulina fortress, and of the survivors who built a village of their own. She told of the happy years there, of Cabeto and of Kwate, but also of the slavers who came and forced them all away. She told John about Cabeto and the other villagers who were chained up and forced aboard the slave ship, and of her promise to Cabeto that she would find him and they would be together again. She told of her year in London, and of the treachery of Lord Reginald Witherham. But she also told of the good people who had risked so much to save her, and to get her to America. Then she told of Captain Hallam, and of the auction block.

" 'Departed for a season,' " Grace wept, "'that thou shouldest receive him for ever.' For a season, it says. And that's what I believed. But the season has been too long. And too much has happened that is too terrible. I do not think I will ever again receive my Cabeto."

John pulled the Bible back over to himself. He traced the words down the page with his finger. When he found the place, he read it out loud: "'. . . that thou shouldest receive him for ever; Not now as a servant, but above as servant, a brother beloved, specially to me, but how much more unto thee, both in the flesh, and in the Lord?' "

For a long time, he sat in silence. Grace wiped her face with her sleeve and waited uncomfortably for him to speak. But still he sat.

Finally John read the verse again, slowly and distinctly: "'. . . a brother beloved, especially to me, but how much more unto thee, both in flesh, and in the Lord.'" He rubbed his hand over his face. "Grace," he said, "I don't think this is speaking to you."

"Why?" Grace asked. "Because I'm nothing but a colored woman? Just a slave?"

"No, no," John said. "It's not that at all. It's because he is talking to Philemon, and I am the one in Philemon's place, not you. This is talking to me."

"What?" Grace asked.

John laid the faded red ribbon in its place and turned back to the Old Testament. He continued to turn back section after section until he found the book of Micah again. He traced down with his finger to chapter six, verse eight, and read:

He hath showed thee, O man, what is good; and what doth the LORD require of thee, but to do justly, and to love mercy, and to walk humbly with thy God?

"Maybe this is my chance to do what God requires of me," he said.

36

"Your porridge is greatly improved," John told Grace.

Grace laughed out loud. "A small touch of salt," she said. "But only a very small touch!"

Those were the only words John spoke to her before he left. He put on a freshly washed shirt and his Sunday shoes, and he yoked the oxen to the small two-wheeled cart. Grace opened the door a crack and watched him drive the cart down the road.

When the housework was finished, Grace went outside to care for the goats and feed the chickens. She collected four eggs in her skirt and brought them in the house for dinner. Her master still had not returned, so she went back to the garden to work until time to cook.

Noon came and went, and John Hull was not home, so Grace continued in the garden, clearing the weeds away from the vegetables. When the sun sank low, she washed the dirt from her hands and went to the kitchen to prepare supper.

By the time John finally returned home, Grace had set boiled eggs on the table alongside fresh tomatoes and a bowl of mashed vegetables.

"Tomorrow you should wash the clothes," John told Grace as he sat down. "And bake bread, too. The day after we will prepare for a long journey."

"Where will we go, sir?" Grace asked.

"Back to Charleston," John said. "To find Cabeto."

Grace put on the baggiest, most faded of the two dresses Lily Ambrose had given her. She didn't mind if that one got dirty, because she had already determined that Cabeto would never see her in it. She rolled up the floppy sleeves, took the bucket of hot water from the fire, and set to work scrubbing the clothes clean. Dirt and mud and cooking stains—she knew how to force them all out. Missus Peete had taught her well.

When Grace finished the washing, she took the wet clothes outside and spread them out over the split rail fences. Not the fences around the goat pen, of course. It would never do to have the goats nibble on Master John's clothes.

After that, Grace fried up a stack of flat bread. She cut slices of cheese and ham, which she wrapped in paper, and she boiled eggs. All the food she put into a box John Hull gave her. She ran out to the garden and plucked off as many tomatoes as she could carry, and she poked them around into the corners of the box.

How would they find Cabeto? And what would happen when they did? He was a slave, after all. Someone else's property. Grace longed to ask her master, but it wasn't her place to question him.

The next day, Mister Chase Ambrose and Missus Lily drove their wagon up the lane to John's house. Missus Lily inspected Grace's vegetable garden while Chase looked over the cornfields and the growing hay. After Missus Lily helped herself to

a basket of fresh vegetables, she moved over to the dirt courtyard and sat down on an upended barrel to wait while Mister
Chase and John Hull disappeared into the barn.

Grace was stirring supper over the fireplace when she heard
the Ambrose's wagon clatter away down the lane. Not too
long after, John stomped his feet on the step outside and came
into the house.

"I will load up the wagon at first light," he said, "and we
can be off."

Grace laid out her master's supper. "Mister Ambrose will
care for the goats and chickens?" she asked.

John pulled out his chair and sat down. "I sold the house
and the farm to him," he said. "I won't be coming back."

✍

Eight days back to Charleston. The trip didn't take as long
as the trip out to Savanna, because this time the oxen only
had to pull the two-wheeled cart instead of a fully-loaded
wagon. John Hull had left the wagon behind with the farm.
They went back across the river, back over the dusty roads,
back past green fields. Grace still sat in the bed of the cart, but
this time she rode more comfortably and unfettered.

One evening, as Grace and John ate a supper of boiled eggs
and bread beside the banks of a river, Grace asked, "What will
you do now, sir, without your farm?"

"I'll be a preacher," John said. "Just as I always wanted.
Now that I can read."

Grace thought for a minute.

"But where will you live?" Grace asked.

"Nowhere," John said. "And everywhere. I will be what is
called an itinerant preacher—one who travels around in the
manner of the great Methodist Francis Asbury. I'll go where

I am needed and stay wherever a home is open to me. It's a blessed life."

"Reverend Francis Asbury?" Grace asked. "Sir Thomas gave me a letter for him. I had it in my sea chest, but Captain Hallam wouldn't let me go back for it. Sir Thomas sent him word asking for help to find Cabeto."

John Hull shook his head slowly and smiled. "Should I ever meet the good reverend, I will tell him about you," he said.

On the eighth night, John stopped the oxen in a grove of trees alongside a small pond. "Wash yourself tonight, Grace," he said. "And put on your good dress. Tomorrow we will be in Charleston."

❧

"A slave, name of Caleb," John Hull said to a white man who waited as two slaves loaded sacks onto his wagon. "Would you know of him?"

The man shook his head.

"Thank you kindly," John said.

He asked the same of an outdoor vendor, and of a fishmonger, and of two colored men who worked on the road. All shook their heads "no." He asked an overseer with a group of slaves, and a man and his wife on their way to St. Philip's Church. He asked and he asked and he asked, but everyone gave him the same answer: "No, I know nothing of that slave."

John asked two men sitting at tea in a small eating establishment, "My good sirs, would you know anything of a slave name of Caleb?"

"Macon Waymon's Caleb, would it be?" the pudgier of the two men said. "The one who works the cotton gin?"

John was so used to people shaking their heads "no" that he was momentarily at a loss for words. He quickly recovered himself and asked, "Lame, is he?"

"Yes," the pudgy man said. "That be the same slave."

⁂

When John Hull approached Macon Waymon with an offer to buy Caleb, Macon laughed out loud.

"*You*, sir?" Macon said. He looked John up and down with a most critical eye. "I do believe my price for such a slave as Caleb would be far beyond your reach."

But Macon Waymon happened to be in the company of his business partner, Samuel Shaw, at the time, and Mister Shaw found an immediate pretext to call Macon aside.

"This is an excellent opportunity for you to separate a foolish man from his money, and to chasten a careless slave at the same time," Samuel said to Macon.

"I don't want to sell Caleb," Macon said. "He knows how to keep my cotton engine running."

"He's a smart Negro, all right," Samuel said. "But he knows a lot more than how to work with his hands. He also knows how to work you."

Macon, color rising in his face, turned on his friend.

But before he could argue, Samuel said, "You are losing control of that slave, Macon. I see it, and the other slaves see it, too. They know he steals chickens from you just like you know it . . . and he takes whatever else he pleases, too, I have no doubt. He sleeps when he should work. The slave quarters rumble with rumors that he will run away, but you don't hear those rumors because you choose to close your ears to them."

Samuel brushed off Macon's blustered denial.

"Use your head, man," Samuel said. "You have two advantageous opportunities laid out before you. Do you know who this John Hull is? He's the fool farmer who bought Pace Williamson's slave that can read. Sell Caleb to him, but don't give him a receipt. That way you can insist the purchase never was completed and refuse to allow Caleb to go with him."

"Get the money for Caleb, and keep him, too?" Macon asked.

"Show your slaves that no one can outsmart you."

⌇

Macon Waymon furrowed his brow thoughtfully and rubbed his hand across his jaw. "Caleb is a valuable slave, Mister Hull," he said to John.

"I am prepared to give you a fair price for him," John said.

"Well, now, in my estimation, seven hundred dollars would be a fair price."

John gasped. "Seven hundred dollars? That is much more than I anticipated."

"As I say, Caleb is a valuable slave."

Macon glanced over at Samuel Shaw, who stood off to the side in the shade of the magnolia tree.

"What amount did you have in mind?" Macon asked.

"Well, I didn't know," John said. "I thought perhaps three hundred."

"Three hundred!" Macon exclaimed. "Even five hundred would be too little for such a one as he."

John Hull shook his head. For several minutes he said nothing.

"I can give you four hundred right now," John finally offered.

Macon sneaked another look at Samuel.

"Four hundred fifty," Macon said. "Not one dollar less."

John took his purse from his vest pocket. Carefully he counted out four hundred and fifty dollars, which he handed to Macon Waymon.

"Thank you kindly, sir," Macon said to John. "Go on down to the slave quarters. I shall get the receipt ready and meet you there shortly."

❦

Grace straightened her dress and fluffed out her skirt. She ran her hands through her hair. She took a deep breath as she waited, rubbing her hands together nervously.

Then Caleb stepped out.

Grace couldn't move. Tears blinded her.

Without a word, Caleb walked over to her and took her in his arms.

John Hull turned away. He spent several minutes inspecting the freshly swept dirt in the courtyard before he sauntered back to Grace and Caleb and drew two documents from his coat pocket.

"Your papers of freedom," he said. "To Grace Hull and to Cabeto Hull. My final gift to you is the bequest of my name. Wear it well."

Grace reached out and laid her hand on her former master's arm.

"You answered my prayers," she said.

"No," John responded. "God did. He just used me to do it. Like he used you to answer my prayers."

"Thank you," Grace said. "Thank you for everything."

"For my whole life, de white man be my enemy," said Caleb. "How can it be dat my great enemy now be my great friend?"

"Not just a friend," John Hull said. "You are my dear brother."

37

Samuel Shaw raised a glass to Macon Waymon. "Congratulations, my good man!" he proclaimed with a confident cheer.

But Macon was not yet ready to celebrate.

"Might just as well let the two of them have some time before I send the colored girl away," Macon said. "Her master, too, of course."

"Do not concern yourself about the colored girl," Samuel assured him. "She will forget soon enough. Negroes always do. They don't have feelings for each other the same as white folks do."

"I have to feel a bit sorry for that poor old farmer, though," said Macon. "Where do you suppose he got the money to pay for Caleb?"

"If he can be tricked so easily, he should not be a slave owner," said Samuel Shaw. "He should not be a landowner, either."

Caleb bid a fond farewell to the old women who worked in the quarters and cared for the littlest children. They were the only slaves around. All the others were at work in the fields.

"I does hate to see you go," Prudie said. "Still more lines of sorrow plowed on dis poor old face of mine."

John Hull couldn't say when he first began to feel that something wasn't right. It might have been the matter of the receipt of sale—he should have gotten that as soon as he laid out his money. Or maybe it was that judge, Samuel Shaw, who pulled Macon away for counsel and never let him out of his sight. Certainly it was before the long and fruitless wait at the slave quarters.

Something most definitely was wrong. A great dread welled up in John. Somehow Macon Waymon must have tricked him.

"Go!" John said to Grace and Caleb. "Keep your papers safe lest someone should try to take them from you."

"Go where?" Grace asked. "Back across the river? Back to your house?"

"No, no!" said John. "Go north. Far north, where slaves are free—Pennsylvania or Ohio or Massachusetts. You must use your wits and take great care. My prayers will follow you."

"Sir—" Grace said.

But John cut her short. "Go! Now! Make all haste to get as far as you can before Mister Waymon gives chase."

☙

"Caleb is gone?" Macon Waymon exclaimed. "Whatever do you mean! How can my slave be gone?"

"My slave, sir," John Hull corrected. "Except that Caleb is no longer a slave at all. I gave him his papers of freedom."

"What? You cannot do that!" Macon fumed.

"Oh, but I already did," said John. "At this very moment, he is on a wagon bound for Mexico." *Forgive me, Almighty God, for telling such a lie. Please accept it as a deed of justice and mercy, offered in all humility to thee, my God.* "And, sir," John added. "You did promise to provide me with a receipt of sale for the four hundred fifty dollars I paid you for Caleb. I am certain you wish to retain your reputation as a man of honor, faithful to your word."

Macon tried to speak, but his anger bubbled over into incomprehensible babble.

John said, "Surely you do not intend to break your word, sir. If you do so, I shall not hesitate to take this matter to the authorities."

"You do that and I shall be forced to inform them that you are nothing but a fool and a troublemaker!" fumed Macon. "Those slaves will be found, and when they are, I will petition to have my slave—Caleb—returned to me!"

"They are not slaves. They are free," John said. "They have their papers to prove it."

"Forged papers, is what they have!" Macon roared. "I will testify that you knowingly bought a slave who could read, and therefore could undoubtedly write. I submit that it was she who forged those papers. A perfect example of why Negroes should not be trained in such skills, by the way. As you can see, sir, this entire situation is of your making."

Macon glared from John Hull to the gathering of slaves who had begun to come in from the fields. It was impossible to read their blank faces. Fury seethed inside Macon. He owned those slaves! Their lives lay in his hands. But would a single one of them reach out to catch Caleb for him? No! He was certain not one of them would do that.

Because Macon Waymon owned so many slaves, and because runaways were a never-ending problem, at the first of every year he paid two poor white men thirty-five dollars each to stay ready to chase after runaways from his plantation. Each of those men had two dogs—vicious, tenacious hounds, trained to track and attack.

"Juba!" Macon ordered. "Run and fetch my slave chasers. Now!"

"Yes, Massa!" Juba said, and he set off running. But as soon as he was out of Massa Macon's sight, Juba eased back to a slow walk. The more of a lead he could give Grace and Caleb, the better.

✐

All Caleb knew of the outside world was the distance he had walked from Macon Waymon's rice farm to his cotton plantation. "Go north," John Hull had told him. So Caleb looked at the sinking sun and figured from that which direction was north. No road lay that direction, which was all the better. But no woods lay there, either. Only a great field that stretched out as far as Caleb could see.

"Run!" Grace said. "I can keep up with you!"

But she could not. First she slowed, then she stumbled. When she fell, Caleb pulled her up and they did their best to keep running, but she fell again, and again.

"De corn be high enough to hide us," Caleb said.

Before they could make it to the cornfield, though, two slaves stepped out in front of them. For a moment all four stared at each other.

"You best get you'sefs to de river before dem dogs come sniffin' for you," one of the slaves said.

"Which way?" Caleb asked.

"Just de other side of dem trees."

Grace and Caleb spent the rest of their first day of freedom dripping wet. They jumped into the river and hid among the reeds, careful to hold their feedom papers out of the water. When they could no longer abide the cold, they climbed back out and onto the bank. Hunkered down low, they ran close enough to the water to dash in and out.

"We can't let dem dogs get our scent," Caleb warned.

*

With the darkness, Grace and Caleb left the river and headed north. All night long they kept moving.

The first shafts of light dawned on nothing but still more flat farmland. Not the least protection was in sight. In desperation, Caleb clawed out a depression in the middle of a hay field. They both squeezed into it and Caleb did his best to pull clods of earth and growing hay back over them. Exhausted, they fell into a sound sleep.

"Dost thou run away?"

Caleb jumped up, sending dirt clods flying.

"I heard the dog howl this morning."

A white man stood before him, a hoe in his hand.

"They do not be far away," the man said.

Caleb's eyes darted from the man to Grace, who was still on the ground, and out to the expanse of field.

"Thou canst not outrun them," the man said. "Not out here. Thou hast no place to hide thyself. Come, I shalt hitch up the wagon and I shalt take thee away."

"No!" Caleb said.

Caleb pulled Grace to her feet.

"Come," the man urged. "In the least, I canst give thee a chance."

In the distance, a dog howled.

"They come closer," the man said. "We must make haste or it will be too late."

"We have no choice, Caleb," Grace pleaded. "We must trust him."

Amos Bligh already had his wagon loaded for a trip to town. Grace and Caleb dug out a space for themselves at the bottom of a pile of sacks while Amos hitched up the horse. As he turned onto the road, Amos saw two men on horseback mounting an incline far behind him. He urged the horse to a gallop.

✒

For two hours Grace and Caleb bounced along in the back of the wagon, practically suffocated by the heavy sacks. Suddenly, the wagon stopped. Grace hardly dared to breathe. But no one came to the back, and soon they started to move again.

When the wagon finally stopped again, Grace heard voices. She heard another sound, too. It was sacks being pulled off the wagon. Grace squeezed her eyes shut and pleaded, *Please, God! Please, please, please, please . . . !*

"Come on out," Amos Bligh called. "Thou shalt find safety here, for a short while, at least."

They were at a small farmhouse, set far off the road in what looked to be the middle of a field.

"Thou shalt find rest and food here," Amos said. "On the morrow we will pray thee on thy way."

After a wash and a welcome sleep on one of the many mats spread across the floor in a large back room, Grace straightened herself up as best she could. It was pleasant to sit and watch Cabeto as he slept beside her.

He was not the slave Caleb any longer. He was Cabeto again. He was her Cabeto.

"Come, please, and sit at table with us," Amos called after Cabeto awoke.

Grace and Cabeto stared uncertainly at Amos. Sit at table with white folks? He led them to the kitchen, where a large table was spread with pottery plates and mugs and iron spoons.

"Our working guests are cleaning themselves up," said the other man, whom Amos called Jed. "As soon as they join with us, we shall sit together and break bread with them."

To the surprise of Grace and Cabeto, the working guests were all colored. But what truly shocked them was the tall man near the back of the group. The one with the lame arm.

"Sunba?" Cabeto breathed. "Sunba!"

Between twilight and candlelight, Grace, Cabeto, and Sunba prepared to leave the Quaker safe house. Each carried a leather sack of provisions. Everyone gathered together, white and black, to join hands and ask God's blessing and provision on the travelers.

Jed picked up a stick and drew a map in the dirt. "This is South Carolina," he said as he pointed to the first block. "Thou shouldst go north here, through Virginia and up here all the way to Pennsylvania, and on through that state, too. From there thou canst go by boat to Upper Canada."

"How long will it take us to get there?" Grace asked.

"Most of three months," Jed said. "Maybe more if thou encountereth troubles."

"Watch thyself hard until thou crosseth over into Pennsylvania," Amos warned.

"And even then, keep a watch out," said Jed. "It used to be, thou wouldst be safe there. But a new law was passed a couple of months back that sayeth slave owners have the right to go into free states and grab back slaves for themselves. Thou wouldst do well to move on through with all haste."

Cabeto shook his head. "I don't know de way," he said. "How can we keep our path straight all dose weeks and months?"

Amos pointed to the fading stars in the sky. "Over there. Doest thou see the shape of the water dipper? Some call it 'the drinking gourd.'"

"Yes!" Grace said. "I see it. Its handle points upward."

"The two stars in the dipper's bowl, the ones farthest from the handle," Amos said. "They point directly to the North Star. Every night, thou canst see it in the same place in the sky. Follow that star, and it shalt lead thee all the way to Canada."

"The brightest star of all," Cabeto said.

"A gift from God, to show us the way," Grace said. "Like the star of Bethlehem that led the kings who searched for baby Jesus."

Amos smiled. "Go with God," he said. "We shalt meet again in heaven."

38

$\mathcal{W}$hat's dat?" Sunba whispered.

"Nothing but an old hoot owl in the trees," Cabeto said with a laugh. But it was a nervous laugh, because he had been thinking the same thing as Sunba, which was the same thing Grace had been thinking: *Maybe it's the slave catcher's hounds, crawling through the brush.*

"I saw dem dogs get a man one time," Cabeto said. "Dey bit him all over his arms and legs, den dey chewed off his ears."

"Did dey kill him?" Sunba asked.

"He wished dey did," Cabeto said.

The three pushed on in silence. Soon, Sunba said, "We could head to de swamp. Dem dogs can't follow us dere. And de slave catchers won't."

Worse than the slave catchers, worse even than the slave catchers' hounds, was the dark unknown between Charleston and Canada. All the three travelers had to help them along their journey was the rough map sketched in the dirt, a star in the sky, and the promise of prayers from strangers. At least in the swamp, they knew the dangers that lurked.

"No," Cabeto said. "We got to go north. We got to go to freedom."

They had passed through fields heavy with the goodness of early summer and were gratefully in the protection of heavy overgrowth when Sunba pointed to a settlement of log houses in the distance.

"I know dat place over dere," he said. "Dem darkies be French."

"How does you know?" Cabeto asked.

"I be livin' out here a long time," Sunba said. "Dem people come from de French island where de big slave rebellion be."

"Is dey slaves?" Cabeto asked.

"No, dey's all free," Sunba said. "Dey helped me once."

"Be careful," Grace warned. "We cannot trust anyone."

✐❧

They wouldn't stay, Sunba told Josephine, the first refugee from the island of Saint Domingue to see him coming across the field. They only needed a place to sleep through the day. Just until dark, and they would be on their way.

"The dogs, they be chasing after you?" Josephine asked.

"Yes," said Sunba, "but dey be far back."

"Dogs come fast," Josephine said. "Hide your *odeur* so they cannot track you."

"You mean the way we smell? How can do we do that?" Grace asked.

"Ah, but it is an easy thing to do," said Luc, who came around from the back of the small house. "Come out to the edge of the woods."

A large plot of ground had been cleared of all brush, and that's where the freed French slaves took Grace, Cabeto, and

Sunba. Luc and two other men dug dirt out of the barren patch and threw handfuls of it at the three.

"What's this for?" Grace asked.

"It be grave dirt," said Luc. "Rub it all over you. Especially your feet bottoms. Before you leave tonight, rub it all over your feet again. The dogs can't catch your scent no more."

The three rubbed the dirt on their hands, on their feet, on their arms, on their legs, and for good measure, on their faces. That day they slept soundly.

At dusk, Grace and the two brothers left—their bodies rested, their stomachs filled with warm soup and fresh baked bread, and their feet rubbed with grave dirt. The freed French slaves pointed them to a safe trail through the woods.

"Colored folks live all through dese woods," said Sunba. "We could make us a drum and send dem messages like in Africa."

"What if some colored folk turn us in to the slave catchers so they can collect the reward?" Grace asked.

"Colored folks don't turn other colored folks in to white folks," said Sunba.

"Sometimes dey do," said Cabeto. "Sometimes dem dollars just sound too good to dem."

For a long time they walked in silence.

"How do you know so much about French slaves?" Grace asked Sunba.

"Dat's where I been livin'," Sunba said. "I know all about de rebellion in dat Saint Domingue Island. Everyone murdered everyone over dere. Dey got dere heads cut off and stuck up on sticks to warn everyone else to stay in dey place and not try to start a slave rebellion of dey own."

"Like Zulina," Grace said.

"Yes," said Sunba. "De white man is losin' de battle and de slaves is winnin'. Dat's why de white folks around here be so scared of us. Dey done seen what we can do."

Most days Grace, Cabeto, and Sunba took to the woods or the deep underbrush to sleep through the daylight hours. Sometimes, when the land was especially barren, they risked walking in the daylight. It was always a dangerous proposition, though.

One evening, Cabeto fashioned a makeshift net from a sleeve of his shirt and took it to the river. He had no luck catching fish, however. So at daybreak, after Grace and Sunba had settled themselves to sleep, he slipped down to a pond situated closer to the road than was safe. He had just snared a good-sized fish when a hand clamped down hard on his shoulder.

"What you doing down here?"

Cabeto swung around to see a craggy-faced white man in muddy clothes and with no shoes on his feet.

"Fishin' is all," Cabeto said.

"Where your master be?" the man demanded.

Cabeto broke into a cold sweat.

"I don't have a master," he said as calmly as he could manage. "I be a free man. Gots my papers to show it."

"Show me them papers," the man said.

Cabeto dug in his pocket and pulled out his freedom paper from John Hull.

"See?" he said. "I be a free man."

The white man squinted at the paper.

"Hmm," he said. "Well, then."

He looked at the fish in Cabeto's hand.

"You wants dis fish?" Cabeto said.

The man nodded. He took the fish and walked away. He did pause for an instant—even turned to glance back—but in the end he just gripped the fish more tightly and walked on.

"Wake up!" Cabeto said. He nudged Sunba with his foot. "Come on, Grace! We've got to go away from here."

An occasional friendly house . . . sometimes a boat in the water that could carry them down the stream . . . at times, a helpful slave willing to point out a secret route through the woods. Now and again a partially filled wagon going north and a driver who would look away while three dirty colored folks jumped on.

More often, an uneasy sleep . . . frightening encounters . . . suspicious warnings. And endless weeks of walking, walking, walking.

"What are you colored folks doing out here?"

Grace gasped out loud and dropped the berries she had collected in her bandana. A young woman, her bucket half filled with the wild berries, stepped out from behind the tall wall of vines.

"Are you runaways?" she demanded.

"No," Grace said. "We're free."

"You all got papers to prove it?"

Grace paused just the tiniest bit before she said, "Yes . . . all of us."

"You can sleep in our barn tonight," the young woman said. "My father will allow it if you're free."

"We like to walk at night," Grace said. "The weather is cooler."

"In that case, you can sleep in our barn today."

Grace lay on a bed of hay, safe in the crook of Cabeto's arm. Sunba stretched out on his back beside them. Suddenly Sunba sat bolt upright.

"I heard a dog," he said.

"You dreamed it," Cabeto mumbled.

But a howl echoed through on the still, hot air, and all three bolted up.

"She betrayed us!" Grace cried. "That white woman called for the slave catchers!"

They leapt up and were out of the barn.

"We must hide our scent," Sunba warned.

Sunba headed for the pasture where oxen grazed and stomped his feet through a pile of manure. Grace and Cabeto tramped after him. Then they were off through the field, and on across the next one.

Just when Grace felt she couldn't run another step, she spied a lone tobacco barn in a barren pasture.

"Look!" she cried. "We can hide inside there, at least for a short time."

Panting, Grace stumbled through the door. Immediately she was greeted by screams and moans and pleas for help.

"What is this?" Grace cried in alarm.

Inside the barn was another, smaller building—a log hut. But this one was fitted with barred windows and iron rings bolted to the walls. And the shackles had manacled slaves chained to it.

"It be a slave jail!" Sunba said. "De slave catchers ain't comin' for us. Dey be comin' for dese folks!"

Grace pulled at the chains, but they were locked.

"Grace!" Cabeto called. "We can't help dem. Run! Run! Run to de river!"

39

*Y*ou be in Culpeper," a scrawny Negro woman who called herself Cisley informed Grace. Cisley plucked pieces of hot fried corn bread from the skillet and shuffled them over to the fugitives.

"We made it to Virginia, then?" Grace asked.

"This be Virginia, all right," said Cisley. "You best watch yourselfs here, too. Slave runners be about. But if you keep on going north, up to the Rapidan River and Black Hills, people there be more free than they be here."

"De Bull Run Mountain," Cabeto said with a nod. "Dat's what we is lookin' for."

"Keep on going," Cisley told him. "The east side of the mountain is what you wants."

"You be from Carolina lowcountry," Cisley's husband, Big Jim, said to Cabeto.

"How'd you know dat?" Cabeto asked.

"Your talk," Big Jim said. "They's the ones with gullah talk."

Grace smiled and dipped her corn bread into a tin cup of hot bark tea. She looked around at the community of colored folks.

"What about all of you?" Grace asked Cisley. "Are you free?"

"Yes'm," said Cisley. "That we be. Law here says so. Nobody don't bother us on this mountain, neither."

"How 'bout you stay here with us?" Big Jim said. "We could cut some logs and build you a place here."

Cabeto didn't answer him immediately. But when he did, it was with a couple of questions of his own: "Are you free to go anywheres you wants? Can you roam far from your home?"

Big Jim shook his head.

"Best not do that," he said. "But we has no need to go nowheres else, neither. We lives here off this mountain just fine."

"Thank you kindly," said Cabeto, "but I think we will keep followin' de star to de north."

"Suit yourself," Big Jim said. "Negro Mountain ain't far from here. Many free colored folks live over there. After that, you just needs go on another day's journey and you gets to the Potomac River."

"Watch out for other groups of colored people, though," Cisley warned. "Some ain't really free like they says. They's just runaways hidin' out. You don' want to be with them when slave catchers come pokin' around."

Cabeto nodded. "De Potomac River just beyond Negro Mountain—dat be Leesburg, den?"

Big Jim nodded.

"Leesburg be a city?" asked Cabeto.

"It do," said Big Jim. "But it's no good for night travel. Colored folks has to be in under cover by the time the city bells chime ten o'clock or else they gets throwed into the lock-up house."

"Even free colored folks?" asked Grace.

"Slave or free, makes no difference," said Big Jim. "And come morning, if you has no money to pay the fine, it's off to the workhouse with you. Best go wide around Leesburg and on to Edward's Ferry."

✑❧

Virginia summer days were hot and sticky. And although the hours of daylight had begun to grow steadily shorter, the span of darkness was still not long enough to suit the travelers. The sunny open didn't matter quite so much while they trekked along secluded mountain paths. But whenever they neared a town, they sought the cover of thick brush—or, even better, of darkness.

Which was why Negro Mountain was such a blessed relief. There, Grace and Cabeto and Sunba did not need to hide themselves, not even in full daylight. They could talk out loud, and cook real food over a real fire. Grace begged to stay for an extra day of rest.

A small woman by the name of Lavinia brought Grace a dress she could borrow so Grace could bathe herself and wash her hair. She washed her dress, too, and spread it out in the sun to dry. Cabeto and Sunba cleaned themselves up, as well.

A huge, woolly-haired bear of a man by the name of Tom handed the newcomers tin cups of a cool sweetgrass tea.

"You got papers?" Tom asked in a surprisingly gentle voice. "You needs papers to cross over the river on the ferryboat."

"Grace and I do," Cabeto said, "though my old massa objects to my freedom. He sent the slave catchers after me, anyway. But, Sunba here—he ain't got no papers at all."

"That's bad," Tom said. "That's very bad."

Tom sat down between Cabeto and Sunba and took a long draught of sweetgrass tea.

"I got a empty paper," Tom said. "Took it from a white man. But none of us here knows how to write on it."

Grace's eyes opened wide. "May I see it?" she asked.

Tom went into his cabin and came back out with a folded paper.

"Have it if you wants it," he said. "All of us here be free already. It won't do you no good, though. It be empty of names."

Eagerly Grace unfolded the paper and spread it out on her lap. It was just like the ones she and Cabeto carried, except that it had no slave name written in the blank space and no signature at the bottom.

"She can write," Cabeto said. "Except she got no quill and ink."

"I can make a quill," said Grace. "All I need is a good, long feather and a sharp knife."

"A big dead crow be layin' out in the corn," a young boy said. "I can bring you its feathers."

"I'll whet my knife to shavin' sharp," a man offered.

Grace took the largest of the crow feathers the boy brought her, and with the newly sharpened knife, she sliced off the lower part. She made a small slit in the middle of the back of the trimmed feather. With the knife's point, she carefully cut above the slit and into the feather—first on the left side, then on the right.

"The hole on that side be bigger," Tom said, pointing to the left of the feather.

"So it is," said Grace. She cut more from the right side.

Grace took the cleaned-out feather over to the remains of the cook fire and plunged the nib into the cooling coals.

She quickly pulled it out and tested it with her fingernail. She shook her head and thrust it back in, and left it a bit longer. When she was finally satisfied that it had baked to the proper hardness, she scraped the barrel of the quill with the back of the knife blade. Slowly and carefully, she shaved the hardened nib to a sharp point.

"A right fine writin' quill that be!" Tom said in admiration.

Lavinia handed Grace half a gourd filled with a blue-black liquid. "We made berry ink for you," she said.

Grace took out her own freedom paper and scrutinized it. She turned it back side up, dipped the nib of the crow quill into the berry ink, and drew a line.

"Just to make certain my pen works," Grace said.

The line was far from perfect, but it was clearly a line.

Grace turned her paper back over and laid the empty form beside it on the table. She dipped the crow quill into the berry ink once again and slowly scratched the name "Sunba Hull" on the blank line. At the bottom, she very carefully did her best to scratch out a signature that resembled John Hull's barely legible name.

⚮

Grace, Cabeto, and Sunba left Negro Mountain as three free colored folks. True, one had a forged paper and another was being hunted as a runaway. But they all had freedom papers in their possession.

They left the mountain in the morning, walked clear through the day and through the moonlit night, and arrived at Edward's Ferry in the middle of the next morning. It was the church-going hour on the Sabbath day, so many people were out on the streets, both colored and white. No one seemed to notice three more Negroes.

Grace was the first to spy the river landing.

At the ferry, the three cautiously followed others who were boarding the boat. They didn't get on, though. They had their papers, all right, but unfortunately, Tom hadn't told them they also needed money.

"Maybe we can do some work to earn money," Grace said.

"No," said Sunba. "We has no place to stay. And we don't know how to act around dese folks. Dey will be suspicious of us."

"We need to get back to de mountains," said Cabeto.

"But how will we get to Pennsylvania?" Grace pleaded. "We don't know any way except across the river."

"We has to find another way," said Cabeto.

They wasted a good bit of the day arguing the point, but finally Grace gave in. Reluctantly they turned up the road and headed back toward the mountains. Evening was fast coming on, yet the sky was still light. They had not walked far when a wagon rumbled up the road behind them. The white driver slowed his horse to a trot.

"Good evening," the white man called out.

Caleb and Sunba exchanged glances.

"Evening, sir," Grace answered.

"Care for a ride in the back of the wagon?" the man offered.

"Thank you kindly, but we ain't goin' far," said Cabeto.

"Jump off whenever you desire," the man said. "Has you a place to lay your heads this night?"

"Dat we do not," Sunba said.

"That being the case, may I offer you accommodations?"

"We has no money to pay for your generosity," Cabeto said.

"Please, do consider yourselves my guests," said the man.

After some hesitation, they climbed onto the wagon. The white man drove the horses up the road a fair ways, but after a while he turned off the road. The horses wound around through a wide open meadow, heading in the general direction of the setting sun.

"We best jump off," Sunba said nervously.

Grace and Cabeto squinted around them into the gathering darkness.

"No place here to hide if he wants to chase us down," Grace said.

"I don't even know where we be anymore," said Cabeto.

Finally the wagon headed up a narrow driveway, and the man pulled the horses to a stop.

"The river's close behind my house," the white man called out to the travelers. "If it wasn't already dark, you could see it. I have a secret ferry back there. I'll haul you across first thing in the morning."

The man's house had several rooms. He told the three that they were welcome to sleep in the one in back.

"I don't like dis," Sunba told Grace and Cabeto. "Why is dis man bein' so helpful to us?"

So they slipped out the window and slept in the thick brush on the hillside.

Still, the white man was as good as his word. With first light, he called out to them that he had the ferry ready. It was actually just a flat wooden platform rigged with wooden beams, ropes, and a pulley. The man had two boys with him, and the three of them tugged the platform across the river until Grace and the men were able to splash out onto the other side.

"Where are we?" Grace asked.

"We'll know when we sees de drinkin' gourd," Cabeto said.

"But it's still early morning. We can't waste an entire day!"

"Better than spend de whole day walkin' de wrong way," said Cabeto.

So they compromised. Cabeto guessed the direction, and they walked—but at a leisurely pace, in case they were wrong. The summer sun was hot, and the river water fresh and cool. Berries grew heavy on the vines and vegetables thick in nearby gardens. Ears of corn, tiny and tender, stood thigh-high in fields alongside the country lane.

After the sun had passed its zenith, something on the far side of a small skirt of brush caught Grace's attention. Two unpainted houses stood side by side, each with a few chickens pecking at the ground around them.

"Colored families," Grace said. "See the little black children out back?"

"Maybe dey just be slaves," Sunba said.

"Or maybe we are in Pennsylvania," said Grace. "Maybe we are in a state where colored people live free."

That thought brought them all such joy that they agreed they would make a camp up the river and relax for the rest of the day.

As twilight gathered, Grace settled herself in a comfortable brush nest, determined to eat her fill of ripe berries. Cabeto lay his head in her lap and nodded off to sleep. Sunba, always the restless one, moved farther on up the river.

"I'll find a fat rabbit," Sunba said. "Maybe we can make us a fire and cook it."

Sunba wasn't gone long before he crashed back through the brush.

"Run!" he hissed. "Men be comin' with guns. Get to de coloreds' house! Quick!"

Cabeto grabbed hold of Grace and pulled her toward the skirt of brush where they first saw the houses.

"Where is Sunba?" Grace cried.

"He's with us," Cabeto said. "Go quickly! Hide yourself!"

A horse snorted from somewhere down river.

Not far behind them, a deep voice shouted out, "Stop!"

"Over there!" someone else called. "I see them!"

"Go! Now!" Sunba ordered from behind. And he was gone.

Cabeto stopped and stared back into the darkness. He could see nothing.

"What do you want with us?" Sunba yelled.

Now Sunba's voice, too, came from down by the river. He was running in the opposite direction from Cabeto and Grace. The horses turned and galloped after him, thundering wildly through the brush.

Something crashed. Two voices rose up together in angry shouts. Accusations, it sounded like. Furious demands. Wild threats.

A gunshot rang out.

The first man screamed, "No! No . . . ! What have you done?"

At the same moment, Cabeto cried, "Sunba!"

Grace grabbed Cabeto's arm and strained to hold him back.

The voices by the river bellowed with angry shouts.

"You fool!" the man with the deep voice yelled. "You stupid fool! Freedom fighters and abolitionists are everywhere. If you've gone and killed a freed man, they'll be after us!"

"Go! Go!" the first man ordered. "Leave the others!"

The horses galloped off in the opposite direction. Then all was silent.

"Sunba!" Cabeto cried again.

He pulled away from Grace. Fighting his way through the darkness, Cabeto headed back toward the river.

"Sunba!" Cabeto's voice was wild and frantic. "Where are you, Sunba? Answer me, brother!"

Grace ran, too, and sobbed out Sunba's name. Cabeto was already far ahead of her. Grace tried to feel her way in the dark, but she stumbled in the thick brush. She turned away toward the river. Where the berry vines met the river, she kicked up against something, and she knew.

"He's here!" Grace called. She fell to her knees and lifted Sunba's too-still head into her lap. "Oh, no! No, no!"

Just as Cabeto reached Grace's side, the brush seemed to come to life. Unfamiliar arms took hold of Cabeto and pulled him away, even as he shrieked and fought.

"I be Canaan, brother," said a deep, rolling voice. "Come away. Please, come away. We'll see to him."

At first Cabeto fought against everyone. But the deep voice continued to roll words of comfort and assurance. Grace soothed him, too. Finally Cabeto hushed his screams and stopped fighting.

A woman who called herself Hetty took Grace's arm and led her to the closest of the unpainted houses. Canaan and Cabeto followed, and several other men came after, carrying Sunba's body.

Cabeto, dazed and confused, asked, "What happened?"

"Mister Peters done got you," said Canaan. "He do it all the time. Pulls someone across the river so nice and friendly. But he tells the slave catchers about it and collects their money, and they be ready and waitin' on this side."

"But we have papers," Grace said.

"It don't matter," said Hetty. "The catchers still pay him."

"We thought . . . if we was in Pennsylvania—" Cabeto began.

"No, sir," said Hetty. "No, you not be in Pennsylvania. You be in Maryland. You still be in slave country."

"Sunba saved our lives," Grace said as she wiped at her tear-streaked face. "He called to the slave catchers and led them away from us."

"He did love you," said Canaan, "That's what the Good Book say."

Grace looked at him in confusion. "What?" she asked.

"The Good Book say no man can love more than that," Canaan said. "Than he lay down his life."

40

The next morning, Canaan hitched a donkey to his cart and took Cabeto and Grace far up the road until it ended at a wide river. He forded the water in the wagon, expertly search-ing out the shallowest places. On the other side, Canaan continued on until he crossed the state line into Pennsylvania.

"Many colored people be up here," Canaan said as he bid the two farewell. "Pennsylvania folks don't much like slavery. You be safer here than most anywheres else."

Grace and Cabeto walked north, right along the road and in the middle of the day. Mostly they walked in silence. When they did talk, it was not of Sunba. Cabeto couldn't bear it. Grace sneaked glances at her husband as they walked together. His limp was bad and growing worse. A gray pallor had settled across his face.

"We could stay in Pennsylvania," Grace suggested. "Other colored folks live here. We could settle in with them. Canaan said white people look more kindly on colored folks up here."

Cabeto shook his head. "We could never rest easy," he said in a voice flat and weary. "Tolerated ain't the same as free."

So they walked on. Every night they judged their path against the bright star, and with the dawn, they walked.

One afternoon, a white woman offered them a meal of ham and beans, but they had only started to eat when she heard her husband's carriage roll up to the house. She shooed them through the back door quick enough and out to the garden, and she pointed them away through the tall corn. With just a little food in their stomachs, they were off again.

Grace and Cabeto slept in the brush that night, the same as they did most other nights. But the nights were definitely growing cooler, and as they traveled it was pleasant to occasionally be offered a mattress for the night, or even just a warm pile of straw in a barn.

⟋⟍

"My, my, but you look dreadful!"

Grace gave a guilty start. Plump red apples scattered across the ground had attracted her over the rail fence. Now she was caught, her skirt filled with the apples.

"Oh . . . I am just . . . I was only—" Grace stammered.

Grace looked guiltily at the small, gray-haired woman who stood in the adjacent garden, a large basket clutched in her hand. Grace had not seen her on her knees, pulling up turnips and carrots.

"Don't worry yourself about those windfall apples," the woman said with a gesture to Grace's skirt. "You are welcome to them. Only, it looks to me that you could do with a good bit more than just wormy apples."

Grace mumbled her apologies and started to back away.

"Please, come into the house," the woman said. "My sister Louise has a pot of venison stew simmering over the fire and a round of freshly baked bread just out of the oven."

Grace hesitated.

"Don't tell me that doesn't sound good to you," the woman said with a smile.

When Grace still held back, the woman said, "It just may be that Louise and I can be of further assistance to you. Are you alone?"

"No," Grace said. "My husband . . . he is out by the road."

"Do give him a holler," the woman said. "Surely he is hungry for venison stew, too."

❧

Fanny and Louise Pentecost. Those were the names of the two sisters. Their father had built the house, they said. It was roomy and comfortable, and before darkness fell, they offered Grace and Cabeto more than venison stew. They poured warm water into a washtub so the two could clean away the travel dirt, and Fanny showed them to a feather bed where they could sleep the night.

"I believe I have an extra dress about your size," Fanny said to Grace. "It is blue with yellow and white flowers. Would that suit you?"

Grace looked down at the tattered dress in which she had walked all the way from Charleston, South Carolina, to Pennsylvania, and smiled appreciatively.

Grace and Cabeto were not the only guests in the Pentecost sisters' house. Two colored men, August and Sim, occupied the room next to theirs. Fanny Pentecost introduced the newcomers to them at supper.

Neither Grace nor Cabeto was in much of a mind to talk. But they need not have worried. August most certainly was.

"The halls of freedom is proclaimed to all the world from these here United States," he said between spoonfuls of stew. "All the world exceptin' for the African race, that is."

Grace and Cabeto looked at each other. Cabeto reached for another piece of bread.

"Conflictin'. That's what I would say of this here country's high-soundin' words," August continued. "There surely is no freedom for a colored person here."

"Dese good ladies has been mighty kind to us," Cabeto said.

"Yes, and I would not speak a word against them," said August. "But kindness, now . . . that ain't freedom, is it?"

Grace shifted uneasily. Cabeto resigned himself to his bread.

"What I say is this—every sober-thinkin', hard-workin' colored man in this country ought to leave and head for Canada," August stated.

Grace set her mug down on the table and pushed back her chair.

"I do thank you kindly for the supper, Madam Pentecost," Grace said. "By your leave, I ask that you graciously excuse me now, for I really am quite tired."

But Fanny's reply was not to Grace. It was to August.

"While your observations may not have been made with the greatest delicacy, sir," she said, "there is truth in what you say. Colored people often come along this road. Some of them are hungry and dirty, and look as though they have been traveling for a very long time. Sometimes they intend to do exactly what you suggest—continue on to Canada. Yet that is not so easy a task as some would imagine it to be. A river must first be crossed. On the other side, still more land lies between them and their goal. When they get close to the waterway that divides the two countries, slave catchers lie in wait, so it is not easy to get safely through to the boats. And, of course, there is the tiresome matter of the high cost of passage."

Grace stared at Fanny Pentecost.

Panic passed over Cabeto's face, too, and he looked around for a way to escape just in case it was called for.

"But many good people in Pennsylvania stand ready to assist such travelers," Fanny quickly added. "Is that not so, Louise?"

"It most certainly is so, Fanny," said Louise. "You and I are willing to assist. So are the goodly fellows who transport travelers through the gauntlet to the boats. And the merchants who carry folks hidden in their wagons. And those who look the other way when it is time to collect the fare on the boat."

"Why?" Grace whispered. "Why would all those people do such things?"

"Because there are those here who believe the colored race in the United States should live with the same freedoms the white race enjoys," Fanny said. "Many of us long to see that day come."

For two days and nights, Grace and Cabeto stayed with the Pentecost sisters, as did August and Sim. The outside doors stayed closed and the windows shuttered against prying eyes. On the morning of the third day, a man with his hat pulled low over his face—a man introduced only as Robert—hustled all four of them into his carriage, and he drove the horses on a three-hour ride to the lake crossing. No sooner had Grace and the men alighted than an energetic man in work clothes stepped forward. He nodded to the men and tipped his hat to Grace, and he signaled to a woman in a grove who was busily shepherding three young children. The woman and children immediately moved to join him.

"Your boat passage," the man said as he handed each of the four a slip of paper. "Follow us and do as we do."

Once on the boat, August and Sim drifted away to sit apart from the white family. But Grace and Cabeto stayed with the man and his wife throughout the journey. The couple's two little boys scrambled around together on the deck, but Mary, their young girl with golden curls, sat up straight and tall.

"I'm afraid of the water," Mary said to Grace.

"Oh, don't be!" Grace assured her. "Many wonderful adventures happen on boats."

"Have you been in a boat before?" Mary asked.

"Oh, yes!" Grace said. "One time, I—"

Suddenly Grace thought about August, and how much he talked. So instead of finishing her sentence, she asked Mary's father, "What is Canada like, sir?"

"A British colony," he said. "Although until a few months ago, it was actually French. Now, however, it is firmly under English law."

"And there are other people there . . . like us?"

"Oh, yes," he said. "Many hundreds, I should say. Brought in as slaves, they were. No more, though. Slaves cannot be brought into North Canada now."

"It is truly a land of freedom, then?" Grace asked.

"I do not know," the man replied. "I pray it is. I also pray that our land will one day be a land of freedom."

❧

When they arrived in Canada, August and Sim promptly set off for the city of Toronto. But Grace and Cabeto headed for the countryside, where they were welcomed into a community of others who had escaped from slavery. Already the northern night winds blew up a chill. Cabeto and Grace set to work piling up branches they intended to use to build themselves a temporary shelter. But before they had gathered enough, men began to trickle over their way, saws and hammers and knives in hand. Women came, too, bearing baskets of vegetables from their gardens and apples off their trees, and parcels of dried meat and cured ham.

Cabeto chose the site for their house—a grove of oak trees, nestled under a shady canopy of leaves.

"You doesn't need cover from the sun up here," Daniel, a muscular man with one drifting eye, pointed out.

But Cabeto insisted it would remind him of times worth remembering.

"Come to the meetinghouse on the Lord's Day, won't you?" Calliope asked Grace. "Daniel preaches for us."

Grace smiled. "I am partial to preachers," she said. "We surely will do that."

Cabeto wanted to immediately prepare a garden beside the house, but Daniel laughed and said no, not in Canada with winter on the way. Instead, Cabeto accompanied the men to the stream, where he caught many fish, and he went with them to hunt for rabbits. He joined the men around the community fire, and under their tutelage he worked for days in the smokehouse.

Grace gathered walnuts and wild onions and herbs, and she gratefully received the plump squash and potatoes and carrots that Calliope and the other women gave her to store away for the cold weather.

"The winter is the hardest," Daniel said. "But it won't last forever."

One day the green leaves began to fade and change. In days, it seemed, the woods were a sudden blaze of yellow and gold and red. Cabeto hurried to report this to Daniel.

"Something is happening to the trees!" Cabeto exclaimed in alarm.

"Enjoy the sunshine while you can," Daniel told him. "Winter is not far away."

🖉

Winter was cold, and snowy, and very long. But spring came again, as spring always does. And one day—when the world was once again sunny and warm and Cabeto's garden lush and full—Cabeto stood tall and proud in the courtyard of his log house. It was the 27th day of June, in the year of our Lord, 1794. Grace stepped out of the house and stood beside him, their newborn baby cradled in her arms.

"My son!" Cabeto announced with great pride.

In the way of Africa, Cabeto took the baby from Grace's arms and held him high in the air.

"John Freedom Hull!" Cabeto announced. "That will be his name!"

Grace smiled.

"May the Good Shepherd carry our son on his shoulders all the days of his life," Grace said. "And may he dwell in the house of the Lord forever."

Epilogue

Through the budding of spring, the glories of summer, the harvest of fall, and the snows of winter, freedom prospered. Even so, memories danced in Grace's head. She spoke of them to her child from his earliest days, so as John Freedom grew, those who had peopled Grace's past became a part of his life, too.

One day a white man clomped, clomped on horseback into the colored settlement.

"I'm from the Hudson Bay Company and was out this way on other business," the man said. "Several months past, the company received a letter in our mail packet addressed to one Grace Winslow."

"That's me," Grace said. "Though my name is now Grace Hull."

Grace took the letter from the man and turned it over in her hand. She recognized the fine writing. It was from Lady Charlotte.

"How did you find me?" Grace asked.

"Seems you have influential friends, madam," the man said. "Your friend, John Hull, works alongside a Methodist preacher name of Francis Asbury. Just about everyone knows who he is. Seems the two of them asked after you all over Pennsylvania and New York, and everywhere else they went."

After a bowl of soup and a cup of tea, the rider took his leave. Before he was out of sight, the entire village gathered around the fire to hear Grace read her letter.

Dearest Grace~

Friends of Sir Thomas in Pennsylvania shared their home with the Reverend Francis Asbury, and from him learned that you and Cabeto arrived safety in Canada. Since that day, our entire group has offered unceasing gratitude to Almighty God. Oliver Meredith is now employed by the Hudson Bay Company in Canada, and it was he who discovered your location.

Our group is stronger than ever, and we have gained much support throughout London. With the help of Prime Minister William Pitt, we do believe that the African slave trade will soon come to an end. We pray for that day.

Your father is a changed man, Grace. He is a firm member of our group. We appreciate the passion and experience he brings us.

As for me, I remain with Reginald, for I have nowhere else to go. But my heart is with you. I am at liberty to come and go as I please, for Reginald hardly notices me. That is a mercy, I suppose. His business in Africa at Zulina has fallen off terribly and it causes him no end of distress. He vows to discover who is at fault and make that person pay.

I remain your loving friend,
Charlotte

J-o-h-n . . . F-r-e-e-d-o-m . . . H-

John Freedom, a strapping four-year-old, practiced writing his name by carefully tracing the letters in the dirt with a sharpened twig. It was he who first saw the tall white man coming down the road.

"Mama!" he called. "Mama, come quick!"

Grace stepped outside. She didn't recognize the man on the horse until he doffed his wide-brimmed hat. When she did, she caught her breath.

"Mister Meredith?"

"Yes, Oliver," said Oliver Meredith. "A letter arrived on the ship from London, and a packet marked important, both addressed to you in my care. I decided I should ride out and deliver them in person."

This time the villagers didn't wait for the white man to leave. They immediately gathered around the fire and sat impatiently all through the day while Grace talked with Oliver, made him a cup of hickory tea and dished him a plate of dinner, and finally saw him on his way.

"Read your letter, Mama," little John Freedom insisted before Mister Meredith was even out of view.

Dearest Grace~

I think of you often and remember you fondly.

Last year, I wrote a letter to my father. This week, when the ship arrived in port with a mail packet aboard, I was overjoyed to see a letter from him. There was news included that I thought would be of interest to you.

Your Mama Muco left my father's house. She would not be his slave anymore. My father did not chase her down. He said he recently learned that she had gone out to the distant villages and gathered up children abandoned by the slave catchers. She learned about your work at the Foundling Hospital from my letters to my father and she wanted to do the same thing in Africa.

My father is a man haunted by the ghosts of the captives he sent away. He refuses to work with your mother and her brother the king, and trades with a rival nation farther down the coast instead. Princess Lingongo has disappeared. Talk is, she has been taken as a slave herself. This is all my father's doing, of course, but Reginald blamed Jasper Hathaway. Reginald fired him and spoke so ill of him that no one else of any repute will associate with him. Mister Hathaway lives in a small house on the next street up from your Missus Peete, who spits at him whenever she sees him.

The packet contains a gift my father sent to me. It seems more appropriate for you. Oliver will see that you receive it.

In loving friendship,

Charlotte

Grace tugged the string off the package and unwound the layers of heavy paper.

"Look!" she said. "It's a turtle and it's made of solid gold!"

❧

"The supposed necessity of treating the Africans in such a way gradually brings a numbness upon the heart and renders those who are engaged in it indifferent to the sufferings of their fellow human creatures. In treating them as less than human, we become less than human ourselves. How else could we act in so uncivilized, so unchristian a way?"
~John Newton~
Slave ship captain turned preacher and abolitionist
Author of the hymn *Amazing Grace*

❧

March 25, 1807—A bill passed in Parliament and signed by King George III banned the transport of slaves into or out of England or any British territory.

Slavery Act of 1839—Made slavery illegal in England and its colonies.

September 22, 1862—Emancipation Proclamation by United States President Abraham Lincoln

December 6, 1865—The 13th Amendment to the United States Constitution officially abolished slavery in the United States.

2010—Three times as many slaves live in the world today as in Grace's day. When the first abolition bill passed in 1807, an estimated four million people were enslaved. Today, UNICEF's conservative number is more like twelve million people of all races.

Discussion Questions

1. Do you think Grace could have done anything differently to protect herself under British law as it existed in the eighteenth century? Have you ever felt that the American system of justice leans too far in the defense of the accused (i.e. the guaranteed right to legal representation, presumed innocence, and so forth)? Why or why not? Why do you suppose the founding fathers took such pains to include these in our Constitution?

2. In the eyes of many in genteel eighteenth-century England, America was populated with lawless gun-toting wild men. The English were not so impressed with the influence of foreigners on their own shores, either. Yet when Grace sees the sailors licking their plates, when she recalls the horror wrought by those who plied the slave trade, she wonders who truly are the uncivilized ones among them. How might this be a commentary on our different societies today? Can we really look at other cultures and judge them impartially?

3. African characters in the book, from Cabeto to Tempy to Grace herself, talk about their native religion—ancestors, spirit trees and so forth. Is it possible for such deeply held beliefs, such as a belief in the creator and in a mediator between God and humanity, to serve as a pathway to Christianity? Was this so for Grace? Why or why not?

4. Macon Waymon considered himself to be "a different kind of slaveholder," especially kind and benevolent. In what ways was this opinion justified? In what ways was it not? So he felt a singular sense of betrayal when Issum ran away, and Waymon applied a gruesome punishment. In the cool reason of the next morning, do you think Waymon felt his actions were justified? Do you suppose his treatment of his slaves changed after that? Why or why not?

5. What did you think of the contrasting viewpoints of slavery as alternately expressed by the slaves in the grove

and the French slaveowners in their mansion? Is it possible today for two groups of people to look at the same incident and see it so differently? Why or why not?

6. Today, in the cool, clear view of history, it is difficult to accept the varied defenses of slavery expressed by these characters (although all were actual arguments). Which do you think was the more persuasive defense, financial or ideological? Why? What are your thoughts about the biblical arguments offered?

7. Sir Geoffrey Phillips contended that it was counterproductive to "speak with a voice of thunder, abhorrence and condemnation," even about matters that truly are a blight on mankind. Do you agree? Why or why not? Ethan Preston insisted that speaking the truth in a calm, rational voice would help the nation recognize the true cost of slavery. Might that be a word of advice for us today? Why or why not?

8. It is difficult to comprehend what it would mean to be so severely punished for the sin of using one's bith name, or clinging to pieces of one's language or culture. Or to face possible death for the sin of learning to read. Why do you think Grace's life was so affected by what she read in the Declaration of Independence?

9. Although there are people of faith who touch Grace's life, her faith comes about almost entirely by reading the Bible. Is this realistic? Why or why not? In what ways did John Hull answer her questions honestly? In what ways were his responses colored by his own prejudices and background?

10. Were you surprised to learn that more than four times as many people live as slaves today than in Grace's day? There is plenty of room for twenty-first-century abolitionists! Come and visit www.GraceInAfrica.com to see how you can help and to share your ideas. You can make a difference!

Blessings in India: Book 1

The Faith of Ashish

❧

1

South India
March, 1898

*Y*ou know what you must do," Lata said to her husband.
Virat knew. Though it could cost him his life, he knew.

On the mat in the far corner of the hut, little Ashish moaned in his sleep. Virat could not bring himself to look at his son, so battered and broken. Instead, he busied himself adjusting his dusty *mundu* skirt. He untied the knot at his waist, stretched the long, wide strip of cotton cloth out as far as his arms would reach, and, as tightly as he could, wrapped it back around his thin body. The garment must be flat and smooth, with no folds. Untouchables were forbidden to wear folds. It was a caste rule, and caste rules must never be broken.

"I wove a new broom for you," Lata said to her husband.

"Put it in place," Virat answered. "I am ready."

Lata struggled to force the wrapped bundle of twigs down the back of her husband's tightly wrapped *mundu*. Even on this terrible day, she took care not to snag a hole in the worn cotton of his only garment.

"Do the broom bristles hang down far enough?" Virat asked anxiously. "They must brush against the ground. Do they brush against the ground?"

Lata knew each crease on her husband's dark face, every cadence of his gentle voice. They had walked side by side through sorrow and disaster, through want and despair. But never before had she heard the hoarse tremble of raw fear that tinged his words this day. With all her might, she gave the broom another shove. Jagged twigs clawed into Virat's bare back. Blood trickled down his brown skin. He winced, but made no complaint.

Padding silently on bare feet, Virat moved across the dirt floor to the sleeping mat he had dragged inside to keep his son from curious eyes. Damp locks of black hair framed the boy's swollen face. Virat reached out and tried to bend over his child, but the broom on his back wouldn't allow it. So he stood stiff and straight, like a brown tree that cannot bend in the wind.

"Be a good boy," Virat whispered over the sleeping child. "Remember, you are Ashish. You are a blessing. Always and forever, remember who you are."

When Virat left the hut, Lata did not follow behind him in proper Indian fashion. Instead, without apology, she walked by his side.

"The cup," Virat said.

Lata plucked a dirty string from her husband's outstretched hand and looped it around his head, positioning it just above his ears. Careful to leave it loose, she tied it in a knot. Virat slipped a flat tin cup over his mouth and secured it in place with the string.

"Take it off!" Lata insisted. "Do not wear that awful thing here! This is *our* side of the village! Our house!"

Do you have questions or comments?
Would you like to learn more about author
Kay Marshall Strom?

Visit her at her website www.kaystrom.com
and on www.GraceInAfrica.com

You are also welcome to join in the discussions on her blog:
http://kaystrom.wordpress.com

Abingdon Press has many great fiction books and authors
you are sure to enjoy.

Sign up for their fiction newsletter at
www.AbindgonPress.com
You will see what's new on the horizon, and much more—
interviews with authors, tips for starting a reading group,
ways to connect with other fiction readers . . .
even the opportunity to comment on this book!